BLUE COLLAR
BOSTON COOL

BLUE COLLAR BOSTON COOL

SCHRAFT STREET SHENANIGANS

Michael A. Connelly

iUniverse, Inc.
Bloomington

Blue Collar Boston Cool
Schraft Street Shenanigans

This is a work of fiction. All of the characters, names, incidents, organizations, and dialogue in this novel are either the products of the author's imagination or are used fictitiously.

iUniverse books may be ordered through booksellers or by contacting:

iUniverse
1663 Liberty Drive
Bloomington, IN 47403
www.iuniverse.com
1-800-Authors (1-800-288-4677)

ISBN: 978-1-4759-5564-4 (sc)
ISBN: 978-1-4759-5567-5 (hc)
ISBN: 978-1-4759-5566-8 (ebk)

Library of Congress Control Number: 2012919120

Printed in the United States of America

iUniverse rev. date: 10/23/2012

Schraft Street
Bradford. 10 Miles North/Northwest of Boston
Population 15,000
Retail, Three-Deckers, and Apartment Buildings

	l	Herlihy's Hardcore Gym
	l	
	l	
	l	
	l	
	l	
	l	Herlihy's Three-Decker
Schraft Street Diner	l	
	l	
	l	
Schraft Street Sports	l	
	l	
	l	
	l	
	l	
	l	Schraft Street Shenanigans
	l	
Schraft Street Market	l	
	l	
	l	
	l	
	l	Schraft Street Clothing
	l	
	l	
	l	
	l	
	l	Fat Frankie's Three-Decker (Bill)
	l	
	l	
	l	
Apartment Bldng ('Strippersville')	l	
	l	

CHAPTER ONE

Eking Out a Living

JIM HERLIHY HURRIED WEST ON Schraft Street, hustling the few hundred yards from his renovated three-decker (featuring a three-bedroom modernized apartment on each of the three floors of the big wooden house originally built in 1920) to the neighborhood gym he owned, thoughts bouncing from how achingly cold, windy, and abjectly gray it was for early November to how crazy Big Bill had been acting lately.

Schraft Street was a long, narrow but busy East/West thoroughfare in the small Boston suburb of Bradford, population fifteen thousand, about ten miles north/northwest of the city's downtown. Lately Schraft Street had become just about Jim's entire world—albeit a somewhat chaotic and challenging one. He'd inherited the old three-decker he'd grown up in along with several hundred grand when his seventy-two-year-old father had died suddenly of a heart attack a few years ago. He'd used the inherited money and the advance from his gritty Boston 'Cops, Gangsters, and Strippers' novel to set up Herlihy's Hardcore Gym; to buy the nearby small neighborhood watering hole called Schraft Street Sports; and to fix up the old three-decker. He'd done an exceptional job on the third floor apartment he lived in himself, but had also modernized the first two floors enough to command decent rents. When he could collect them, that is. Perhaps renting the first floor to three Boston cops and then the second floor to three strippers/sometime hookers hadn't been his best business decision. It wasn't his worse either though, primarily because of all the stiff recent competition.

Lately he'd started thinking that distinction might just be allowing Big Bill Donnelly to buy a 25 percent interest in Herlihy's Hardcore. He'd met Big Bill when they were both working out mornings at Powerhouse Gym in nearby Chelsea, and, with the gym nearly empty at that time in the morning, Big Bill had asked Jim to spot him on his heavy benches. Heavy as in over 500 pounds, for reps. *Plenty* of reps. Big Bill wasn't really big, he was head-turningly huge even among serious lifters, at 6' 6," and 350 pounds, and back then was competing in national powerlifting competitions. Donnelly was also a most intimidating Boston Cop, who looked as mean as he lifted. Facially, Big Bill reminded Jim of Lee Marvin in his *Liberty Valence* days. But, Jim soon realized, Big Bill, appearances strikingly to the contrary, actually had the easygoing manner of those (at least the reasonably well-adjusted of the lot) who are so obviously bigger, stronger, and tougher than everyone else that they have absolutely nothing to prove.

Big Bill had left the Boston Police Force to manage Herlihy's Hardcore, and, nights, to bartend at Schraft Street Shenanigans, a neighborhood Strip Club not far from Schraft Street Sports, and almost right across the street from The Schraft Street Market.

Schraft Street Shenanigans was, of course, the eminent choice of employment for Jim's somewhat troublesome second floor tenants. The most notable of these was by far the youngest, Amy Jordan. Notable because she was sweetly attractive bordering on downright gorgeous, surprisingly witty and usually upbeat and good-natured, at least for a stripper/sometime hooker . . . and had a 'thing' for Jim, while Big Bill had it bad for her. Bad news all around, as far as Jim was concerned.

But what was weighing on Jim's mind this particular dismal bitter Boston fall afternoon was the gym's finances, and especially his meeting with his grossly oversized partner to review those finances. Jim was a relatively serious workout guy himself, at age thirty-five and 6 feet, 210 benching slightly over 400 pounds.

The gym—like the bar and the three-decker and even his writing—had of serious financial necessity recently become strictly, intensely all business for Jim.

But for his partner and manager the gym was almost entirely a labor of love. Increasingly, Big Bill was displaying a virtually obsessive fascination with the latest fitness equipment, constantly beleaguering Jim with colorful catalogues displaying technological marvels accompanied by blisteringly painful prices. Bill was now insisting on leasing the newly available space next door to set up a special 'heavy-duty-room' just for hardcore young builders and lifters. He'd regale Jim with passionate accounts of the progress of those worthies, while—much to businessman and 75 percent owner Jim's dismay—generally ignoring the frustrating struggles of the ordinary members, who accounted for well over half of the gym's revenues.

As Jim, preoccupied and leaning into a very cold, brisk wind, approached Herlihy's Hardcore, he was dismayed to see the self-described "Famous Fat Foursome" getting out of their new Ford Expedition, all four waving wildly to him across the small parking lot. Overweight people aren't really unusually jolly, but you'd never guess *that* being around these four bouncing burlies. To make matters much worse, the slimmest and most attractive of the group—this of course damning with faint praise indeed—was forever telling Jim how much he resembled her strange choice for a dreamboat—relatively obscure actor Ron Eldard. This exuberant but genetically-challenged exercise enthusiast—Linda—had been enthralled by Eldard's dark portrayal of 'Westie' gangster John Reilly in the movie '*Sleepers*' starring Brad Pitt and Robert DeNiro.

Linda had said to Jim, "You have the same dreamy eyes and smile and mustache and dirty-blond hair as my Ron. Plus you have just the right amount of raw-boned muscle. You can park your shoes under my bed anytime. Meanwhile, you're inspiring *me* to get to my perfect weight."

Jim had thought but certainly *not* said, "Anything remotely resembling perfect is just not in your genes, Linda. Diet and exercise are great, but they're not miraculous. Please keep joyously doing the best you can anyway."

He'd managed his usual bright, friendly smile, and just said, "That's what we're here for, Linda. The perfect weight part, I mean." Jim genuinely felt quite bad—and as gym owner even somewhat responsible—that The Famous Foursome weren't improving faster and more dramatically.

This afternoon Linda practically sprinted over to him, gave him much too enthusiastic a hug, and exclaimed, "Perfect timing! You can work out with us!" For the first time today Jim was glad he had that meeting with Big Bill.

After disengaging from Linda and the rest of the gleefully energetic Famous Foursome as diplomatically as possible, ("Wow, how absolutely off-the-walls would these amazing ladies be if they'd had the good fortune to be genetically *blessed?*") Jim proceeded to the gym's tiny but neat and well-equipped office, where he was very happy to see that his accountant, Lloyd Dolson—who also kept the books for Schraft Street Sports, and did Jim's taxes and provided him with investment advice, not that Jim had much money to invest beyond the gym, bar, and three-decker—was already there.

To Jim's chagrin, though, Lloyd still wasn't comfortable discussing the business's dicey finances one-on-one with uber-formidable Big Bill, so instead the two were now deep into an animated conversation regarding the relative merits of the most elite entertainers at Schraft Street Shenanigans. Lloyd was 5' 6," 130 pounds, wore thick glasses, and definitely did not share Jim's problem of unsought attention from the likes of The Famous Foursome and young stripper Amy Jordan. Lloyd also did the books for Schraft Street Shenanigans, and was a semi-regular at the bar, and no stranger to lap dances. And, Jim also knew, at times no stranger to even stronger after-hours fare from some of the moonlighting dancers.

In fact, Amy Jordan had indiscreetly confided to Jim, "You'd think Mr. Dolson would have a plain ol' little dick. Boy was 'Suela surprised."

'Suela was Consuela, one of Amy's roommates, and her best friend. Consuela was in her mid-thirties to Amy's very early twenties, and Jim was both amazed and comforted at how Amy and her 'Suela supported each other. Young Amy actually did very little and very selective hooking; Consuela, realistically nearing the end of her prime earning years, somewhat more, but Jim thought she was almost as good-hearted as Amy, and he liked her anyway.

He'd replied to young Amy's innocent indiscretion, "Oh, so poor little Lloyd has a big dick going for him, at least. Excellent!"

"No, no. It was even *smaller* than 'Suela expected. We're talking really tiny, maybe the smallest she'd ever seen, and she's seen some. Child-abuse small, she was fretting the whole time, even."

"Amy, please don't tell anyone else that. Don't ya think poor Lloyd has enough problems, young lady? You're supposed to be Schraft Streets' resident 'stripper with a heart of gold,' remember?"

"I'm sorry, you're right again, Boss Love Of My Life. I'll tell my sweet 'Suela to shut up about it too. By the way, 'Suela said he came really, really fast too, even though he was pretty drunk."

"Amy!"

Jim really liked the bright and hardworking and impeccably honest little Lloyd, felt bad that he was so physically disadvantaged, and had been momentarily cheered to think that he had at least one positive physical attribute going long and strong. Then, alas, hope dashed.

Walking in today and overhearing Bill and Lloyd, Jim growled, "Alright, Mutt and Jeff Dickheads, some strippers *are* pretty sexy, what a surprise. Lloyd, show me the money."

Lloyd brought up onto the computer screen:

Latest Monthly Gym Cash Flow

Members	800	
Monthly Dues	$25	
Monthly Gross Dues Income		$20,000
Avg Monthly New Members	15	
Sign Up Fee	$50	
Total Sign Up Fees		$750
Avg Mnthly Spend @ Protein Bar	$5/Member	
Total Protein Bar Revenues		$4,000
Subtotal Gross Revenues		**$24,750**
Big Bill Discounts/Credit		($2000)
Net Monthly Gym Revenues		**$22,750**
Big Bill Monthly Salary	$3500	
Other Desk Clerks	$3500	
Maintenance/Cleaning	$2500	
Interest on Equipment Notes	$2800	
Property Taxes	$1000	
General Supplies	$1000	
Heat, Water, Utilities	$1800	
Protein Bar Supplies	$1800	
Total Monthly Gym Expenses		**$17,900**
New Equipment/Major Repairs Fund		**$3,000**

Net Cash to Split	**$1,850**
75% to Jim Herlihy	**$1,388**
25% to Bill Donnelly	**$ 462**
Other Notes	
Cumulative Delinquent Accounts	$15,000
Balance in New Equipment/Repairs	$45,000
Invested: Jim Herlihy	$550,000
Bill Donnelly	$185,000
Total Investment	**$735,000**
Annual Cash Flow	**$ 22,200**
% Net Cash Return	**3.0%**

Jim said, "I need another grand a month in my pocket; and not at the expense of building up the Equipment Fund. You're the expert, Lloyd."

"Ah, ah, raise the monthly to thirty and pick up $4k right there, *if* you don't lose any members. Maybe sell more protein drinks and energy bars, and that type of nasty-tasting but sweetly profitable nonsense?"

Jim said, "That's a pretty big freaking *if*, to be recklessly bandied about by such a little fella."

Bill added, "Miniature Lloyd, that nasty nonsense might bulk you all the way up to an impressive 140 if you'd partake."

Lloyd replied, "What can I say? This business ain't all that complicated. And I'm an accountant, not a magician, sorta smart big guy and not so smart huge guy."

"Monstrous Bill, ya gotta collect the past due, and stop with the credit to the young muscleheads," said Jim, while getting up to see if he could tell what The Famous Four were laughing so hard at now; but, as usual, no way to tell from a distance. While he was up, Jim took the opportunity to mock whisper loudly right into Bill's ear, "The normal-looking members all pay *on time!* Ya not *afraid* of the puffed-up young welchers, are ya?"

"They pay what they can," Bill replied calmly, while wiping the abused big ear with his handkerchief. "I ban 'em we get nothing. It's good business to have guys and gals around the joint who look like they're actually getting something for their money and their hard work."

"Boink strippers out of ya own pocket instead of workout girls out of mine, ya oversized horndog."

Bill growled, "One babe, that was one babe. How'd I know she was gonna split for LA before I could really put the arm on her?"

Jim muttered, "Yeah, yeah, makes it a little hard to put the big arm on after you've had the little dick in."

Lloyd pulled up the 'Aged List of Monies Owed by Gym Member,' with the offender's picture next to his or her past-due balance. Jim waited while Bill perused the list. Jim could tell by the almost comically pained look on Bill's huge face that he was honestly considering the particulars of each problem case.

Then Jim said, "Lloyd, give us a damn column for target Big Bill collections over the next couple weeks, musclebound welcher by musclebound welcher. I'm broke. I need a couple grand quick, Bill, even if it's gotta come out of your end—salary included."

Bill suddenly got 350 power-lifting-pounds worth of scary looking—all the more daunting because he almost never looked at Jim that way. "*Salary* cut ain't happening, Little Jim."

Bill then proceeded to identify about $3k in specifically targeted delinquent collections, which Lloyd duly noted in the new column, and then Bill said in ultra-formidable quiet voice, "There ya go, Mr. Herlihy. Twenty-two-hundred bucks to you, eight-hundred to Monstrous Bill."

Bill suddenly slipped back into normal Big Teddy Bear, and began passionately regaling Jim and Lloyd with his latest plans for the special 'Heavy Duty Addition,' as if they hadn't just had a contentious discussion of the gym's financial struggles and the collection problems with the blue-collar youthful hardcore.

Jim listened as long and politely as he could bear, and then diplomatically tabled the discussion by saying that he and Lloyd had a financial meeting with Schraft Street Sports' Manager and Head Bartender Fat Frankie Leonnetti the next day, and would revisit the overall gym situation in a couple of weeks. *With* that $3k in past-due collections then in hand!

Jim had been planning to work out right after the meeting, but decided he'd had enough Monstrous Bill for one dismal afternoon. Plus, the bouncing burlies were still doing their level best to work out, and at their usual painful decibel level. The chances of them letting Jim lift in peace were about as good as for Big Bill actually collecting that entire three grand in the next couple weeks, as Bill had finally agreed. Jim slunk out the back door of his own gym, into an ever darker and bleaker frigid Boston November early evening.

Shivering, worrying Jim was now further dismayed to see local marginal gangster Hoary Harry Annunzio parking his aging, dented BMW in the small gym lot, right by the street.

As Harry exited his car, Jim walked towards him, calling out, "Whoa, Schraft Street's own Hoary Harry Annunzio joining Herlihy's Hardcore. Who'd a thunk that?"

"No one ever, Boss Hoss. Heading for The Diner, no easy spots over there; and I already had too many at the titty bar to be testing my parallel parking right out in the open. Need some fresh air and a short walk anyway. You wouldn't begrudge an ol' pal, now would ya?"

The lot for Herlihy's Hardcore was somewhat problematically small, and there were big signs threatening towing of non-customers; in addition, Monstrous Bill had been known to put a very deep dent or two in an interloper's car from time-to-time, and what was anyone gonna do or even say about that?

But Hoary Harry Annunzio could be quite unreasonable when he was drinking, and Jim had other things on his mind. So he wordlessly scribbled and signed a "Do Not Tow or Bludgeon" note, and stuck it under Harry's right windshield wiper.

The Diner was almost directly across the street from Jim's three-decker, so Jim had no choice but to walk with Harry, whose unsteadiness was just barely noticeable.

Bookmaking Harry said, "You a betting man today, Boss Hoss . . . Celtics . . . Bruins . . . Pats . . . me eventually nailing that gorgeous little slutsker Amy, one way or the *damn* other?"

Harry parking where he oughtn't was one thing. Jim stopped, grabbed Harry's thin, wiry arm, and effortlessly turned him so he'd have no choice but to look into Jim's eyes. "Best never be any 'damn other' viciousness with my sweet little Amy, Harry."

Harry didn't seem cowed or embarrassed at all, though. He just gave the much bigger Jim a sneering, "You got me for now, Pal, but that don't mean much," look, shook Jim's hand off easily—Jim had grabbed Harry firmly enough to turn him, but had stopped well short of bruising Harry's small arm—and sauntered casually across Schraft to The Diner. A car had to slow significantly for him; tipsy, jaywalking Harry gave the driver a filthy look, and Jim could almost hear Harry say, "Hey, I'm walkin' here, I'm walkin' here." Harry actually did remind Jim of Dustin Hoffman in his thirties, except Harry was thinner, wirier, oilier, and more naturally threatening.

But not threatening enough to keep Jim from standing there staring at Harry until he disappeared into The Diner.

Jim didn't know what he'd do if the likes of Hoary Harry Annunzio ever hurt little Amy Jordan. And he surely didn't want to find out . . . but at the moment he couldn't deny that he had precious little idea how best to keep from having to find out.

CHAPTER TWO

The Lay of The Land

JIM RETURNED TO HERLIHY'S HARDCORE at 8 PM, when he was sure Bill would be off to his bartending at Shenanigans, and of course The Famous Foursome would be long gone. A quiet, solitary but intense upper body workout would be the perfect antidote to the frustrating affairs of the afternoon.

But then he had decidedly mixed feelings to find that Dale O'Dell, Doug Ballard, and Jay Arnold were there, working out together. They usually trained between five-thirty and seven-thirty; and Jay Arnold—by far the most accomplished bodybuilder to have ever trained at this gym, and who had competed in several Mr. Olympia contests, although always finishing out of the top ten—usually worked out with a couple of other competing builders, rather than with Dale and Doug.

Arnold drove Jim nuts. Although Arnold generally trained at night because he wanted suitable workout companions and to be seen and admired by the young and attractive members who had day jobs, Arnold made his living at bodybuilding with some personal training thrown in, had no day job, and spent a ridiculous amount of time at the gym even during the day, some of it joyously talking weightlifting and nutrition with an engaged and admiring Big Bill, and too much of it bothering an oblivious and thoroughly bored Jim Herlihy.

Because Jim owned the gym and possessed an impressive physique himself due to a combination of excellent genetics and reasonably consistent training and nutrition, Arnold expected him to be an ardent physique enthusiast. And, to critique Arnold's physique and posing routines, which he prominently practiced daily in front of the gym's huge mirrors.

But, as far as Jim was concerned, Arnold was (a) indeed absurdly muscular, and (b) an obsessed, cartoonishly one-dimensional and intolerably boring knucklehead, and that was as specific about Arnold as Jim ever cared to get. Whether Arnold's arms and calves were more symmetrical now than in his last contest, or how the definition in his quads compared to that of his most bitter rivals, Jim had absolutely no opinion nor interest. But, Arnold felt that he should have, and was obviously not going to go away easily.

Worse, the living that Arnold was able to eke out from fulltime bodybuilding was marginal, and he was forever pestering Jim that not only should he not have to pay for his membership, Jim should be paying him for gracing the place with his Herculean presence. Big Bill seemed to agree. And Arnold was an awful, even dangerous personal trainer. He was certified, but still chose to ignore the fact that the first priority for out-of-shape forty-year-old men and women was that they not get injured and forced right back onto the couch. Or, far worse, right into a lawyer's office.

Arnold had even complained bitterly when Jim had banned the 'balls-to-the-wall' builder's steroid connection from the gym, the pusher had moved on, and Arnold now sometimes had trouble tracking that all-important guy down.

Dale O'Dell was a different story entirely. Early on, Jim and Bill had hired personal trainer extraordinaire Dale to work the desk part time while she studied to be an orthopedic physicians assistant. Jim had taken Dale out several times, and been enthralled by her looks and lean, reasonably muscular but still decidedly feminine physique; knowledge of exercise, nutrition, physical therapy, and orthopedics; and especially by her sweet nature and common sense. Or, what appeared to be common sense . . . until Doug Ballard came along.

Ballard had been a very successful Newbury Street hairdresser, until he got into male modeling and became even more successful at that. Ballard had met Dale when he went to the eminent orthopedic surgeon she worked for to be treated for shoulder tendonitis. Taken with the attractive and substantive Dale, Ballard had applied the charm that had won over the wealthy matrons at his salon on Newbury Street and, of course, the unusual good looks that had spawned that increasingly successful modeling career.

Dale had then—somewhat casually—just told Jim she'd met someone else. After all, they'd only had a few dates, with barely a goodnight kiss . . . and Jim hadn't even thought of yet telling her how she'd affected him.

Ballard lived in a luxury waterfront condo on Atlantic Avenue in downtown Boston, where of course he had access to a fancy gym that suited his high-living style; but he'd been sufficiently smitten by Dale that he'd taken to working out with her at the comparably low rent and somewhat gritty Herlihy's Hardcore, a half-hour drive under the best of Boston traffic conditions.

Jim was heart-wrenchingly biased, he knew, but still was soon convinced that the uber-charming Ballard was essentially made of cardboard. The naturally big-boned, symmetrical, and muscular Ballard worked out at semi-speed, spending half his energy charming the young workout girls and female personal trainers. (Actually, Jim thought perhaps Dale was not the only Herlihy's Hardcore attraction causing Ballard to eschew the fancy Spa right there in his luxury waterfront building.)

Outwardly, Ballard was as pleasant to The Famous Foursome as he was to everyone else, and they were suitably enthralled. But Jim had overheard Ballard make a shockingly disparaging comment about them, far more mean-spirited than the worst that Jim had ever thought and never dreamed of saying aloud. When Jim reflexively snarled at Ballard as a result, he was amazed at how the formidable-looking Ballard instinctively shrunk, and then slunk away. Sure, Jim himself had no doubt he'd bury the guy, *with* prejudice . . . but how could Ballard know that? And even so, why wouldn't Ballard at least pretend to have a backbone? After all, he was a customer . . . and Jim was known to be a businessman, and far from a hothead.

Dale and Doug just waved to Jim half-heartedly, but Jay came over. Jim was now, out of the corner of his eye, suffering through an agonizing view, from the rear, of his gorgeous, leotarded Dale doing light high-repetition full squats, with her Doug distractedly encouraging her. But mostly the heroic-looking Doug was checking himself out in the mirror, rearranging his thick blond hair with his hands. (Dale had told Jim that she thought Doug looked like a young Fabio. Jim's unstated opinion was that Fabio did indeed also look like a self-important non-entity.)

Arnold proudly showed Jim an absurdly thick album of photos from his fourteenth-place finish in the Mr. Olympia a couple months ago, saying,

"Mr. Gym Owner, you know I moved up two spots this year. Only guy training in Massachusetts that's competed in The Big O in years, and Herlihy's Hardcore has me. Pick as many as you want to blow up and hang on the walls . . . but it's *gotta* cost ya. How I make my living, ya know."

There were literally hundred of photos in the album, the majority of them looking exactly the same. But Jim knew if he made that observation, Jay would gleefully start explaining the minute differences, and where he was focusing on flexing his delts versus his pecs versus his biceps versus his abs versus his quads versus his calves.

Jim said, "Bill has a much better eye than I do, Jay . . . and more time. I gotta work out now. Plus we already have about a hundred pictures of you from the last couple adorning the walls."

Jay's eyes widened, and he exclaimed, "Those all gotta come down, down! Right away! I was way, way better this year, Jim! You know I was, I was! Moved up two fuckin' places I did!" The amazing veins in Jay's neck looked like they might actually burst.

"Yeah, Jay, yeah, you surely were. Work it out with Big Bill."

In fact, Jim had a rule that only pictures of members were allowed on the gym walls. No Mr. Olympia's, past or present, even if they visited the gym to give seminars, or for a workout when they were guest posing in Boston, all of which several had done. There were plenty of impressive members besides Jay who had made noteworthy progress working out at Herlihy's Hardcore, and it was motivational for them to have their picture hanging in plain sight. There were even a few pictures of Big Bill hoisting monstrous weights in powerlifting competitions. But Jim himself had always declined to pose for any appropriate pictures. It was bad enough that he'd let Big Bill talk him into the alliterative 'Herlihy's Hardcore' instead of his preference, 'The Schraft Street Gym' . . . better to just be blandly consistent with the other businesses on the confounding street.

Jim glanced over at Dale and Doug, where Dale was now working on the ladies' amazingly-in-demand new hi-tech glute machine, while Doug chatted up another sexy female personal trainer, who was laughing loudly at something Doug said that, considering the source, couldn't possibly have been funny.

Jim actually considered bagging the workout and slipping over to the small neighborhood bar he owned—Schraft Street Sports—to watch the Bruins game with a few half-drunk casual acquaintances who would undoubtedly be in attendance. But he also knew that his bar manager—Fat Frankie Leonnetti—would be tending tonight. He had a meeting with Frankie tomorrow afternoon, and Christ, that would be plenty soon enough to deal with that particular overly burly and generally recalcitrant fella. Besides, Jay was back deep into his intense heavy-duty leg workout, and was unlikely to bother Jim for a while.

Not only did Jim then get through his upper body workout unscathed, the sexy new personal trainer Ballard had been chatting up—who obviously knew that Ballard was unavailable, at least tonight—took the bench next to him for her light dumbbell work, and volunteered to spot Jim when he loaded the bar to 315 for his heavy sets of eight.

Having an attractive young workout girl spot always injected a nice little shot of adrenaline into any healthy young man's exercise routine.

He didn't know her well at all, but as they chatted and lifted, he eventually realized she was there for the asking. Vulnerable from the frustration of the day, and actually from the last few weeks, Jim was severely, severely tempted. But he knew she was becoming a regular at the gym—both with clients and with her own workouts—so in the end his intense need to reduce not increase complications in his life sensibly carried the day.

Walking out of his gym, Herlihy was surprised that the wind had died down, and that—with him still warm and pleasantly quivering from his long, hard, workout-girl-fueled session with the heavy iron—the November evening now felt more invigoratingly crisp than painfully raw. So he'd stroll some Schraft Street, before calling it a night.

Jim loved walking The Street when it was crisp like this, and quiet, and especially after a hard upper body workout. He didn't normally walk after lower body, because he did a lot of intense squatting, his legs would be rubbery, and he'd be more than ready to sink into his high-end Lazy Boy and let them start recovering.

Schraft Street had many small retail businesses and a lot of lights, but also plenty of fully-grown oak trees lining the sidewalks. Jim loved the view looking up and down the long and narrow street, and with the help of the visually challenged Little Lloyd Dolson, he'd realized that one thing making that view especially pleasing was that Jim had unusually sharp eyesight, 20/15, almost as good as Ted Williams' 20/10 in his .406-hitting, long-ago prime.

Lloyd had told Jim, "Even with my humiliating coke bottles, the best they can get me is about 20/25, which is livable, but nothing is crystal-clear to me like everything must be to you. And for some reason, my screwed-up eyes can't tolerate contacts, hard or soft. Some guys have all the luck."

Jim had put his big arm warmly around Lloyd's narrow shoulders, and said, "Sorry, little bud. But at least you're one smart, energetic, good-natured little fucker."

Lloyd grinned broadly. "Yeah, I should be miserable, but I really am pretty happy; happier than most knuckleheads around here, best I can tell. Can't help myself. Actually, if I was a big, muscular, good-looking blond-headed bastard like you with all the broads comin' round, I'd probably be so happy my heart would burst and I'd be fuckin' dead."

Yup, Lloyd's genetics on the outside were plain awful; but at least he'd been blessed with some pretty darn good wiring inside that little skull.

Walking tonight Jim's thoughts soon turned to his father—dead these three years—as they often did while he was strolling the busy, intriguing street he'd grown up on, after it had finally quieted down for the night.

Jim's mother had been killed and his father badly injured in an auto accident when Jim was four years old. He could just barely remember that brutal night; and just barely remember his mother. The accident had been caused not by a young and immature drunk driver, but by an eighty-year-old, half-senile, half-blind, overly medicated guy who had no business driving slowly on a sunny day, never mind speeding on the dark rainy night it had been.

To make truly awful matters even worse, that befuddled old guy's wife had of necessity been the one who handled the bills and all paperwork, she'd recently died, and he'd let their auto insurance lapse, among all kinds of other things, including subsequently ignoring the letter from the state informing him that since his insurance had lapsed his driver's license was cancelled.

Hank Herlihy's own insurance had covered his medical bills and his wife's funeral expenses, but there hadn't been anything of substance to recover from the elderly at-fault driver, also badly injured, and who passed away not long after the accident.

Hank was a working supervisor in the produce markets in downtown Boston just north of the famous Fanueil Hall Market Place, and he'd had no choice but to continue with that physical work, despite the fact that he now had permanent leg and hip pain to contend with.

The car had of course been totaled, and Jim's father never got another one. He just took the MBTA to work from then on.

Hank's cousin and his wife lived on the second floor of that three-decker, and Jim's mother and father had been very close friends with that couple. The wife was conveniently home with an infant daughter, the kindly woman had always paid plenty of attention to cute little Jim, so she was now happy to watch him after school until Jim's father got home, limping, aching, and tired.

The neighbor's infant daughter had become like a beloved little sister to Jim, helping to instill in him to this day a very soft spot in his heart for all little girls. The couple and that girl had moved away when she was twelve and Jim sixteen—easily able to fend for himself when Hank was working—but Jim still talked to her on the phone every couple of months.

Although Jim was comfortably independent by then, and of course his 'adopted' little sister and substitute mom hadn't died, and he knew he'd see them several times a year, he still had a very painful sense of loss—enough to give him notably better insight into what his father had gone through. That made Jim appreciate Hank even more, and to resolve to forevermore be as little a burden to his dad as possible—in terms of time, money, and, especially, worry.

Earlier, despite the discomfort from his injuries, Hank had still managed to teach Jim plenty of baseball, football, and hockey, and later to come to most of his games, as long as they were at night or on weekends.

About the only time Hank regularly took for himself was Friday night, he and the neighboring cousin habitually spending hours eight-to-twelve at Schraft Street Sports—the very neighborhood bar Jim would later buy with the money his father left him—slowly drinking beer and watching whatever Boston professional team was playing.

Despite the semi-debilitating injuries, Hank was, like his son would turn out to be, a pretty well-built, good-looking guy, and there was the occasional woman around, although never anything particularly serious.

All in all, Jim soon realized that his father had suffered a very bad break and had a pretty tough life; but like Lloyd Dolson, Hank was also considerably blessed with a naturally upbeat and resilient nature.

And Hank clearly enjoyed being around his son, and his son surely enjoyed being with him.

How Hank had managed to save the money Jim had inherited Jim had no idea. And if he had known about that money, he'd have done his level best to convince Hank to spend it on himself before it was too late. But then, of course, Hank's death at seventy-two had been sudden and unexpected, so neither Jim nor Hank himself had any idea that it was getting too late.

At any rate, walking The Street and thinking of Hank now often helped Jim cope with the considerable ups and downs of his struggling, mini-entrepreneurial life on Schraft Street.

The one unsettling moment for strolling Jim tonight was that as he approached Shenanigans on his way back to his three-decker, he saw Hoary Harry outside on the sidewalk having a cigarette. Jim met Harry's eyes, and on the spur-of-the-moment decided he'd stop for a clarifying word relative to any inappropriate intentions regarding sweet little Amy Jordan. But Harry just gave Jim a quick hard look, and headed unsteadily back into the club.

Jim stopped for a few seconds, considering following him in. But, knowing Harry, he was undoubtedly now pretty damn drunk; and, unfortunately, sweet little Amy was undoubtedly in there running around pretty damn naked.

Jim had now totally cooled down from his workout, the wind had stiffened again, and the night had definitely slipped from invigorating back to painfully raw. So he headed on home.

To get his head ready for bed, as he walked he pushed away all thoughts of Harry, Amy, Big Bill, Fat Frankie, and those troubling finances, by replaying his most excellent upper body session, as spotted by the sexy new personal trainer. He grinned. He'd lifted hard and heavy tonight, without a hint of injury . . . just the familiar, healthy, growth-promoting gentle soreness now settling in to help him sleep.

CHAPTER THREE

Editors, Accountants, Tenants, Bartenders, Strippers, and Gangsters

JIM AWOKE REFRESHED THE NEXT morning, thrilled that the stripper/hookers renting the floor below him not only hadn't knocked on his door—which they sometimes drunkenly/druggedly did after work looking for booze or just to talk or to complain about their apartment or solicit him for paid or even unpaid sex of which he never, ever partook or even a couple of times to pay a portion of their overdue rent—but they hadn't even made enough nonsensical noise to wake him up in the wee hours of the morn.

He was also, of course, equally glad that he hadn't taken up the sexy new personal trainer on her obvious if unspoken offer, or to even have a few too many beers at Schraft Street Sports. The brief, unhappy late afternoon encounter with an already half-hammered and vaguely threatening Hoary Harry was again something of a potentially distracting dark cloud; but Schraft Street had long been providing Jim with practice in pushing such distractions aside, and again this morning he was readily able to do so.

He was reviewing the latest financials from Schraft Street Sports on his PC in preparation for his meeting with Fat Frankie at 1 PM when his editor Steve Chadwick at Scribner called.

Chadwick said, "Sooo . . . how's it going?"

"Life sucks, Steve. Cummings said the world is puddle wonderful, but for me it's asshole awful."

"You wallow in bars, strip clubs, gyms, hookers, cops, and gangsters. The hell ya expect. So write another damn book about it already, *you* asshole. Why I called, of course. Musclebound Dickhead."

"Trying, but they're really getting to me lately, Steve. Just struggling to keep my fool head above water. Worst of all, an exceptionally worthwhile woman is now haunting my gym and my dreams. Gave me just enough of a tumble to screw my skull up, and then moved on to the worst asshole of all. Prick works in New York City sometimes, too, with all you *real* pricks."

"Yeah, women do that sometimes; happened to my second cousin on my mother's side, coincidentally, about fifteen years ago. But, it is just so, so wrong that it happened to such a special guy as you. *Hey*, everything about you screams 'One-book mini-wonder.' You got a name and a foot in the damn door. You know how many far, far better writers than you would give their right arm for that? Ya got money problems, just write the freaking sequel! Cookie cutter bullshit, and we both pay the rent for a few more months!"

"Christ, it's depressing enough living it never mind analyzing it."

"*Analyzing?* Are you actually trying to write some serious literary shit or something? 'Cause that'd be like Tim Wakefield trying to resurrect his career by becoming a power pitcher . . . or me trying to become a musclehead like you."

"It's nice to have such an inspirational editor. I will try, Steve."

"Seriously, Jim, if you can *promise* a decent draft in six months, I'll get you a fifty grand advance this very week. Get your head above water, free you up, *and* light a fire under your procrastinating ass."

"Would if I could but I can't. Got some decent notes, but I need more to commit. Plus I gotta get the gym and the bar and even the house on the right track. Pretty soon, though, Steve."

"Yeah, I've seen that gym and that bar and that house and the strip club and those strippers. Tried to clear the images from my skull, but haven't quite made it. Good luck, knucklehead." And Chadwick hung up.

Jim took his notes for the sequel out of the drawer, and reviewed them. He resolved to make a real effort to chat up the young cops renting the first floor—as well as a few of the shady characters who haunted Schraft Street Sports and Schraft Street Shenanigans—for some updated ideas.

He'd written the first book based on observations, neighborhood stories and rumors, Fat Frankie's remarkable catalogue of colorful tales, relatively casual conversations with cops, strippers, and shady characters; and of course, his own reasonably fertile imagination. Including research and countless rewrites, with much help from an unusually patient Chadwick—who, truth be told, had spent much more time than he normally would because he and Jim had really 'clicked'—the book had taken Jim over two years to complete, while balancing gym, bar, and house. After the book came out with its modicum of success—Jim figured all told he'd made around a hundred grand from it—he'd certainly bought plenty of drinks, but that had been the extent of it.

But now if the tenant cops—particularly Sergeant Carlton Carrollton, who Jim actually considered a friend—had anything they knew was good, they'd want very generous discounts on the rent. If the shady characters had anything good, they'd want a few bucks in hand, and probably for him to spring for some after-hours hardcore shenanigans with his second floor tenants. Some of these guys had a very literal interpretation of the boast, "*I* never had to pay for it in my entire life."

After he organized the notes, he thought about the phone call, and grinned. He wished Steve Chadwick lived around Boston instead of in New York. An actual friend with half a brain.

He'd only been back prepping for Fat Frankie for a half hour when there was a loud, repetitive knock on the door, and a bubbly little-girlish voice was sweetly calling, "Open up, Mr. Sleepyhead! Rise and shine, Mr. Jimmy!" . . . Then, well before he could get to the door, Amy Jordan shrieked, "I'm a busy girl, sir, a very busy girl! So open the Christ up, willya, ya fuckin' asshole!"

When he opened, Amy was shyly looking down, and giggling like the sweet little twenty-year-old waif she should have been, absent extremely cruel if not uncommon circumstance. Jim had yet another painful flash of feeling helpless and totally out of control. Amy had once shown him a color photograph of herself at age six, and he'd been shortsighted and self-oblivious enough to really look at the amazingly adorable damn thing. Naturally, the picture was also strikingly reminiscent of his memory of his 'little sister' when she'd been six, and Jim himself had been ten.

Now, big-eyed, mildly freckle-faced, 5'3" Amy reminded Jim of one of those bouncy sixteen-year-old Olympic gymnasts, in both physique and energetic, enthusiastic comportment. Amy was, in fact, universally recognized as far and away the most athletic and entertaining pole dancer not just now, but in the venerable twenty-year-history of Shenanigans.

Amy also still had a big-eyed, adorable look of vulnerability that reminded Jim of many cartoon renderings he'd seen of heart-wrenchingly cute little girls.

Amy wouldn't tell Jim much at all about her background growing up in a very poor area of Brockton, about fifteen miles southwest of Boston. But once Amy's roommate and best friend Consuela had become certain that Jim had Amy's best interests at heart, Consuela had told him that Amy's father had left the family when Amy was a baby and then spent most of the rest of his short life in jail, and that her mother had been an alcoholic and an OxyContin addict. Of course, not surprisingly, those afflictions had led to the typical hideous choices in men; and accompanying maternal neglect. Amy had suffered through both physical and sexual abuse from not one but two stepfathers.

Consuela figured that what had 'saved' Amy—to the extent she was saved, and Amy certainly did have a kind heart, lack of bitterness, and remarkably good sense of humor, for having grown up in such tragic circumstance—was that Amy had had a surprisingly sane and supportive circle of girlfriends through middle- and high school.

Jim had taken to paying Amy every week for buying his groceries and cleaning and other household supplies at the nearby Schraft Street Market, as well as for periodically cleaning his apartment. It actually hurt his soul when, virtually every time he paid her—on time, as opposed to her and her partners in debauchery relative to paying their second floor rent—Amy would sweetly say something like, "And, Mr. Jim, how would you like a blowjob with that maid service? I'm running a special this week, just for muscular, blond-headed and mustachioed nice guys upon whom I have a serious crush." Jim would just give her a big, brotherly hug, and affectionate peck on the cheek.

But, on the other hand, the mischievous Amy would invariably forget the toilet paper, telling Jim, "I'm barely twenty. I certainly have had my humiliating ups and downs in this miserable life, but I must have a subconscious aversion to participating in any form or fashion with middle-aged guys' bowel movements. Because in general I have a pretty *good* memory."

On far more than one occasion, Jim had caught Amy giggling and peeking at him from the barely-cracked second floor door as he made his way up the stairs with a huge bag of nothing but a months supply of toilet paper—and one six-pack of light beer for appearances. Amy and everyone else knew that Jim never drank in his apartment. In fact, whenever those untouched six-packs came anywhere near accumulating, Amy would confiscate them, so she and her equally mischievous—albeit older, harder, heavier, wrinklier, and far less witty—roommates could yell up at three in the morning, in gleeful and top-of-lungs unison, "We're drinking *your* excess beer tonight, Boss Jim. Happy shopping . . . and even happier wiping!"

This morning Jim—sporting the normal broad, bright grin that Amy always inspired no matter how Jim was otherwise feeling—said, "Hey, little girl, you cleaned the apartment a couple days ago, and about all I've done since is sleep here. And I been gettin' all my meals at the diner, bar, and gym, so the cupboard is still full."

Amy sashayed in, sat at the kitchen table, and said, "Hoary Harry was drunk at the bar last night, bought me a bunch of drinks I didn't even want, wanted to buy a bj but was way too drunk by the end of the night. Woulda taken me two hours just to bring up a boner, never mind settin' little Harry a'spittin.' But he told me a funny story about you . . . but Harry actually didn't think it was funny. He was getting mad about it, actually."

Amy already seemed concerned, so for the moment Jim decided against telling her about his own contentious encounter with the already half-hammered Harry late yesterday afternoon.

'Hoary Harry' Annunzio was a marginal gangster—bookmaking, a little loan sharking, pimping, selling coke—who had a very small financial interest in Schraft Street Shenanigans, and was in there every night. He probably spent more drinking at the bar, buying lap dances, and paying for sex than he made from his minor ownership. He was a small, wiry, dark-haired, dark-complexioned guy with oily good looks.

Jim and Harry had played high school football together—Jim as running back/linebacker, Harry as wide receiver/free safety—and at a post-game party Harry had a few too many beers and decided it would enhance his considerable reputation as a tough little guy if he beat on Jim Herlihy, who everyone knew could bench press 330 pounds, an impressive feat for a 180-pound high school senior. Harry got in the first punch, but after that it hadn't been close. Jim had the good sense not to hurt Harry or hit him nearly as hard as he could have, but he'd had a couple beers himself and that first sneaky punch had been seriously irritating. Jim ended up hoisting the beaten Harry and depositing him very gently in a nearby dumpster. The contents of the dumpster turned out to be far nastier than Jim realized, and Harry had never forgiven him, despite the fact that Harry picked the fight and Jim apologized profusely for the unhappy ending.

No one but Harry ever spoke of the incident, and Harry only did when he was depressed and very drunk. Why he would ever tell Amy Jordan about it Jim had no idea, but he knew immediately that was what Amy wanted to tell him. She was concerned, and now so was Jim; much more than he had been yesterday. Harry didn't have the reputation as particularly violent, but he was undoubtedly connected in some fashion, he did seem able to collect his loan sharking and other debts, and most people were wary of him.

The only thing Jim now liked about Harry was that, in connection with his sports book, he was a genuine expert on baseball and football in general, and on the Red Sox and Patriots in particular. Harry could talk about them not only knowledgably, but also with flair and wit.

Harry talked a lot about women, too, but always with an undercurrent of condescension, resentment, and even general dislike. Jim hated that. Somehow Jim saw an element of 'little girl' in most all women, even the older, battle-hardened stripper/sometime hookers. He had a real worry that someday the flash of blind anger he felt when he saw a woman being mistreated was going to get him into serious trouble. It had already caused him some relatively minor problems. And Amy—well, Jim surely wished Amy hadn't shown him that picture of herself at age six.

Jim didn't really understand Harry's attitude on women, either, because Harry had always had reasonable success with them. Maybe it was because although Harry had good luck with many women, he hadn't had good luck with the right woman . . . which just happened to be exactly the boat Jim himself was in right now. Which was, of course, a painfully disappointing boat, but Jim didn't feel an ounce of resentment towards Dale O'Dell herself, never mind womankind in general.

On the other hand, women absolutely loved the handsome, charming Ted Bundy, who'd then proven pretty damn unappreciative indeed, so who knows?

Amy finally said, "Harry scares me, Jim. He's always asking me to go away with him for the weekend, up to New Hampshire or down to the Cape. Says he'd wine and dine me, treat me like a queen the whole time. Fat fuckin' chance of that, and even fatter fuckin' chance of me going. But he doesn't like it when I turn him down, even though I stand on my fool head trying to be polite about it. Not even once have I told him that if it was up to me I wouldn't even be sitting at this bar with ya, you greasy, oily, smelly, perverted, small-dicked lowlife sleezeball guinny cat fucker! I guess now another thing I'll be thinking but will be too polite to say is that I wish my sweet Jimmy had left you in that stinking dumpster to be ground all up into tiny Harry-bits and deposited in a rat-infested landfill."

Amy was laughing and crying at the same time, so Jim hugged her and gently kissed her on top of her head, as if she still was the six year old in that photo. And, of course, he silently resolved to be both very wary and very observant of Hoary Harry Annunzio, whenever he ran into him at Shenanigans or around the neighborhood—for his own sake as well as for Amy's.

Jim finally got back to reviewing the latest Schraft Street Sports financials—as compiled by Lloyd Dolson—and thinking about Fat Frankie Leonnetti. He knew Frankie was skimming and giving out free drinks—hell, Lloyd kept the books for several bars, and had told him it was inevitable and happened in all of them, and all you could do was review the financials, carefully chart the 'take' in comparison with booze bought and changes in booze inventory, and fire people when the numbers got notably out of whack. Lloyd somehow figured Frankie was dinging Jim to the tune of about $400 a month or $5k per year, and advised Jim to just consider it part of Frankie's salary.

The gregarious Frankie knew all kinds of guys from Bradford and the surrounding towns, and he was a good enough conversationalist and enthusiastic enough cheerleader for the Sox, Pats, B's and C's that Jim had to admit that the personality of Fat Frankie Leonnetti was a key ingredient in the modest success of Schraft Street Sports.

At a very big-boned and burly 5'11" and 250 pounds, Frankie was also a formidable presence keeping order among the bar's generally hard-drinking, blue-collar clientele. Frankie had kept both a baseball bat and a .22 caliber pistol behind the bar, until Jim told him to take the pistol home. Jim figured Frankie hadn't done that, he'd just done a better job of hiding it.

Frankie was a master at genial passive resistance—Jim Herlihy actually had a hard time getting Frankie to do anything that Frankie didn't want to do. It was basically Frankie who decided what beer and booze they'd sell, the prices they'd charge, who got credit and who didn't, who got banned from the place, what part-time help they needed, what time they opened and closed, what needed fixing and what needed replacing. When Jim and Frankie disagreed, Frankie would invariably just wear Jim out. Frankie loved to debate and to negotiate. He was forever haggling with the booze and beer salesmen, and he'd wear them out too.

Jim had offered Frankie a chance to buy 25 percent of the place, but Frankie had declined, saying he didn't want the worry. That made no sense to Jim since Frankie already seemed to live and die with the joint, but of course Jim had absolutely no interest in debating the point.

Frankie also had his own three-decker at the other end of Schraft Street, which he'd meticulously outfitted himself, even nicer than Jim's. Big Bill Donnelly rented the first floor from Frankie, and a couple of the owners of Schraft Street Shenanigans rented the second floor, while Frankie lived on the third floor with his formidable wife, who was a nursing supervisor at Massachusetts General Hospital.

Frankie was a truly gifted handyman, and did most of the maintenance in the bar himself, while charging Jim the full going rate. On his days off, Frankie did what he called "side jobs," generally modernizing kitchens and bathrooms with cabinets, countertops, tile, faucets, showerheads, and other materials he bought at Home Depot or Lowe's. Frankie had done plenty of work on Jim's three-decker and at Herlihy's Hardcore, with Jim acting as his assistant, and trying to learn so in the future he could do his own maintenance.

At the end, Frankie said Jim was the worst handyman he'd ever had the misfortune to try to train, and that Jim should just bite the bullet and forevermore pay Frankie for all his maintenance needs, "even changing light bulbs. That gorgeous little downstairs stripper Amy would make a better carpenter than you, Jim."

Jim couldn't get the overly burly Frankie to join Herlihy's Hardcore, but Frankie was always going in there to plot with Big Bill on expensive improvement projects that Frankie could do, like the special addition next door for the serious young muscleheads.

Jim winced at the agonizing memory of Big Bill and Fat Frankie ganging up on him. That was worse than Jay Arnold, Doug Ballard, and the bouncing burlies combined.

He managed to push Frankie out of his mind, and looked at the little summary of his personal cash flow he'd jotted down:

Average Monthly Gross Income

Herlihy's Hardcore	$1500
Schraft Street Sports	$2000
Net Three-Decker Rents	$1200
1st Book Royalties	$500
Other Investments	$800
Gross Monthly Income	**$6000**

"What an entrepreneur," he thought. "Three pretty major assets, constant attention and headaches, and I'm struggling to gross seventy k a year." And that was, of course, Jim's primary Schraft Street quandary—he just couldn't figure out how to get by without bouncing madly from gym to bar to house to writing, such as it was. They all contributed marginally to his meager living, so he had no choice but to spend time and worry on all of 'em.

His secondary but still quite significant Schraft Street quandary was the people—from Dale O'Dell to Hoary Harry to Amy to his employees to his customers to his tenant cops to, well, the whole neighborhood. Jim was a friendly fella with a very ready and engaging grin and he'd been living in the same house on Schraft Street every single day of his entire thirty-five years, so he knew virtually everyone on Schraft Street. Given the denizens of very rough and tumble Schraft, that was definitely a mixed blessing, at best.

Lloyd Dolson then called, saying that he had an emergency with another client and would have to beg off helping Jim with the relatively routine meeting with Leonnetti. Lloyd's parting shot as he hung up was, "Anyway, Jim, I know how you relish your quality one-on-one time with Fat Frankie."

Schraft Street Sports was diagonally across the street from Jim's three-decker, just beyond The Schraft Street Diner. There was light-colored cedar paneling throughout, and the long, straight bar—which was on the left as you entered, seated twenty on fixed stools, and extended about two-thirds the length of the place—was also light wood. There were a few tables in the back, a few more in the center, and booths comfortably seating four along the right and back walls. Carefully selected photos of the Red Sox historic heroes whose uniform numbers line the roof of Fenway Park adorned the walls, along with photos from the Sox 2004 and 2007 Championships, and from the Pats 2002, 2004, and 2005 Superbowl wins . . . along with pictures of Tom Brady from the heartbreaking losses to the Giants in 2008 and 2012, because Jim considered just getting to the Superbowl a major accomplishment—and absolutely loved the way Tom Brady threw a football.

Jim had also, of course, had no choice but to invest painfully in a number of oversized high-definition TVs, as part of the remodeling he'd paid Frankie to coordinate immediately after Jim bought the place.

Wide-rangingly-sociable Frankie had somehow managed to scrounge up a fair number of autographed baseballs, bats, footballs, and jerseys, and these he kept in a couple of big glass cases behind the bar . . . so those seated at the bar would have something besides paneling and Frankie's own big butt and even bigger belly to stare at.

When Jim walked in, the young part-time bartender was behind the bar, and Frankie was on the phone in the small back office.

Frankie said into the phone, "Boss Jim just got here, I'll get back to ya."

Then he said to Jim, "Trouble, Boss. Best have a seat."

Frankie usually took the ups and downs of the bar totally in stride, or at least did around Jim. Jim winced. This he did not need today.

Frankie said, "Last night 'The Big A' slipped in it turns out hiding a heavy 'foreign load.' You know he usually does all his drinking right here. Place was busy 'cause both the B's and C's were on, and Young Tony called in sick, so I'm running ragged here. No time to talk to 'A' and no reason to think he's already thoroughly juiced. I serve him his usual quick couple doubles, and then he goes down, slipped right off his favorite stool he did. Regulars usually see it coming and catch him he does that, but the guys sitting beside him last night weren't regulars, and they were watching the Bruins anyway. Bottom line, he hit his fool head hard on the floor, knocked out, blood, concussion, commotion, ambulanced off actually. Cop I don't know came by later with questions."

Jim had, over the years, suggested banning 'The Big A' (more formally Andy Andrews) from Schraft Street Sports many, many times, because the guy obviously had a huge problem. But Frankie always protested that The A was harmless, a thoroughly amiable drunk, had many friends among the regulars, paid for his drinks and bought his fair share for barmates, lived right down the street and didn't even own a car, and would be thoroughly lost if he had to do his drinking elsewhere. Frankie didn't think banning The Big A would be anywhere close to doing the guy a favor. Jim didn't like the idea of making money off of someone else's severe problem . . . but short of firing Frankie, he knew he was not going to get The Big A out of Schraft Street Sports.

Jim just said, "Admitted to the hospital?"

"Overnight. I personally picked him up and brought him home this morning. Nurse cussed me out as a dickhead for over-serving him, doc thought I was family and told me A's got a decent case of 'Mickey Mantle Liver' and I gotta get him to quit drinking as of right now. 'A' told me his head hurt but he's a gamer not a quitter; and will be at his assigned post on time at the usual six PM; have the stool empty and waiting for me, please, Frank. Told me that yesterday a couple co-workers at the factory took him to The Ninety-Nine and then Shenanigans down the street for his birthday, hence the unusual 'imported load.' Apologized profusely for cheating on Schraft Street Sports, and swore up and down he wouldn't dream of suing his absolute favorite place in the world. 'Least he does have good Blue Cross from the factory, so no unpaid medical to worry about. My wife is off today, and she said she'd check in on him a couple times this afternoon, plus give him the 'next drink could be your last,' spiel, not 'cause we have any real hope it will take, but out of her strong sense of nursely duty. And love of ballbusting in general, I s'pose."

Jim said, "Yeah, you won't buy into the joint, I should see if Marnie will. *Then* you'd listen to ownership."

"No, Jim, then I'd work at Shenanigans with Big Bill. I already spend way more than enough time around my Marnie . . . yeah, and I'm sure you'd love having *her* for a partner. But Jim, something else happened last night."

"Give me a fuckin' break."

"Cannot believe the bad luck. Eddy Harcharik got drunk and stayed past his curfew, that crazy wife of his stormed in, grabbed his big beer and poured it over his head, and then threw the heavy mug at the wall. The amazingly bad luck is that the stranger cop came in to bust my balls 'bout The A hittin' the damn deck was just about to leave, 'cept that freakin' mug just missed his skull. I can't believe how hard Harcharik's skinny madwoman of a wife threw that big mug, she must have been a softball player or somethin.' Anyway, cop said he's gonna go check our incident history, see what kind of blood bucket we been running here. Somehow we have had an unusual number of dust-ups lately. Bottom line, you better have a word with Sergeant Carrollton."

Boston Police Sergeant Carlton Carrollton had played high school football with Jim and Hoary Harry, and was now one of the three Boston Police Sergeants renting Jim's renovated three-bedroom first floor apartment. Carlton was the senior of the three sergeants, the one Jim knew best, and the most friendly and reasonable of the three. Carrollton competed in local powerlifting competitions, was a member of Herlihy's Hardcore, and liked to work out with Big Bill, although he wasn't nearly as strong. Actually, although Carrollton worked much harder at lifting and weighed about thirty pounds more, he really wasn't all that much stronger than Jim.

Shortly after Carlton and his cohorts moved in, Jim had said, "Hey Carl, ya know Shenanigans dancers adorable Amy Jordan and her friend very, *very* curvy Consuela?"

"I've had professional cause to visit Shenanigans a time or two," replied Carrollton. "That gorgeous little Amy is kinda hard to miss. You're too old for her, Boss; and she'd be *way* too much trouble for you. Whatever you got in mind, I'd advise against it."

"Amy, Consuela, and this other dancer I don't know are willing to rent my second for the full asking; and I need the dough quite badly . . . unless you know someone more appropriate."

Carrollton considered this mildly surprising idea for a few seconds, shrugged, and then said, "I have asked around for ya, and come up empty. As you know all too well, appropriate ain't all that prevalent here on Schraft. Well, no law against stripping. And we're not vice. Minor drugs and occasional very discreet hooking . . . what we don't know won't hurt them—or you. Anything thrown in our face will . . . including excessive noise."

"So noted. I like home life reasonably calm and quiet myself. Amy and her 'Suela are, underneath it all, surprisingly reasonable. If not, out they go . . . and they're willing to give me a decent security deposit, too."

Jim collected the rent from Carrollton and—although he was the most reasonable of the three first floor tenants—that rent was often late. When Jim's 'Cops, Gangsters, and Strippers' novel had made some money, Jim had cut the rent for a couple months, as well as buying all those drinks.

Jim *never* gave discounts on gym memberships . . . he didn't want to set any dangerous precedents, or, especially, confuse Big Bill in any way.

Overall, Jim knew Carrollton had expected more for the stories and cop's viewpoint he'd provided Jim as background for the book. And now Jim was planning a second book . . . and apparently, to ask Carrollton for help with this new cop who was undoubtedly going to be some kind of a thorn in the side of Schraft Street Sports.

Jim now said, "Gotta watch these knuckleheads closer, Frank."

"Explained the unusual 'A' situation, Boss. Harcharik was sitting at a table swapping rounds with four other UPS guys, pretty freakin' hard to monitor individual intake when I'm running ragged. I do hear ya, Boss, but you know this is competitively-priced Boston blue-collar neighborhood; guys don't drink, we're outta business."

Jim sighed, wondering what had possessed him in the first place. "Do the best ya can, Frank; tell young Tony too."

Jim then decided to wait 'till later in the week to review the bar numbers with Frankie. That was always torturous, and he'd had enough Fat Frankie Leonnetti for one day.

CHAPTER FOUR

The Schraft Street Diner, Schraft Street Clothing, Herlihy's Hardcore—And The Four Grannies

Jim had been thinking of an intense mid-afternoon leg workout to blast that bad-news-fest with Frankie right out of his mind, but he was suddenly very hungry, and The Schraft Street Diner was just down the street. The Diner had a small strip steak on the menu, and over the years they'd learned to season it and cook it just the way Jim liked it. It was now right between lunch and dinner crowds, The Diner should be empty, so Jim went in.

The Diner *was* mostly empty, but still not even close to empty enough. Amy Jordan and her roommates were having a late, pre-shift lunch. And they were hardly going to let Jim eat alone. Worse, Fabulous Faye—a stripper/not hooker who'd finally gotten too old for that business and had transferred her talents (and loud Fran Drescher-voice) from Schraft Street Shenanigans to The Schraft Street Diner—was on duty.

So, accepting the absolutely inevitable (which he realized he'd been doing a lot lately) Jim sat in the booth beside Amy, facing the other two, who were grinning wickedly. Undoubtedly figuring they'd be able to finesse Jim into picking up their check. Probably just by getting up and walking out the door, since they'd already ordered and would undoubtedly finish their food before he did.

"We were just talking about you, Bossman," said Amy, with a wry, very cute grin. "Living right in the same building, we get to see your comings and goings. Speaking of comings, though, lately you're *always* alone. And lucky little me has the privilege of cleaning up after you, and I never find any sticky tissues, if you catch my nosy perverted drift. What's up? Had your testicles removed or something?"

Truth be told, Jim had been feeling more than a little anxious lately. And truth be even further told, he did find his greedily wanton booth mates very sexy indeed. Amy in her adorably sweet-but-still-sexy-waifness, the other two in their very shapely-butted sluttiness. But 'little sister' Amy he just wasn't gonna do, period—and the other two were now strictly off limits because that would be just too painful for the smitten Amy.

"My life is complicated enough lately without letting my dick start getting me into trouble, too, thanks for asking; and no offense meant to thee or thine."

Amy said, "Yeah, that damn Dr. Dale at the gym. I know, Jimbo, I know. Uppity bitch. Although I do like her anyway."

Jim said, "She's not a doctor yet, the designation is P. A. She hasn't even started med school. She will be a doctor eventually, though, of that I have no doubt."

Amy did periodically work out at the gym, and Dale O'Dell had tried some 'big sisterly' counseling that hadn't worked, surprise surprise. They were friends of a sort anyway.

Amy said, "That rich modeling guy Doug is a total babe, can't deny that. Somehow I still think he's a phony asshole. Plus he looks at me like he's expecting a few freebies, even though he has to know I'm both a pro and a friend of Dale's. Conceited cocksucker."

Amy's sexiest roommate—a very shapely thirty-five-year-old Italian named Consuela who would be Jim's first choice had he been so inclined—said, "That Doug Babe drives a fuckin' Ferrari; I'd give him some freebies wouldn't turn out so free."

"I bet," said Jim, unable to suppress a broad, agreeable grin.

Consuela continued, "Bossman, you got a gym, a bar, and a three-decker, but we still know you basically ain't got a pot to piss in. Don't even own a car, for Chrissake. Any one of us be more than happy to give you a couple freebies as samples, that really *would* be free."

"Samples. Then I get addicted to your considerable charms just one floor down, be pretty freaking far from free in the long run, methinks. I'd end up paying you rent."

"If either of you fat old sluts boink my sweet Jimmy, I'm gonna stab ya in your sleep," proclaimed Amy, albeit still sporting an adorable smile that took every bit of the sting out of the insult and mock threat. "But the idiot's being faithful to an uppity bitch now won't give him the time of day. Although I do still like her anyway."

Consuela said with a surprisingly sweet laugh, "Boss Jim, we know how you feel about that damn Dale, but ya could at least jerk off once in a while."

Jim winced, shrugged, finally grinned at his booth mates, and replied, "I'm not admitting a damn thing at this advanced age, but I did figure out when I was twelve that there are *discreet* methods of disposal. Patton Oswalt should have known better. No one wants to hear their mother say, 'You're disgusting. No one has a cold every single day for twenty-five years.' Especially don't wanna hear it while driving. Point being I'm sufficiently savvy that Amy's forensic investigations are forever futile."

Amy said, "I don't know who Patton Oswalt is but now I feel bad for his mother anyway. I'm gonna join your gym again, Jim, so you have to raise my maid pay."

When Amy was drinking too much (actually she always drank too much by Jim's standards, it pretty much went with her job, so when she was drinking *way* too much) Jim had promised her a discounted gym membership to help her cut back and generally get things under control. But then he remembered he didn't want to encourage or confuse Big Bill, so he'd just increased what he paid her for doing his cleaning, laundry, food shopping, and little bit of surprisingly palatable cooking.

Amy was in workout mode more often than not, partly because she really did want to stay in virtually perfect shape, and partly because she enjoyed the considerable attention paid to her by the studly young workout guys at the gym. These guys weren't exactly Harvard grads, but some of 'em were a clear cut above most of the clientele at Shenanigans. On the other hand, of course, some of 'em were the clientele at Shenanigans.

Best Jim knew, though, Amy didn't give out freebies to any of them either.

Fabulous Faye came to take his order, laughing, and saying too loudly in Drescher-voice, "The lovely ladies caught ya again, Jim. You look overwhelmed, and who could blame you? The usual steak, salad, and big class of ice-cold milk?"

Jim just muttered, "Yeah. I'm always overwhelmed, here, there, and everywhere. Hell, Faye, *you* overwhelm me even when I have the great good fortune to be eating here alone."

Amy pouted, pounded his thigh, kissed him on the cheek, and said, "You lie. You love to see us coming. And I'm gonna get ya yet."

Faye said, now quietly, "She will, Jim, she surely will."

Amy's two roommates did indeed excuse themselves for the ladies' as soon as they'd finished their meals, and Jim knew they wouldn't be back. In fact, how could he not, since they were blatantly laughing and winking at each other.

Amy stayed, and said, "You know, Jim, I bet I could boink that Doug Babe, and then tell Dale about it, and that he's a phony sleezeball cheater. Not that I want you with Dale 'stead of me, but I'll do it for ya anyway. Plus even though I don't like that Doug Babe, boinking him might be fun . . . might not be, though, 'cause he's gotta be selfish and self-absorbed in the rack, just like he is everywhere else."

"Please, Amy, don't be boinking anybody on my account."

Amy then sincerely offered to pay the ladies' check, but Jim just shook his head, smiled a little sadly, and told her to go on and get to work; and to behave herself best she could under the unfortunate circumstances. And, of course, to continue to be very, very careful.

Jim finished his steak in blissful peace, once again marveling at how tasty it was, for a little neighborhood diner like this. They even had good bread. And great breakfasts, always served quick and piping hot.

Best of all, as the dinner hour approached, the place had gotten busy enough that Fabulous Faye for once didn't have time to bother him, or even to sell him one of her own special pies for dessert, that she invented, baked at home, and brought in to work. Just like Keri Russell in *Waitress*; which is where Fabulous Faye got the idea, she'd told Jim about a hundred times. Faye would usually then start blubbering about the tragic fate of *Waitress* Writer/Director/Actress Adrienne Shelley. Thus overwhelmed, Jim would inevitably end up buying several pies to take home. Everyone said the pies really were Fabulous but Jim didn't like pie and had never tried one. He left them on the counter in his apartment for Amy and cohorts, who loved the pies; and, actually, pretty much anything they could get for free.

Waitress happened to be on HBO so Jim watched it. But he still didn't much get the pie thing. Mostly he fumed at Russell's cluelessly abusive husband, and then beamed at the accidental, ill-timed, and unwanted baby upon birth magically morphing into a very much-loved little girl indeed.

But then, before he could slip safely out of The Diner, The Four Grannies came in. Like The Famous Foursome at the gym, The Four Grannies were always together . . . and, also like The Foursome, they loved Jim Herlihy. Jim didn't mind too much, because all four of The Grannies were mothers of kids—three boys and one girl—that Jim had gone to school with, and knew pretty well. Those four old friends had all moved away, a couple to the suburbs and a couple out of state, were married, had kids, and at least half-decent jobs. Jim didn't get to see them much anymore, and genuinely enjoyed getting very enthusiastic updates from the proudly beaming Grannies. Especially since these four old friends were all doing reasonably well—which was, unfortunately, all too rare amongst those Jim had grown up with.

The Grannies even enjoyed Jim's patented schtick with them, which was—even as Jim was sincerely "oohing" and "aahing" over the latest pictures of their cute little grandkids—telling them creative outrageous and/or nonsensical stories about shenanigans their kids had pulled off in the old days, such as streaking sold-out Fenway Park on a sun-splashed Saturday afternoon, getting into Boston's infamous Naked Eye strip club when they were only sixteen, *very* bloodily brawling with drunken young South Boston Irishmen during several Saint Patrick's Day Parades for no reason whatsoever, going down to the very dangerous deeply flooded Quincy Quarries to high-dive and drink beer, briefly stealing a police car, drag racing on The Southeast Expressway at three in the morning, thumbing to New York City when they were supposed to be on a camping trip, running errands for notorious local mobsters, and even swimming with a couple of tiger sharks off Falmouth Heights Beach, down the Cape. Many of the stories weren't true a'tall, but enough were comical exaggerations of notorious misdeeds that the ladies had found out about that they now could never be totally sure whether Jim was pulling their leg or not—and he'd never say. At any rate, The Grannies got a kick out of it all, and today Jim left The Diner grinning.

Jim's three-decker was almost directly across the street from The Diner, and Herlihy's Hardcore was then a couple minute further walk beyond his house. The weather had now gotten even worse—it had started sleeting, for Chrissake. Schraft Street sure looked gloomy under these conditions, and at this time of day . . . but you couldn't deny that there was a lot to do without walking far. Good stuff and not-so-good stuff.

He went up to his apartment and changed into a warm-up suit Amy had picked out for him at Schraft Street Clothing when he'd given her money to buy him workout clothes. It really was a good-looking suit, and, more important, unusually comfortable, his favorite; Amy actually had an excellent sense of style, and seemed to care more about how Jim looked than he did. For the last couple years she'd bought all his clothes—and all at Schraft Street Clothing, which was where most of the young denizens of the gym, bar, and strip club bought their clothes—and everyone told Jim he was finally dressing better. Jim didn't much care about that, he was just happy he didn't have to shop for clothes anymore. One less thing.

The Famous Four were at the gym, training under the kind and empathetic eyes of Dale O'Dell, which they did periodically. They were serious about losing weight and getting generally healthier, but were also always more than happy to seize the opportunity to take a break; the appearance of Jim Herlihy being perhaps their favorite such opportunity.

Despite Dale's ardent protests that they ought to keep up the momentum, all four hurried over to proudly point out to Jim their latest collective progress report, which was now prominently posted on the bulletin board . . . tracking individual and collective weights, accompanied by colorful pictures in their very stylish workout clothes.

All four of the bouncing burlies were experienced paralegals, and Linda was a supervisor; apparently also unusually competent, at least to hear her friends tell it, who also had confided to Jim that her annual income was well over a hundred k, just to make sure he'd know what a catch she was. At any rate, they certainly had enough money to dress well. Jim had, of course, also realized that not just Linda, but probably all four of them made more money than he did.

Dale had carefully weighed them in when they joined the gym and engaged her training services, and it was actually the four ladies themselves who had gleefully publicized the fact that collectively they weighed exactly a thousand pounds, to the gram. The kind-hearted Dale O'Dell certainly would not have done that.

That even-grand starting point did make it easy to track their collective progress, and today they were excited that collectively they'd broken the eight-hundred-pound barrier, coming in at 799. Jim had written numerous articles for *The Bradford Bulletin* about the exploits of gym members such as Jay Arnold, Big Bill, Dale, and even Doug Ballard, among others. The Famous Foursome were now convinced that an article by Jim Herlihy in *The Bulletin* celebrating their collective 20 percent weight loss accomplished over just about a year-and-a-half would cement their legend.

Dale said, "Jim, the ladies would really like it and they deserve it. So far, all your articles have been celebrating the young and super-fit members. But over half your business is ordinary folks just trying to stay in decent shape. So it's not only the right thing to do, it's also the smart thing to do."

Jim was shaking his head but smiling broadly despite himself, so Linda said, "He's gonna do it, I know he is, Dale . . . stop that gorgeous grinning, Jim, you're making my heart flutter again."

Lately Jim couldn't leave the house without being overwhelmed. Hell, between Amy, her roommates, and the three Boston Police Sergeants all living right below him, home was hardly a safe-haven either. Even at three AM.

So now, instead of picking the brains of the cops and strippers and gangsters and assorted lowlifes at Schraft Street Sports and Schraft Street Shenanigans for fascinating grist for that overdue and desperately-needed sequel, he was gonna be interviewing four women averaging two-hundred-pounds-per regarding their passion for diet and exercise. And probably their life stories. Undoubtedly at their hangout of choice—IHOP. None of 'em drank, and they were loudly proud of it. He also knew he'd be forced to rewrite that article several times before it suited 'em.

And *The Bradford Bulletin* definitely wouldn't pay him for the article— hell, they'd probably try to classify it as advertising and charge him.

Jim had worked at *The Bradford Bulletin* as a printer's assistant and then as a printer while in high school, and while studying English and Journalism at the Boston Campus of The University of Massachusetts. After graduation, he continued to work there, as a local reporter and columnist, and then as an assistant editor. He certainly didn't make much money doing that, but he sure did get to know his neighbors . . . and future bar and gym customers.

In fact, he'd never worked anywhere but *The Bradford Bulletin*, only leaving when he'd inherited the money he used to buy Schraft Street Sports and to set up Herlihy's Hardcore Gym. And to buy himself the time to finish his first novel.

Although the bar and the gym and even the writing hadn't quite turned out as Jim had hoped—and the bar and the gym could certainly be most frustrating, and Jim had undeniably enjoyed working for *The Bulletin* for as long as he'd been there—he still had precious little second thought about having left, because his salary from *The Bulletin* and income from the inheritance conservatively invested would have earned him even less than he was making now. And, he had no doubt that he'd have eventually gotten thoroughly sick of the generally repetitive work at *The Bulletin*; and probably sooner rather than later.

As Jim walked towards the Leg Area in general and the squat racks in particular, he saw Jay Arnold warming up his massively muscled thighs and his thick, sturdy knees with leg extensions. Distracted by Dale and The Famous Four, Jim hadn't had a chance to check out the Leg Area for potential problematic conditions. Jay had no workout partner this afternoon, hated to work out alone, and he was absurdly thrilled to have unsuspecting Jim happen along. For a second Jim thought Jay was gonna give him a huge sweaty, tank-topped bear hug.

Jim especially hated to do squats with Jay. It wasn't just that Jay would excitedly recite to Jim all the sets, reps, and weights he'd done in his last workout, and what all his improvement goals were for this one. Or that Jay would loudly curse and stomp around after a set that hadn't gone as planned, as bad as 'The Youk' after popping out with the bases loaded.

It was that Jay squatted with ridiculously heavy weights, in excellent form but with an almost-all-out level of exertion that Jim would never dream of subjecting his own knees to. It hurt Jim's knees just watching him. And Jim was convinced that it was inevitable that sooner or later Jay was gonna hurt himself, and Jim Herlihy did not want to be around when he did.

When Jim or Dale or Big Bill or other members with some knowledge and half a brain would tentatively caution Jay, the professional builder would snarl, "My knees feel fuckin' great and this is how I make a living. You're gonna jinx me with that pussy bullshit!"

They worked up together to 315, Jim doing fifteen relatively easy reps, Arnold an absurdly easy ten. Arnold loaded the bar to 405, and did an almost equally easy ten. When Jim stripped the bar back down to 315 for his next set, Arnold sputtered, "Ya gotta be shittin' me, Boss Jim. You got good legs. That 315 is a fuckin' feather for ya!"

Jim couldn't help but chuckle. "For the thousandth time, Big Jay, I'm just workin' to keep the wheels fit and toned. I need 'em healthy so I can wander up and down Schraft Street dazed and getting my balls busted."

After Jim did the same relatively easy fifteen reps with the 315, Jay loaded the bar to 495 for his next ten. That was no strain either.

After the set he said, "Boss Jim, you got good genetics and excellent natural symmetry, plus the ladies tell me you're a handsome fucker. Not as handsome as that faggot Ballard, apparently, but handsome enough. You could win some contests and look good doing it, ya really busted your balls. Put your own picture on the walls, help business. You say watching me bust it hurts your knees. Watching you pussying around hurts my heart."

"Thirty-five years old, Big Jay. Other priorities, son."

Jim did at least push the reps with 315 up to twenty, which did have his thighs burning, and especially his lungs near to bursting. That mollified Jay a little, or at least got him off Jim's workout, and back to gleefully expounding on the intricate details of his own.

When Jim spotted Jay for his final now 'balls-to-the-wall' set of ten with 625, Jim was really wincing, and holding his breath. He breathed a sigh of relief when Jay, after they'd racked the huge weight, clapped his hands loudly, and exclaimed, "Great set, and my knees feel fuckin' fine, Bossman!"

Jim thought but certainly didn't say—since Arnold would just take it negatively—"Yeah, congratulations, Big Jay; but those risky all-out squats with 625 freaking pounds are definitely one of those endeavors where everything *is* just fine . . . until all at once everything is pretty fuckin' *far* from fine!"

Nearing the end of the bizarre workout, the image from *The Sopranos* of Capo Eugene Pontecorvo twitching after hanging himself in his basement popped into Jim's head, and it stayed until Jay was out of sight; off to work his huge calves for forty-five minutes with a young amateur builder who'd most fortuitously happened along. This young musclehead would be all ears as Jay talked sets and reps and weights, begging for ever more detail, and encouraging Jay to show him those flexed calves from one more angle.

Jim happily went off to do cardio on the stair-stepper, to be followed by hammering the heavy bag. Jim had naturally muscular calves, and was never gonna bother doing any special work for them, beyond running and other endurance work.

But on his way from the stair-stepper to the boxing room Dale O'Dell accosted him.

"You're running the Big Jerk Capital of the world! Why would anyone with half a heart want to spend five minutes wallowing in this retarded macho bullshit? And you . . . just because you're smaller and quieter about it doesn't mean you're not every bit the humongous asshole he is . . . actually, you're even worse, because you're a hypocrite too, who has the power to make it better."

Jim, genuinely dismayed, said, "Yikes. Big Bill was disrespectful to The Famous Foursome? I can't believe it."

"That's another story. But today he made fun of the way the 'Gay Guys' are dressing and acting lately, they protested and insulted him right back, far more cleverly, and Bill got mad and gave them a really bad time. Jay runs around half-naked in here, and no one says a word about it."

The 'Gay Guys' were a group of eight—four couples, it sort of appeared to Jim and he surely wasn't gonna delve into it—who frequented both the gym and Schraft Street Sports. They lived in an apartment building everyone referred to as 'Strippersville' at the other end of Schraft Street, which was also home to many of the employees of Schraft Street Shenanigans. They'd been obvious but muted, and generally no one bothered them at any of these venues, although Jim certainly knew there were plenty of regulars at the bar who'd always been uncomfortable around them. Frankie Leonnetti was definitely in that category.

But lately they'd become increasingly loud, flamboyant, and publicly affectionate. Big Bill and Fat Frankie had, separately, complained to Jim about it. Jim could not trust either of them to diplomatically talk to the GG's about toning it back down, so one more thing for him. Jim had always found them not only absolutely harmless, but funny, intelligent, well informed, and interesting, and had enjoyed bantering with them.

So, although he did it as carefully as possible, their feelings were still hurt, and they responded basically in the vein, "We thought you understood and were our friend. We're gonna be ourselves and stand up for our rights. And we spend a lot of money in your bar and in your gym. We buy more of your protein shakes and fancy juice drinks than anyone, by the way." Which was true, they loved sitting around the juice bar, and watching the young muscleheads (male and female) work out, commenting on the bodies and especially on the workout clothing. Three of them worked at Schraft Street Clothing as buyers/managers, and were undoubtedly a key component of the local clothing store's surprising success, especially in selling to the young, hip, and fit.

In the course of that uncomfortable conversation it came out that they'd taken an eye-opening trip to San Francisco, and joined a prominent Gay Rights Organization whose name Jim couldn't remember. In any event, he hadn't thought he'd gotten anywhere. Jim was amazed and dismayed that one of the guys was actually in tears at the end. But then, they had toned it down some, at least for a while.

Today Jim said, "It's kinda hard to control Big Bill, and the Gay Guys haven't been making it easy lately either, Dale."

"Everyone really likes you here, Jim, and respects you. You can do a better job. With Big Bill, The Famous Foursome, the Gay Guys, the middle-aged housewives . . . and even with Doug. He thinks you don't like him."

Jim internally smiled at the insane concept of him liking Doug Ballard. But he just said, "I only have so much time . . . and mental energy, Dale."

Speaking of Doug, he was now on his way over, and for the first time in his life Jim was happy to see the bastard coming—and to hand the lovely Dale O'Dell over to him.

Jim had done some amateur boxing as a teenager, getting plenty of expert instruction in the process. He'd always loved to pound the heavy bag, and considered it both the most enjoyable and most productive of his cardio work. Today, working off the frustrations of the day and the week, Jim lost himself in a whirlwind of expert hard and fast non-stop left and right combinations. Jim had unusually good endurance from both nature and extensive hard work, and also knew how to integrate smooth, controlled breathing into the flurry of frenetic activity.

When he finally ran down, he realized one of the young MMA enthusiasts had been sitting and watching while waiting for the bag.

The kid whistled, and said, "Boss Jim, I have never seen anyone pound the damn thing so hard and so fast for so freaking *long*. If you ever go off on a person like that, they'll be arresting ya for murder. You in the slammer, Big Bill will *really* be crazy!"

"Don't tell anyone, kid, but the recent behavior of Monstrous Bill was one of my primary inspirations for all that."

But Jim then grinned at that thought, realizing, of course, that it was life in general—as well as Schraft Street in general—that had inspired his especially frenetic session tonight. Actually having Monstrous Bill specifically in mind while pounding on the bag was every bit as absurd as picturing Hoary Harry's fragile-looking little mug at the end of those punches; opposite ends of the spectrum though those images certainly were.

When Jim took off his bag gloves in the locker room, he saw that the hand wraps underneath were soaked in blood. He'd absolutely ripped the hell out of his knuckles, and hadn't felt a thing.

CHAPTER FIVE

Old Friends, Cops, Accountants, Gangsters, and Schraft Street Shenanigans

ON FRIDAY MORNING, JIM GOT a call from Keith Garrity, his closest friend through high school and college, and the quarterback who threw to Jim in high school. Garrity had earned an MBA from the University of Massachusetts. Tall, lean, presentable, and personable, Garrity had put himself through college and grad school working as a popular bartender at several downtown Boston hot spots, first in touristy Fanueil Hall, and later in the new Liberty Wharf section, at the southern end of the city, on the water and on the border between downtown and South Boston. He'd eventually worked himself up to night manager.

Garrity absolutely despised the Boston winters, and after graduation, he'd moved to West Palm Beach, Florida, as a general manager in a trendy nightclub in WPB's downtown City Place. Jim talked to him every few weeks, and knew Keith was doing well and liked Florida every bit as much as he'd thought he would.

This morning Garrity said, "Hey, Jim, they want me to buy into this place, and I got some savings and a loan arranged to do just that. Club is doing good, but one of the older owners wants to take his dough and move to California to be near his daughter moved out there. What are you up to?"

"Up to? My fool neck in crazy weightlifters, gym managers, bartenders, falling-down-drunks, strippers, hookers, gangsters, gay guys, and cops, I guess. Plus the usual gray skies, sleet, general griminess. Let the good times roll, old friend."

"Ouch! Reason I called, actually. I'm able to buy in but the guy who's leaving owned 50 percent of the jumpin' joint, and I can't swing all that right now. Business is good and getting even better, so the ownership ain't cheap. Lately you seem pretty fed up with ol' Schraft Street. You sign a letter of intent for 20 percent of this place, and this fella'd be happy to wait until you'd sold your Schraft Street holdings to get your share of his dough. Seriously."

Jim was taken aback. He whined to Keith regularly, and they'd certainly kicked around the idea of Jim someday moving down there, but it hadn't got past the level of general bullshitting, and swapping war stories . . . Keith about how much fun he was having and how much tail he was getting, Jim about how much Schraft Street nonsense he could absorb without hanging himself.

"Wow. Sell my Schraft Street holdings and actually move to West Palm Beach, Florida. No more Big Bill, Bouncing Burlies, Fat Frankie, Hoary Harry, or Fallen Angel Amy . . . or girl of my dreams Dale. Yikes. I have to think about this, old bud."

"You don't know enough to really think about it, Jim," replied Keith. "Been promising to come down and see the place for three years, haven't left Schraft Street yet. So come down now, check out the town, the club, the numbers, the gyms, the beaches, the warm weather . . . and especially the babes. You can't get laid here, there's no hope for ya."

"I do like the sound of that last anyway, I surely do," said Jim, savoring a solitary big grin. "Nail some taut and tanned Florida dolly, and then two days later you're fifteen hundred freaking miles away from the bitch. Sweet."

"Well, don't come down and *pretend* to be interested just for an out-of-town boink, please. But if you've got half a mind to really look at the numbers and consider it, then let's get 'er planned."

So now, on top of everything else, in a couple weeks Jim would be spending a few days in Florida. And several hundred dollars getting there and back.

Jim had mixed feelings when he hung up. Intriguing possibility . . . but this just might not be the best time for him to be making momentous decisions like this.

Editor Steve Chadwick called to see if he'd made any progress on that front, and Jim was able to tell him he'd made arrangements to buy Sergeant Carrollton dinner that very evening, to search for authentic ideas. He didn't tell Chadwick that the first order of business with the Sergeant would be for help in dealing with potential repercussions from crashing 'Big A's' and smashing big beer mugs.

Amy came up to clean, and for the usual suggestive banter, and other semi-entertaining nonsense, but she also still had Hoary Harry heavy on her mind. He'd been unusually drunk at the bar in Shenanigans every night this week, and she was getting really tired of dodging him all night long.

Then she looked Jim in the eye, and, with lower lip slightly quivering, added, "I think it's now even worse than that, Jim. Last night late he was finally *so* hammered the other owners talked him into leaving before we closed. I was walking home alone at two when I saw him passed out in his car with a damn bottle in his hand, parked on *our* side of the street. I'm worried he was waiting for me—with what intentions I cannot be sure . . . actually, drunk as he was, undoubtedly he had no idea himself."

"Damn!" exclaimed Jim. "Why the knucklehead has to get so stupidly drunk lately I have no idea. Plus, he's one of those pain-in-the-ass idiots whose already marginal personality changes for the worse even after only a couple drinks."

"Why you had to dunk him in that dumpster."

"Well yeah, but back then—and actually even up until relatively recently—he wasn't that bad a guy, 'cause a lot of the time he'd be sober."

Amy thought for a moment, and then said, "Yeah, I guess. I've always been a little uncomfortable around him, but I remember when I first started at Shenanigans I didn't mind him too much. Was never gonna hit the hay with him, though, at anything remotely resembling a reasonable price. Actually, not at any price, 'cause if nothing else I got enough sense not to get indebted to guys like Hoary Harry Annunzio."

"One of these days, Amy, you'll have enough sense to find another line of work entirely."

"Sense I already got, Gentle Jimbo. It's money put back I'm working on."

Jim just sighed and shook his head, and then finally, reluctantly, agreed to stop in after his dinner with Carrollton, and have a diplomatic—but now *very* firm and straightforward—word with The Hoary One.

On the other hand, of course, meticulously planned diplomacy is often wasted, when one is dealing with the totally legless. ("Hold that thought. I gotta go puke.")

Jim would in fact be ready for a few beers tonight, it was just that Schraft Street Shenanigans and Hoary Harry would certainly not provide the soothing surroundings he'd be in need of by then. Not only did he have the good Sergeant scheduled for dinner—undoubtedly with Fabulous Faye waiting on them—but before that he'd have his rescheduled session with Fat Frankie on the bar finances, along with some painfully contentious discussion on repairs and upgrades Frankie was proposing. Which would, of course, transfer yet more dough from Jim's pocket into Frankie's. At least Lloyd Dolson would be available for this meeting.

The meeting with The Fat Fella was as frustrating as expected—both Jim and Lloyd thought the numbers showed Frankie had upped the skimming a little, but Frankie's protestations of total innocence and hurt feelings were as unshakable as ever, and at the end Frankie had his usual daunting list of mandatory maintenance projects he'd be happy to perform, at his usual exorbitant hourly rate. Including a major remodel of the ladies' room.

It was true that the relative handful of women who frequented Schraft Street Sports were loudly critical of their accommodations. (The mantra of the male customers was, "Shut up about it. You should see the men's room.")

Jim's opinion on the matter was that the hardcore little sports bar didn't have that many female customers; the few they did have didn't spend much money; and these particular ladies weren't much fun to look at and even less to listen to. And that, when it came to women, between tenants, gym, diner, and strip club, he was already beleaguered enough. He ardently wished the law still allowed Men-Only Taverns, as it certainly should; *man*kind's inalienable right of refuge, which had been overlooked in The Constitution, proving that The Founding Fathers weren't perfect.

At any rate, Jim wasn't in any hurry to spend money he didn't have to encourage 'em.

Sergeant Carlton Carrollton did have some decent new cop and gangster stories, both funny and scary. Jim took copious notes. And Carrollton did at least know who that new cop was, who'd been snooping around Schraft Street Sports. He said he'd look into the matter, but, depending, there might end up being a cost. One way or the other.

Then Carrollton said, "Perhaps Mr. Leonnetti might offer some timely and carefully conceived counseling to your most overly enthusiastic patrons."

"That, Officer, would entail Mr. Leonnetti actually doing what he was told; right here on Schraft Street. I'll keep trying, but I'm not optimistic."

Carrollton was a good-sized weightlifting guy and he put away two of those tasty little Diner strip steaks at Jim's expense, and then he ate one of Faye's Fabulous Pies all by himself. Watching the interaction between those two, Jim realized that Carrollton was probably eating Faye all by himself too. Relative to both the pie and especially Faye, Jim thought "*way* better him than me."

Harry was at the bar at Shenanigans, there was an open seat beside him, and he was already well on his way; but definitely not there yet.

Jim said, "Buy ya a beer, Harry?"

"Beer? I haven't drunk beer in years. I'll have a double scotch, though, ya insist."

Jim said, "The good thing about beer, especially light beer, is that ya can enjoy a fair bit of it, and still know where you are and who you are. I love light beer for that very."

"Alright, Boss Hoss, you insist, I'll have a beer with ya. For old times sake. Just don't dump my scrawny ass in any nasty dumpsters for old times sake, ya musclebound fucker. And make the beer Stella, at least, not that watery piss you drink."

So the good news was that Harry had agreed to switch, at least momentarily, from scotch to beer. The bad news was that the arrival of his powerful 16-ounce Stella inspired him to much too quickly down the last half of his double scotch. It certainly did not look like Jim would have much time to reason with Hoary Harry tonight.

Jim said, "So how's it going, Harry? And why the hell are you suddenly bringing up ancient high school hijinks?"

"Hijinks? Don't hear that word much in my circles. Hijacks, yeah, those I'm familiar with . . . How come I treat that gorgeous little Amy like a damn queen, she ignores me, you ignore her, and she's all over your ass. And how come you never nail any these sexy bitches? You ain't a normal guy, Boss Jim."

"Never said I was. Got a lot on my plate lately, just tryin' to keep things as simple as I can. You?"

Harry paused a few seconds, took a very big swig out of that 5.2% Stella, and said, "You don't really wanna know, Boss Jim. But let's just say I've temporarily sort of fallen into disfavor. Not soon-to-be-history disfavor, but on the outside-looking-in dis-fuckin'-favor. 'Nuff said on that . . . If I can't fuck that gorgeous little Amy, maybe you should nail her, and then tell me all about it. And I do mean every last fuckin' detail, son."

Jim turned towards Harry, leaned in a little, looked hard into Harry's eyes, and said, "Seriously, Harry, that little Amy is at heart a sweet little girl who was born into very bad circumstance, and evilly mistreated right from the beginning. I'm no fuckin' gangster, but if both her abusing stepfathers weren't already dead I'd beat 'em to death slow, grinning ear-to-ear the while."

Harry slugged down the rest of his Stella, and ordered his usual double scotch before Jim could advise otherwise.

Then Harry said, staring into that new scotch, "I know ya all too well, Boss Hoss, and I believe ya, I surely do. Except what if one of 'em had a gun?"

Then Harry left the bar to go find a lap dance or three.

Jim ordered another Bud Light, and was just beginning to relax when Consuela sat next to him. "So, how's The Hoary One tonight?"

"Troubled."

Consuela said, "Yeah, the other night he didn't get so, so drunk, gave me two hundred to go home with him, nailed me angry 'cept he never could come. Not to get too technical on your celibate ass, he did at least maintain a decent boner for a surprisingly long time, gotta give him credit for that. Anyway, I know he's troubled, dickhead. Who the fuck around here isn't? Including you."

"*Business* troubled. I told him Amy didn't deserve any more problems, firm as I could. 'Course not sure he realizes what a problem he is for her.

He was okay with it all . . . 'cept he did indirectly manage to slip the word 'gun' in there."

"Goddamn guns. No guns around here, guys like you and Big Bill could make *all* the rules. Big Bill can be dumber than dog shit, but he ain't gonna be abusing any women, at least. On the other hand, though, he's no knight in shining armor either . . . I'm worried you might try to be."

Jim chuckled. "Take it from his partner, that 'dumber than dog shit' can be plenty painful in and of itself. But, you're right, Bill's no bully, thank God."

Consuela had to go make a living, best she could. Jim looked over and saw that Harry was on what must have been at least his fifth consecutive lap dance, with yet another new double scotch on the table beside him—Jim didn't understand paying for grinding lap dances, just *looking* at naked young women in reasonable shape made him way hornier than he ever wanted to be if he wasn't gonna get to actually do anything—so Harry was undoubtedly gonna return sometime soon.

Jim finished his beer wondering if it made any sense to talk to Harry any more tonight. Consuela and Amy were now both dancing naked on the big stage in the middle of the huge rectangular bar, smiling at him, and giving him as much special 'show' as they could without irritating the other connoisseurs at the bar. The way Jim was feeling now, having sex with either one of them tonight would probably be the most pleasurable thing he'd ever done in his entire life. And it would be irrelevant whether he paid 'em or not, 'cause either way they'd undoubtedly be into it as much as he was.

But he wasn't gonna do it and Harry was now probably past the point of no return, so he finally decided that it did not, in fact, make any sense for him to wait for Harry *or* to watch the sexy shenanigans of his second floor tenants any more this Friday night.

Before leaving, he watched Big Bill lumbering around behind the bar for another minute, chuckling, and thinking that if the Strip Club Architects had seen The Monstrous One coming, they would have sacrificed a few square feet of stage space, and also rounded the stage corners. Bill was never gonna figure out how to negotiate those sharp corners without coming to a complete stop and then performing an official-looking military right-face or left-face.

Jim chuckled a little louder, now thinking that that might just be the most grossly oversized, out-of-place, and generally ridiculous-looking mini-marching in the history of the world.

He had nursed three light beers, and now had enough of a mild relaxing glow he decided just a couple more before sleep would finally provide a reasonably soothing end to a pretty frustrating week. Jim considered himself a master at maintaining that magical 'three-beer-high.' Better than anyone he knew. Whether he was drinking for an hour or for eight hours, it was second nature for Jim to pace, pace, pace. In fact, just as Jim's dick had never gotten him into any real trouble, neither had his drinking . . . not since that damn dumpster fiasco, anyway.

So he repaired to Schraft Street Sports, where he watched the end of the Bruins game with some pleasant and knowledgeable regulars he knew just well enough to stay totally sports- and surface-level. Thus, that much-needed enjoyable end to the workweek, with just the one minor discomfort being provided by a couple *very* unattractive women complaining loudly but thankfully briefly about his poor, misunderstood ladies' room.

When one of the woman sputtered, "Boy was I happy to get out of there," Jim thought but certainly didn't say, "Yeah, well, I bet my poor shitter was equally happy to see the backs of you two walkin' out the damn door."

Actually, considering the quality of the female clientele of Schraft Street Sports, Jim was happy that the ladies room couldn't actually talk, for fear of the unhappy behind-the-scenes tales it might tell. This was one ladies room that was definitely *not* ever gonna need to be swept for hidden cameras.

CHAPTER SIX

A Connie Parker Saturday

Jim woke Saturday morning feeling fine, not a hint of 'gover. He lay in bed, happily replaying the end of the night. The Bruins had tied Montreal at three with a minute and a half left in regulation, and then won the game with a minute and a half left in overtime. Jim didn't follow the Bruins all that close, not like he did the Sox and Pats, so why should he care . . . but since he'd been watching the game with several Schraft Street Sports regulars who really did care, he'd gotten caught up in their enthusiasm, and then of course the game had ended exceptionally well. It was only November, still the first half of the season, and the Bruins would almost surely make the playoffs as they almost always did, so it shouldn't have been a big deal. But Jim's bar had erupted in cheers when they tied it late, and louder cheers and high-fives all around when they won it with OT winding down.

The bad news was that Jim had to spring for a free round for the house, but the good will was well worth it.

Jim had played high school hockey on the first line as a forward, but hadn't been good enough to be offered a scholarship. He had received scholarship offers to play football at a couple Division 2 schools, but he knew he was never gonna play pro, he'd had four teammates in high school go down with serious knee injuries, so he decided not to risk it.

He wished there was an MDC skating rink within walking distance—hard skating would be an enjoyable addition to his cardio—but there wasn't, and he certainly wasn't gonna rent a car to go skating. Or take a damn MBTA bus with skates hanging over his shoulder. So he hadn't skated in years.

Sometimes in the spring or fall when it wasn't too hot or humid Jim would run all the way into Boston, which he loved to do, except for very diligently dodging the damn cars. (On scene, for all practical purposes, pedestrians *never* have the right of way in Boston. The most important relevant rights that they *do* have are the right to scamper out of the way while swearing at the drivers and pointing to the bright white 'walk' sign; the right to sue from their rehab facility . . . or, finally, the right of their next-of-kin to sue after the funeral.)

A few times he'd run into the Fanueil Hall area in the early evening, hit the hot spots, almost always met a woman, and she'd agreed to give him a lift home when he finally convinced her he really didn't have a car, and had legged it into town. And then, well, they were there, weren't they . . . in the same vein as, "The room's already paid for, so what the hell."

After an excellent, quick breakfast at The Schraft Street Diner—and quiet, Faye wasn't on duty yet and the Stripping Set wasn't awake yet—Jim headed to the gym, ardently hoping that his upper body workout would be equally blessed by peace and quiet.

When Herlihy's wasn't busy and Jim could readily alternate non-stop heavy 'push and pull' exercises . . . benches with chins, incline presses with barbell rows, weighted dips with power cleans . . . while enveloped in the energizing background music he and Big Bill preferred (e.g., Stones, Creedence, Springsteen, Billy Joel, Tina Turner, some Michael Jackson, Jim's all-time favorite workout song, "Loverboy" by Billy Ocean) playing at a clear but not overwhelming volume, Jim would lose himself in a restorative mental and physical focus that he supposed was not too unlike that experienced by religious rivalists. Jim wasn't always in the mood for such intense solitary workouts, but he surely was this morning.

But Big Bill called him over to the desk as soon as he walked in, with a look on his huge mug that reminded Jim of Major Reisman when he was dealing with Telly Savalas playing murderous religious maniac Archer Maggot.

Bill said, "You're not gonna believe this latest, Boss."

"Fuck me and screw you, ya big fucker. I'll hate it, sure as shit, but I'll believe anything these days. Unless someone tried to tell me good news."

"Yeah, I guess this particular madness isn't all that hard to believe, considering the culprit. Crazy Connie Parker got really pissed at Jay again last night, but instead of just calling him 'a fuckin' faggot cocksucking cuntlapper' like she usually does, she totally lost it, and fired a five-pound-plate at his skull. Luckily she missed Jay's empty noggin, but the five-pound-plate hit Linda square in the crack of her ass, and even split her tight pants right down the seam. Man, oh man, did she screech bloody murder all right, at least according to Ronnie Doyle, who was manning the joint. 'Cause I was tending at Shenanigans."

"Yeah, I know you were tending at Shenanigans, 'cause ya served me three beers; or four 'cause I bought one for Harry. Dickhead. Was Linda hurt?"

Bill looked over to the entrance, and said, "Ah, here's Ronnie now, I told him in to come on in and tell us all about it."

Ronnie said, "Linda's very well-padded back there, so mostly just her feelings."

Jim said with an audible sigh, "*That* is certainly a relief, at least."

Ronnie picked back up, "Yes it is. Man, did that Famous Foursome screech though. Crazy Connie didn't even apologize, just kept screaming at Jay, until he and I together got her out of the joint, and wrestled her into Jay's car. That is one strong, crazy, mean bitch. Best ass I've ever seen, but Jay should still have his head examined."

Jim said, "I think it has been but they didn't find anything. Where's it stand?"

Ronnie replied, "Linda said that even though she loves you like all get out, if you ever let Crazy Connie back into this gym she's gonna sue the pants right off your sexy, gorgeous ass. Linda's words, not mine, Boss."

Bill said, "Jay called this morning to plead the crazy bitch's case and how sorry she is and how she loves this place and it's all she's got and she needs her personal training and all that drivel. I'm glad I only own 25 percent of this sumbitch and don't have to decide this shit."

Connie Parker was Arnold's girlfriend, and a very serious female bodybuilder. She did indeed have a great body, especially her ass and legs, but a very masculine and even mean-looking face. She was also a kick-boxer and knew a fair bit of karate. She had been a stripper-but-not-hooker at Shenanigans, but had been fired—and banned—for kicking a regular customer so hard in the groin that he had to go the hospital. Apparently the drunken customer while getting a lap dance from behind had slurred something like, "Man, your ass is so great it's finally driven your face right out of my skull, 'long as ya don't turn around anytime soon."

Amy told Jim that all the other strippers were really glad that Connie had kicked that customer good. First, because he was an idiot who—when he was drunk—would make disparaging remarks to all the girls. Second, because they were all afraid of Crazy Connie, and were "relieved to see such a mean, mean manly bitch go."

Jim knew all too well about the guy's disparaging remarks because he'd been walking by when the knucklehead made one while getting up out of his seat to pinch another stripper's bare ass really hard. Jim grabbed the way-out-of-line drunk and slammed him back into his seat while barely missing a stride.

Connie still lived in the 'Strippersville Apartments' at the other end of Schraft Street. Connie did not own a car either, and Jim would often pass her on the street, or see her in The Diner, along with at the gym all the time. For a while Connie wasn't speaking to him, and would pass by in stony stare-ahead-silence, while Jim just continued with his normal friendly greeting, as if Connie was a sweetheart. She was mad first because before she started dating Arnold she'd invited Jim up to her apartment for drinks or dinner several times, and he'd politely declined, suppressing a shiver while he did so. Second, when she got fired from Shenanigans she'd lobbied him hard for a bartending job at Schraft Street Sports. Jim had passed on that, too. The customers were crazy enough without bringing in even crazier bartenders.

Connie was always shouting the worst obscenities at Jay in the gym. Jay claimed it related to his womanizing, but Big Bill told Jim it more likely was over drugs; both steroids and speed. Now that Jim had kicked out their regular supplier and he'd moved on, supplies could be problematic and expensive, and both Jay and Connie were cash-strapped heavy users.

Jim said, "Well, Connie's banned for now, that's a no-brainer. Brother. Now I guess I'm gonna be talking to Jay about some kind of anger management and drug treatment for Connie before I can even think about letting her back in; and to Linda about taking pity on her—and on me—if she does get help."

"Not just Linda, Boss," said Ronnie, with an ironic smile. "I think most of the members would prefer not to be worrying about flying five-pound-iron-plates if they had their druthers."

Big Bill laughed. "Boss Jim, I see some quality time with Jay, Connie, and Linda in your future."

"You're the manager. You should be handling this, ya monstrous dickhead."

"I would but nobody listens to me. I mean, I'd wallow in it, but then they'd still want to talk to you, you'd decide, and I'd have just wasted my time. I will be happy to tell Jay she's banned, and, as far as I'm concerned, that should be the end of it forever. I can bench over 600 pounds, but that Connie still scares me."

Jim sighed. "That's a starting point, I guess. Now I'm gonna try to get upper body and heavy bag done before Jay or The Foursome darken the damn door." And he did.

Even much, much better, Dale O'Dell came in; and Doug Ballard was back in New York working. So Dale did upper body with Jim . . . restoration of a kinder, gentler, but still plenty energizing sort. He loved talking to Dale, well beyond the romantic interest. She was just so sweetly damn sensible and empathetic. He not only told her all about the Jay/Connie/Linda fiasco, he also told her about his renewed determination to write a sequel, and his conversation with old friend Garrity and his upcoming trip to West Palm Beach.

(Jim knew Dale also really liked—and worried about—Little Amy Jordan, but there was no way Dale could help with the scary Hoary Harry conundrum, so Jim didn't even consider troubling Dale with that dark cloud.)

Jim then said, "Hey, I miss the perfectly fitting leotards. What's with the baggy shorts?"

"Accenting the image as a thoroughly professional trainer, especially with my older female clients. And these shorts fit just fine."

Jim shook his head with an exaggerated grimace. He thought Dale looked like a young Mary Tyler Moore with just the right amount of increased feminine muscularity . . . and that her gorgeously heart-shaped butt was, in fact, even sexier than the far more celebrated Connie Parker's. Now, though, apparently Dale had decided to downplay that slightly exotic asset.

So Jim just grinned broadly at Dale with an ironic, Sam Elliot-sideways tilt of his head, spread his muscular arms out to the side with palms facing forward, and exclaimed loudly, "Shucks!"

The only negative to working out with Dale was that the extraordinarily good-hearted Physician's Assistant was famous throughout Herlihy's for dispensing very knowledgeable free basic orthopedic injury rehabilitation advice, even to members who had never used her personal training services. A couple of middle-aged women tentatively approached her, and, as usual, she graciously interrupted her own workout to help them. Jim greeted the ladies cheerfully—they were after all paying members from his own viewpoint—but then went right back to his own intense workout.

Dale pretty much tried to help everyone around her. She was probably the only gym member who wasn't a total musclehead who had any relationship with Connie Parker.

Dale said, "Connie does need help bad, Jim. Her life's been about as hard as Amy's, and in her own way Connie's even more screwed up than Amy is. Obviously, she doesn't have Amy's preternaturally good heart as an underpinning."

"There's an understatement for the ages."

"You know, Jim, when someone is in here all the time, putting her heart and soul and plenty of the little money she has into the crazy goings-on around here, there is some level of responsibility created for you, as the owner and somewhat sensible center of this place. You can't just casually throw Connie away as if she never existed."

"Speaking of throwing."

Dale said, "Well, yeah, she has to understand how dangerous what she did was, and get help, and vow to never do anything like that again. I'll even call her myself, and see if she'll have dinner with me. Someone halfway sane for her to really talk to."

"You're a saint, Dale." But he did add to himself, "Except for the Doug Ballard thing."

Regarding the trip to Florida, Dale said, "You should get away. And see your friend Keith. But I sure can't see ya moving. You're addicted to Schraft Street. And Schraft Street is addicted to you."

After the upper body, Dale even agreed to alternate with him on the heavy bag. Jim grinned watching her. Dale hit the big bag like she was worried about hurting it. She and Amy Jordan both somehow managed to look like adorably cute little girls while they were throwing punches. Dale did have excellent endurance though, although not as good as his.

No one yet—not even the serious young MMA guys—could hit the bag really, really hard and fast for as long as Jim Herlihy could. Dale could hit it even longer, though, because she did hit it so lightly. One time when Dale finally stopped and they were switching places, Jim impulsively gave her a big, very sweaty hug. Dale looked at him really funny. She had hugged him back pretty good though, he couldn't deny that.

Overall, as an antidote to the Connie Caper, it was an excellent workout.

Except he forgot that his hands hadn't fully healed, and his wraps were soaked in blood again at the end of his extended (and Dale-inspired) session on the big bag.

CHAPTER SEVEN

Watch What You Wish For

Jim started the sequel early Saturday afternoon. Carrollton really had given him some good ideas, he had to admit.

He was rolling along pretty good until Amy came by. She knocked lightly, as if worried about disturbing anyone in the building, and then shouted at the top of her sweet lungs, "Open up, open up, it's good news for you, Mr. Jimmy! The doctor said since you refused to boink me I'm *not* having your baby!"

She then quoted Larry David loudly, "Boy cock, girl cock, ee-i ee-i oh!"

Amy, as usual, sat at the kitchen table, and she said, "Hey, maybe your very brief talk with our Harry did a little temporary good, 'cause last night he still got hammered and pestered the hell out of some poor innocent dancers . . . 'cept for the first time ever one of 'em *wasn't* pool lil' ol' Amy Jordan!"

Jim replied, "Yeah, accent on the *temporary*. Best both continue to be very careful of our very Hoary friend."

She asked if he'd have lunch with just her at The Diner before her shift at Shenanigans. She insisted that she'd had a good week money wise, and would not only pay for her own meal, she really would be happy to spring for his. But he finally had a little momentum going, and told her that.

Without asking, she pulled a couple steaks out of the freezer, put them on the counter to thaw, and said, "Okay, I'll leave you alone for a half hour 'till these thaw a bit, and then come back and cook 'em up just right; being *so* uncharacteristically quiet you won't even know I'm here until lunch is actually served. Meanwhile, I'll run by The Diner and bring back some fries and ice cream. We will have a very nice lunch like the boring suburbanite couple we should have been. Then I'll have a sublime evening showing my freshly unbearded clam to assorted drunken degenerates."

Unusually, she didn't offer any boinking. That surely didn't mean that the subject hadn't crossed his mind. Between Dale and now Amy, this Saturday was really starting to test his willpower.

He did indeed have a nice lunch with Amy, who had cooked those pretty damn good steaks up perfectly, as promised. The Schraft Street Market actually had an excellent butcher. The fries and ice cream Amy had brought back from The Diner were top notch too. And, he'd coaxed out the sensible and empathetic side of Amy by laying the latest Connie Caper on her. Towards Connie Amy had the natural dislike and resentment of anyone who'd been nastily bullied on a regular basis.

But Amy did say, "Yeah, every now and then Connie could be alright, semi-reasonably join in on our stripper bitching sessions. She'd even laugh sometimes, 'course over the years we've had some pretty funny ladies at Shenanigans, ya gotta laugh. You wouldn't laugh, 'cause you're a dickhead guy, even if better than most, but stripper humor can be funny if you know how to listen."

"Hey, I might not join in on the boisterous cackling, but you degenerate madwomen do get me smiling sometimes, despite myself."

"You're alright, Boss. And, yeah, I don't like the growly twat so much, but I'd still sure hate to hear that she'd slit those big veiny wrists. Sure, have that uppity bitch Dale try to help Crazy Connie, better her than me. Although, I do like her anyway. Dr. Dale, I mean."

Jim worked well until he wound down around seven. Well-begun isn't of course anywhere near half-done, but it was enough of a start that he'd at least begun to feel committed to actually writing the damn thing. He even used his outline to do himself up a daily schedule of target word count to complete a 120,000 word fast first draft in about 100 days, allowing of course for downtime when he was in West Palm Beach. So he'd have something to show Chadwick by spring, and maybe pocket that fifty k then. Assuming he wasn't in the middle of de-Schrafting and moving to Florida, that is.

He'd been planning on a relaxing night in with the tube, later watching the Celtics play the Lakers out west. But, after writing all afternoon, he surely felt like a few beers. And last night between Shenanigans and Sports hadn't been half bad, he had to admit. The regulars at Sports were even more into the C's than they were the B's, so if the Celtics could at least keep it close, the joint would be jumping.

So, he headed down to Shenanigans, just planning a couple there, before repairing back to his own bar. He was still pretty anxious, and the thought of Amy's self-described freshly unbearded clam popped into his foolish head before he could suppress it. Well, a few beers should take the edge off all that. Actually, thinking about Dale took the edge off thinking about Amy and her roommates, (he thought, "Man, having three sexy ladies living right downstairs whom you've seen naked in suggestive poses literally hundreds of times sure isn't all it's cracked up to be") but overall certainly didn't make him feel any better.

The first thing he noticed walking into Shenanigans and heading for the big rectangular bar in the center of the place was that Hoary Harry was not in his assigned seat. That was unheard of on a Saturday night. Big Bill then told Jim that Harry hadn't been seen at all since last night. Jim stayed longer than he'd planned—nursing four light beers instead of his usual three—primarily waiting to see if Harry would show. But he did not.

Amy sat next to him on a break, and said, "Christ, it seems like I'm dancing in a different joint, no Harry staring at me nethers like he was goin' for a doctorate in the gynacuntological sciences. I think it's literally been six months since I danced a set without feeling those scary, beady eyes all over me. I'm real relieved but a little worried at the same time."

Jim watched Big Bill lumbering around in back of the bar as fast as his 350 pounds of heavy-lifting muscle would allow, but still finding time to glance over at Amy every now and then. Jim said, "Amy, what have you told Bill about Harry stalking you?"

"Nothing. I'm a desperate little degenerate, but I'm not stupid. I thought you knew that, my Darling Dickhead."

While Jim was nursing his fourth beer, he was replaying his conversation with Harry last night, sitting in this very seat, especially the part about, "Not soon-to-be-history disfavor, but on the outside-looking-in dis-fuckin'-favor." It seemed unlikely that the savvy, long-serving Harry could misread a serious situation that badly . . . but maybe the combination of money worries, his infatuation with Amy, and his sharply increased drinking had gotten the better of him.

Jim had come in seriously worried about Harry vis a vis "Little Sister" Amy, but leaving Shenanigans he was surprised to find himself starting to seriously worry about Harry vis a vis Harry's dangerous friends and associates.

Watching the Celtics game at Schraft Street Sports was, unfortunately, not near as fun or relaxing as watching the Bruins game had been the night before. First, because the Celtics fell behind early, and never made enough of a run to make the game interesting. Second, because all eight of the Gay Guys were there, dressed inappropriately for a blue-collar sports bar, drinking liberally, and, as they got drunk, talking too loudly and well outside the general tenor of the bar. They were paying no attention to the Celtics game, other than irritating comments on who they thought the hottest ballplayers were.

Jim only said something to them once, but he was constantly considering saying more, and generally fretting over how to diplomatically tone 'em down. Even more worrisome was the prospect of Fat Frankie throwing them out, or, worse, a couple of the other patrons doing it. *With* prejudice.

Tonight Jim also had 'The Big A' and Eddy Harcharik to worry about.

Harcharik was once again staying past his curfew and drinking past his limit. Thankfully, Jim was eventually able to talk him out of the bar and headed for home before the skinny wife with the Tom Brady arm stormed in, but it hadn't been fun.

Frankie had been doing his best to slow 'A' down—or at least told Jim he had been— but eventually 'The A' did begin to list badly. Jim ended up walking the poor guy home, listening to A-speak the while, not coming anywhere close to understanding one word of it.

After helping 'A' up the stairs to his apartment, Jim sprinted back to the bar like a madman just because he felt like running.

When it became obvious the Celtics were gonna lose, Jim was ready for bed. But he decided he'd better not leave until the GG's did, and that turned out to be not for another hour. To top it off, near the end, one of 'em came over and sat next to Jim, wanting to drunkenly discuss the Connie situation. His idea was that Jim should let her back in, but require that Connie and Jay not be there at the same time. In fact, this guy thought that since Jim was so reasonable and well respected, he himself should become Connie's new training partner, at least for a while. Jim pictured himself working out with Connie on a regular basis, and the between-sets conversations that would engender, and then Eugene Pontecorvo and his basement popped back into Jim's head.

Actually, though, Jim thought the first part of the guy's idea wasn't half-bad, and wondered why he hadn't thought of that himself.

Jim had breakfast at The Diner earlier than usual Sunday morning, since he was definitely not in the mood for stripper-company. He did have Fabulous Faye as his waitress. The Diner was just about empty at this early hour, and Faye sat playfully in his lap, grinding a little. She laughed loudly, and then, still sitting and grinding in his lap, whispered in his ear, "Yikes, is Fabulous Faye growing on Big Boss Jim? 'Cause I feel not-so-little Jim growing under Fabulous Faye's big ass. And it feels damn good, too."

Faye laughed again, and got up. She smiled seductively down at him. It was absolutely all he could do to keep from saying, "Alright, Faye, ya wanna fuck, throw down that apron, we'll run across the street to my place, and I'll tear ten pounds outta that big ol' ass!"

Instead he just smiled up wanly, and muttered, "Wish I could, Faye, wish I could." She left. Man, he had a huge, painful boner. He stared at the table, half expecting it to start rising. It didn't, but then it was bolted to the floor.

It was good he hadn't grabbed Faye and headed for the door, 'cause he would have run smack into the burly Boston Cop who was already boning her, Sergeant Carlton Carrollton, in uniform. Carrollton sat in the booth, across from Jim. He reached across the table and grabbed Jim's hands and looked 'em over good. The knuckles were still badly skinned, as well as somewhat swollen.

Jim, while he was picking the sarge's brain for story ideas, had—for the moment somewhat casually—mentioned his concerns about Harry, mostly relative to Harry's semi-stalking of Amy, but also regarding how Harry, when drinking, was suddenly, bitterly, bringing up the ancient dumpster dunking.

Carrollton now said, "Boss Jim, I was only kidding when I suggested you might consider a preemptive strike against The Hoary One. As a Boston Police Sergeant, I'm not really supposed to suggest to civilians that they kill each other. How'd you do this?"

"Heavy bag. Are you serious, Carl?"

"You did all this on the fuckin' bag? With hand wraps and gloves? Were you on PCP or somethin'?"

"No, I was on Schraft Street. In more ways than one. Again, are you serious?"

"Harry is missing. Not just from Shenanigans, he had a meeting yesterday afternoon that he would not likely have missed if something wasn't really wrong. And he ain't sick at home, either, no one has seen him there since Friday afternoon. So, yeah, I'm serious about wanting to find Harry anyway. I'm not really serious about you as involved . . . but those are some fucked-up hands for just the damn bag. Especially on a guy who's been pounding on big bags for twenty years, knows how to wrap his hands, and has never banged 'em up like this before."

"Well, Carl, Schraft Street's been working on me pretty good the last couple weeks. Especially the women. You know the company I keep. Believe me, I did it on the bag. How'd ya know about the damn hands anyway?"

"A couple folks from Shenanigans noticed 'em last night, and were wondering. You have the rep as a very sane guy, Boss Jim, but you also have the rep as someone 'could do some serious damage quick with those hands, if it ever got to that. And Harry has mentioned your name some lately, too, as we discussed . . . self-defense is an excuse best served piping hot, Boss."

"Heavy bag, Carl."

Carrollton left, whispering something in Faye's ear. Jim was pretty sure he could read her lips replying, "Yeah, off at three. And then I'll be there directly."

His pesky big boner came roaring back. Jim grinned sardonically: "Sir J. Peter Throbbington The Omnipresent;" at least lately. He thought about Harry, as an antidote. A dead Harry would solve a couple problems. But he'd known Harry since elementary school—hell, they'd played T-ball together—and he really would hate to hear that fringe-player Harry had already met a gangster's end at age thirty-five . . . and while thoroughly broke, at that.

One way or another the case probably would end up providing some kind of fodder for his sequel. He just hoped he wouldn't have too much of an inside view. The cops on his ass for something he'd only briefly thought about doing was a worry he surely didn't need right now.

CHAPTER EIGHT

Perception

JIM WAS ON AN ENCOURAGING early roll with his sequel, and spent Sunday afternoon, and all day Monday and Tuesday writing. The gym was open until eleven, and he didn't get there until around nine, when Ronnie Doyle was manning the desk and the place was almost empty. Big Bill worked at Shenanigans every night except Sunday. Actually, working out at this time of night was a nice change, except it was then difficult to get to sleep until 1 AM or later.

On the plus side, though, was that except for Friday and Saturday nights, after ten, especially in the winter, Schraft Street was really quiet, so Jim's post-upper-body-workout walking contemplations were essentially undisturbed. Other than by intermittent worries over missing Harry, Crazy Connie, recalcitrant Frankie, thickheaded Monstrous Bill, fallen angel Amy Jordan, his overall finances, and especially the unavailability of Dale O'Dell, that is.

Boy did he have it bad for that wonderful woman. He'd started dreaming about her more often, too. Once in a while he'd somehow get her . . . far more often he did not. Usually Doug was the problem, but other times it was murky-faced strangers in bizarre circumstances. He had no control over the dreams, and no idea what they meant—other than the obvious that he was in serious unrequited love, and it was starting to mess with his sleep. On the other hand, it was probably helping his writing, and it was definitely energizing his workouts—especially pounding on the heavy bag.

Jim had agreed to meet The Famous Less-Fat Foursome on Wednesday night at IHOP out on Route One in Saugus to interview them for that damn article in *The Bradford Bulletin*. For some reason, the ladies didn't particularly like The Schraft Street Diner—and Jim was just as happy for a venue where he'd be anonymous. Jim wanted to just take a cab out there, but the ladies insisted on picking him up in front of his place. They were a little late, so he ended up standing out on the sidewalk for a few minutes. No one he really knew happened by, but several people he'd just seen around passed. Jim at least nodded to everyone on Schraft Street, even if they never responded. Tonight everyone nodded back, but they seemed to be looking at Jim differently as they did.

Jim had promised to outline and pitch the article to the editor he knew at *The Bulletin*, but he hadn't gotten around to doing that yet. He told The Foursome that he had anyway . . . he was pretty sure *The Bulletin* would go for it, they were always looking for human interest stuff about local people, and the fitness angle and impressive progress the ladies had made should work. On top of that, they'd all grown up pretty poor, and were all doing quite well in those paralegal jobs, so he'd include plenty of career stuff too. The friendship and mutual support angle would undoubtedly work its way into the article as well.

He certainly would officially clear it before starting on the article. But now he thought he should have cleared it before subjecting himself to this four-on-one interview. He wasn't particularly looking forward to writing the article, but going through what was undoubtedly going to be a long, loud, and semi-painful up-close session with The Famous Foursome for nothing was even less appealing.

But then, of course, the ladies wanted to talk Crazy Connie and flying five-pound-plates first. Jim demurred politely but firmly relative to going someplace private to inspect firsthand the big purple, painful bruise on Linda's butt; or to even look at the picture they offered. Linda's friends did proceed to do a better than adequate job of describing the impressive bruise verbally, colorfully accompanied by plenty of good-natured burly girl guffaws.

Connie had apologized to Linda through Jay, but not directly. Jim pointed out that Connie was banned from the gym, and probably did not know how else to get in touch. Linda said Connie could work out somewhere else, forevermore. Jim said Connie did not have a car, and there was not a suitable alternative nearby.

Linda said, "I can't believe you're sticking up for her. Someone could have been brain-damaged or even killed. You have some liability here."

"Not unless I was negligent, and should have reasonably known she'd turn plate-hurler. I could not. I can swear in court that I honestly believed she was only half-crazy, not nearly as nuts as she looks, and was as shocked as everyone else."

"But now you *do* know, Jim," said Linda. "We know more about legal liability than you do. Be very careful here."

Jim was more than ready to table Connie, and get into the article.

But now Linda said, "There's surprising rumors flying around, too. Something about a missing Hoary Harry guy . . . and you and bloody hands, even."

"Yeah, I know Harry, and I'm a little worried about him myself. I bloodied my hands on the heavy bag. End of story."

One of the other ladies said, "It's amazing what people will say . . . and think. Everyone on Schraft Street knows everyone's business, and has an opinion. On Connie, Jay, this Harry, us, the Gay Guys, Big Bill, the Shenanigans girls . . . you. 'Don't mess with Jim. He has a dark side. And now he's laying low.'"

Linda said, "Schraft Street has twenty-four-seven eyes, ears, and tongues. Of course, we can't deny being just about the loudest busybodies of 'em all. We heard you were sprinting up Schraft Street Saturday night like the devil himself was after ya . . . but then you suddenly stopped and casually strolled into your Sports, not a care in the world. Strange behavior, Jim."

Then, for some reason, all four decided that was just about the funniest thing ever, and laughed about as exuberantly as 800 pounds of good-natured womanhood could . . . which was pretty damn exuberantly. They even managed to get Boss Jim chuckling himself.

Jim, still trying unsuccessfully to suppress a smile, looked 'em all in the eye, and said, "Come on, ladies, I'm innocent, I'm not laying low or losing my mind or anything else, I'm just holed up getting back into writing; and my dark side isn't any darker than most people's. Let's get into discussing your amazing collective accomplishments."

Just like they did when they were working out, The Foursome encouraged each other and played off each other, loudly building momentum as they did so. Jim didn't get all the humor, but he did have to smile at the energy and enthusiasm and joyfulness, and the obvious affection they had for each other, even when they were mutually busting burly booty. They didn't stay on subject too well, and it certainly went on too long—and, Jim was sure, too loudly for the other patrons, at least for those who didn't know The Foursome, who were boisterous regulars here—but in the end Jim didn't mind it too much, and he certainly had more than enough background info to write a good article.

Or at least a good first draft, because he knew right well that they'd all be back here discussing The Foursome's proposed "enhancements" to what they'd surely consider his comparatively mild-mannered first effort.

The fitness goal to which they were now passionately committed was a collective 600 pounds, and Jim decided he'd be able to say in print that he had little doubt they'd get there. And have fun doing it. And probably not look half bad when they did get there. A full 40 percent down from that starting collective grand.

They all had to give him long, hard hugs as they were dropping him off, and Linda kissed him, and said quietly, "I know it wasn't you set that Hoary guy off missing, Jim. And that you'd never hurt anyone if you didn't have to." Jim had his first ever Linda-inspired sexual thoughts. And, he realized, yet another vexing visit from the enthusiastic but painfully undiscerning Lord J. Peter Throbbington. Man, he was in a bad way.

CHAPTER NINE

Schraft Street Gets Deadly Serious

FRIDAY MORNING AT THE UNGODLY hour of six AM there was a loud knocking on Jim's door, that woke him from a sound sleep. The knocking wasn't followed by shocking obscenities shouted in sweet girlish voice, so it could not be Amy Jordan. It could be and was Sergeant Carlton Carrollton, accompanied by a handsome little guy who looked like Peter Falk, but who was wearing, instead of a rumpled overcoat, a very sharp and well-tailored pinstriped blue suit.

The Falk-looking guy was in fact a detective, and Hoary Harry had in fact been found dead, very badly beaten, and finished off with a broken neck.

The coroner set the time of death at very early last Saturday morning between two and six, sometime after Harry had stumbled out of Shenanigans alone and grumbling. He'd had words with a stripper—not any of Jim's tenants—about what he considered a lackluster lap dance. She'd responded that he was three-quarters passed out, and in no condition to judge lap dances.

Jim was genuinely stricken to hear the worst about Harry. If the cops could see that, they sure didn't say so.

Jim even had an absurd thought that it was a real shame that probably the last thing Harry experienced in life—except for that horrific beating—was a really lackluster lap dance. Amy had once told him that the girls felt particularly stupid doing lap dances for very drunk guys, and generally got them over with as quickly as they could . . . unless the drunk was an unusually good tipper.

They sat around the kitchen table as Jim—temporarily a little dazed—dispassionately recounted his Friday night, at Shenanigans and Sports, and finally celebrating the thrilling Bruins win. But, of course, he'd left Sports around eleven, and essentially just walked across the street to get home. He hadn't seen anyone between eleven Friday night, and eight Saturday morning, at The Diner.

Jim then steadied himself, and said, "You know I don't own a car, Carl. Whatta ya think I was doing, lugging dead Harry over my shoulder, three streets over to those woods?"

The Falk-looking guy said, "Your stripper friends have a car, Big Bill has a car, Fat Frankie. And Harry's old Beemer was found between Shenanigans and the wooded area where he was found, could have ambushed him and used that. Harry was punched in the face about fifteen times by a guy who, apparently, could hit very hard. He was unconscious when someone—probably a very strong guy—grabbed his head and twisted it violently, breaking his neck badly. All of this you could do. You had remarkably banged-up hands, and Harry allegedly was giving both you and *especially* your gorgeous little stripper friend Amy a hard time. So, yeah, Mr. Herlihy, you're well into the mix."

"Yeah, well, my DNA won't be on Harry's face. Although, I did shake his hand a couple times at Shenanigans; that drunken dance when a guy's alternating between telling ya he hates ya fucking guts with good reason; but then you're still my best friend ever, put 'er there, ol' pal."

Detective Falk said, "There probably isn't any DNA on Harry's face. You say you bloodied your mitts all the way through gloves and wraps, I say you could have easily banged 'em up on Harry's mug through thin gloves, hittin' him as hard and often as he was. The way Harry was killed and dumped is not the way his gangster friends would have done it."

Jim got up, went to his hall closet, brought back his oversized gym bag, and pulled out his bag gloves and bloody wraps. He said, "Here's the blood. I'd look pretty fuckin' suspicious *and* even more stupid than normal making my appointed Schraft Street rounds sporting this bulky get-up. Ya want this sweaty, bloody, nasty shit for your evidence room?"

"Yeah, ya wise-ass fucker," snapped Detective Falk. "We always immediately clear anybody who can show us at least one gun that *wasn't* the murder weapon."

Carlton leaned well back with a funny grimace on his big-cop's face, and said, "Damn, Boss, that is *nasty*, you should wash those wraps; or better, throw 'em away in a medical waste bag. The leading citizen of Schraft Street should not have something like that percolating in his hall closet."

Jim shrugged and said, "Well, I already told you guys all I can about me. You know Harry's drinking recently got worse, as did his obsession with little Amy, and he drunkenly told me he was on the outs and it was hurting his cash flow, but that he wasn't in physical danger. He's been notably different lately, and I did mention it to you, Carlton, but that's *all* I know about my poor old friend Harry."

Falk said, "We also heard you performed a mad dash half the length of Schraft Street Saturday night. What's up with that?"

"I was running on Schraft Street from Schraft Street. Your silent partner there understands perfectly."

Carlton said, "Yup. Be doing it myself sometimes, 'cept with my luck I'd pull a hammy."

Falk said, "Yeah, well, don't go anywhere, Boss."

"Actually, I have a three-day semi-business trip to Florida planned next week to see an old friend, Keith Garrity, who you know well, Carl. Gotta go, but what's three days."

Falk leaned in towards Jim, and said, "The BPD strongly prefers that you stay on Schraft for now."

Jim silently thought, "Christ, this guy looks like Detective Columbo and talks like Sergeant Friday."

Jim then leaned in a little himself, looked the detective in the eye, and said, "I'm innocent, Detective, and accordingly you do not now have—and never will have—evidence with which to charge me. Right here on Schraft I own this house, Schraft Streets Sports, and 75 percent of Herlihy's Hardcore, all free and clear. They don't throw off all that much cash, and admittedly they and especially those who run 'em for me are major pains in the ass; but between 'em the assets gotta be worth at least a mill and a half, given enough time to find another Bradford-born-and-bred idiot clueless enough to buy them. I gotta go, but, unfortunately, after three short days I also *gotta* come back, totally independent of you two misdirected knuckleheads."

The Detective sneered, "Long-winded, wiseass son of a bitch."

Carlton chuckled and said, "Not entirely, Lou. I know the guys he's talking about."

Lou shrugged, and replied to Carlton, "Your ass, would-be detective."

Carrollton said, "Jim, say hi to Keith, and keep me posted on any travel." Then he half-chuckled. "Those bloody mitts and you holed up in your apartment the last couple days have Schraft Street buzzing, Boss. Now when you lam it, you will be convicted in the court of public opinion anyway . . . at least until ya get back."

"Public opinion I can deal with, 'least 'till you geniuses clear me one way or the other . . . but what about Harry's friends and associates? What if they really didn't do it and start thinking maybe I did?"

"Hmmm, there's a worry for ya," sneered Falk.

Carlton said, "Shut up, Lou. We'll get the word out that you're a very marginal suspect. And that we'd frown on anything premature and rash. And by far most important, that, in fact, you owe *me,* Sergeant Carlton Carrollton, money. Or soon will, that book comes out. Your heirs probably don't realize all the free rent you owe me . . . who are your heirs, anyway?"

"Cousins who don't live around here. Until I get married."

Carrollton was a regular at the gym, and as a cop kept his eyes and ears open. He said, "Yeah, maybe that classy Dale babe will come around eventually. 'Course, you do have other options . . . but they're not very good ones . . . and, right, who am I to talk."

After they left, Jim wished he'd gotten Harry to open up about those business troubles . . . but then had some serious second thoughts. Did he really want to be the guy feeding the cops potentially incriminating info on Hoary Harry's business associates?

There was a familiar light knocking on his door . . . accompanied by a most unfamiliar silence.

Amy entered in tears. "I desperately, desperately wanted him to leave me the Christ alone, Jim. But not like this. Goddammit, not like this!"

Jim hugged her, and said, "He was seriously, seriously troubled, Amy, it happens to guys live like he did. There is absolutely nothing you could have done . . . maybe I could have done something, though."

"I wish I hadn't said that evil bullshit about Harry-bits, I really do . . . I think about him sober when I first met him, and I sort of even miss him, or think I do . . . I think about him lately, I can't help but be so, so fuckin' relieved . . . and then so, so goddamn guilty . . . What could *you* have done, 'cept maybe get yourself hurt or killed too?"

"I dunno. Maybe talk to him about something besides the Sox and the Pats, before he went off the deep end and it was too late. Realistically, though, probably nothing. Probably nothing at all. Besides, my time is way, way better spent trying to save *you*, little sister. And that's not going too good either."

"Yeah, well, I gotta make a living while I can, Jim; get a few bucks put back, too, I surely will while I'm at it. And I ain't no damn charity case neither, kind sir!"

Jim made it a point over the weekend to take some breaks from the writing—he was now finding it hard to concentrate for too long anyway—to take his normal turns at the gym, diner, sports bar, and strip club. He even went into The Schraft Street Market to buy some fruit, vegetables, Ensure, and skim milk. The girl behind the counter was a faithful and fit gym member who knew Amy always bought Jim's groceries, so she chuckled, and said, "Uh oh, Boss Jim, you walking down Schraft Street with a big bag of groceries under each arm is only gonna fuel the speculation that you've gone off the deep end."

"I didn't do it, spread the word, please." She just gave him a big, very friendly smile. She was pretty sexy, that smile really was pretty friendly, so on the way out he had yet another opportunity to think the usual frustrated, "Man, I'm in a bad way."

The cashier at The Market had laughed off the Schraft Street Speculation, but, as Jim pursued his normal Schraft Street wanderings, it was obvious that many people had not.

At the gym and at Shenanigans Jim observed Big Bill carefully. The immensely powerful guy still had an intense interest in Amy, he knew—both amorous and protective. Jim also knew Amy had let the big fella down gently but firmly, both because she'd told him she had and because he knew Amy. Neither Jim, nor Amy, nor Amy's roommates had let on to Bill that Amy was becoming seriously frightened of Harry, and Amy had told Jim that she hadn't discussed it with anyone else. What Bill might have picked up from observing their interaction at Shenanigans he wasn't sure, but he did know that Bill stayed extremely busy bartending. Bill was far from the fastest at mixing drinks, although he tried hard . . . Jim thought Fat Frankie was literally twice as fast. Actually, Bill wasn't fast at anything . . . including on the uptick.

So Jim was fervently hoping that Bill hadn't somehow gotten it into his huge head that Amy was in real danger from Harry, and reacted. That wouldn't be in character, nor would the extreme viciousness of the solution. On the other hand, who really knows? People Jim had known for years were certainly wondering about him. And then if Harry ever had hurt Amy . . . Jim couldn't help wondering about himself.

The morning before Jim's trip to West Palm Beach, there was yet again a light knocking on his door. That sweet little girlish voice said, "Open up, love of my life. Please open, My Darling. Then she shouted, "Jim Herlihy is the best guy ever, and I don't care what any retard around here says or thinks about it! Cops *or* cocksuckers!"

Amy stormed in, now starting to cry.

She stammered, "Christ almighty, now Carlton and that asshole Columbo-looking partner are coming in Shenanigans, bugging the shit out of everyone, customers *and* entertainers, and taking me into the back and implying that I used the power of my freshly unbearded clam to get you to beat Harry to death. I told the dumb bastards a hundred times that you'd never do anything like that unless you absolutely had to, there's no way you had to, and anyway my freshly unbearded clam has no power over you whatsoever. Shown it to ya a hundred times at the club, up close as I'm allowed to get, and still haven't been able to get ya to give me even one neighborly boink, even though I'm in your apartment here all the time."

"Carlton and Columbo or mostly just Columbo, Amy?"

"Columbo's the boss, I guess, so mostly him . . . but my good friend Sergeant Carrollton ain't helping much at the moment."

"I'm sorry, Amy. All we can do is keep telling the truth. And stay strong. And support each other, and stay close to the other girls."

"Even some of them seem to think you did it. And did it for me."

"The truth is the truth, little girl. People that know you and care about you will believe you."

"Big Bill keeps telling the cops and everyone else to back off me. And he's worrying over me like a monstrously big brother . . . sometimes I wish I was in love with him instead of with your heartless ass. But I guess how I feel about him is how you feel about me. And how I feel about you is how you feel about that uppity bitch Dale. Although I do like her anyway."

Jim chuckled and gave Amy his usual brotherly hug, and gentle kiss on the top of her head. "I think I'm starting to get the point that you think Dale's an uppity bitch but you like her anyway, Amy. Does Dale know you think she's an uppity bitch, by the way?"

"Hell yeah she knows! I have never once seen Dale without I didn't say, "Hi, you are one uppity bitch Dr. Dale. But I like ya anyway."

"She's not a doctor yet, Amy. She's a P.A."

"Yeah, that's what she says; but then she goes right on *acting* like a damn doctor. So I always tell the uppity bitch I'm gonna keep calling her doctor anyway. I don't have much in life, please don't deny me my small pleasures. Like swearing my head off at your fuckin' door."

Jim grinned. "I'm not sure I feel about you exactly the way you feel about Monstrous Bill, Amy. I love you like a little sister, but I also think you're nothing short of absolutely gorgeous. I'm just in love with that uppity bitch Dr. Dale."

Amy again smiled shyly like the sweet little waif she should have been, and said, "Yeah, I love Bill like a monstrously big brother, but can't say I like the way he looks. I wish I could but I can't."

"So I do love you in a way, little sister, but I sure do hate the dreadful way you make a living."

"Hey, I'm basically down to boinking only one guy. You probably know who he is, but I'm not gonna tell ya anyway. He gives me money in a general way, not every fuckin' time. So now I've sorta promoted myself from hooker to kept woman. Hooray for me."

"Yeah, hooray for Amy."

"So I don't actually do that much boinking lately. Mostly now I use this great new vibrator Consuela gave me for my birthday, generally thinking of you the whole time, and your wonderful dick that I've never even seen, even though you've seen my freshly unbearded clam literally one thousand times. How is that fair?"

Jim could but shake his head and smile, sadly but lovingly.

Amy pulled out her cell phone camera and said, "The least you could do is let me give you an HJ, take a picture of your beautiful dick at its angriest, which I could then print and paste on this great new vibrator that Consuela gave me for my birthday."

"I just can't do crazy stuff like that, Amy . . . What if Dale someday asked me if you had a picture of my dick on your great new vibrator that Consuela gave you for your birthday. Dale would know I was lying."

"I wouldn't tell a soul. Not to mention ever dream of lending out *that* specially decorated beauty. How would she know to ask?"

"She'd know. After all, like you said, the uppity bitch is a damn doctor."

CHAPTER TEN

West Palm Beach

JIM HAD HAD KEITH GARRITY Email the financial numbers for his nightclub, which was called, "The Meeting Place at City Place," shortened by one and all to just "The Meet." Garrity also included pictures of the club inside and out, of the waitresses and bartenders, and of a sample of the regular customers. The place was trendy and modern, and most of the staff and customers were young, fit, and attractive, which jived with Keith's description of the clientele over the phone.

Garrity also included pictures of two attractive women in thong bikinis, along with a note that said, "My two toned and tanned 'tappees,' both of whom are perfectly happy with our casual relationship, and just sort of generally know about each other. Your particular problem and Schraft Street both seem a million miles away . . . do note, though, that my relationship with these two is not so casual that I lend 'em out to friends. Not to worry—there will be other opportunities down here."

Between his writing and other responsibilities and distractions, Jim hadn't had time to study the numbers for The Meet. (He had found time to temporarily ease J. Peter's pain with the help of Keith's thong-bikinied-photos, not just because he had become far too anxious to sleep and had to do *something* and those pictures were as suitable as anything else he had handy, but also so he'd be able to tell Keith he had done so without lying. Keith would ask, and he *would* know if Jim hadn't been and wasn't now appreciatively forthcoming. Jim had flushed the evidence, so Sweet Little Amy would be none the wiser. If he *hadn't* taken such clever care to hide his tracks, Amy would ask if he'd been thinking exclusively of her *during*, and would also know that he was lying.)

Jim would never dream of thinking of sweet little sister Amy *during*; but, despite the fact that he was an English major and aspiring writer, and that Amy was intelligent way, way beyond her birth circumstance, Boss Jim had zero confidence that he'd be able to explain any of this to her.

So on the flight down (direct, almost on time, coach, completely full, aisle seat, exit row, uncomfortable but could, of course, have been much, much worse) Jim studied the numbers carefully. Bottom line—as long as they could *keep* the club as trendy and popular as it had been for the last three years—it would be a good investment, with a far better cash return than his Schraft Street holdings were providing. Problem being, of course, how much could he get for those holdings—and how long would it take to get a fair price.

Wallowing in this kind of detail got him to seriously start thinking about everything that such a move would entail. Sure, in a way he was addicted to Schraft Street. But then he thought about Linda and The Famous Foursome. Big Bill, Fat Frankie, Carlton, Ronnie Doyle, Jay, the regulars at the bar and the gym and the strip club, even Lloyd Dolson . . . sadly, he had to admit that although he knew almost everyone on Schraft Street, he did not have any friends on Schraft Street in the close, unremittingly supportive, and very special way that Linda and her cohorts were friends.

There were also, of course, people on Schraft Street like Hoary Harry . . . and this damn Detective Lou . . . and, maybe the brutal murderer of Hoary Harry *wasn't* some out-of-town mobster punishing Harry for seriously stupid drunken and easily avoidable transgressions, but someone far, far closer to home.

Jim then decided he definitely needed to stop thinking about Harry. He was starting to have a real problem focusing on free-falling Harry's murky threat to Amy rather than on his own surprisingly clear and even more surprisingly fond memories of playing T-ball with Harry as little kids. He couldn't believe how bad he now felt about Harry's brutal demise, right after half-wanting to kill the stupid SOB himself.

And, of course, then there were the Schraft Street women . . . Dale, Amy, Amy's roommates, Fabulous Faye, The Famous Foursome, many others . . . he'd hate to leave them forever . . . on the other hand, maybe never seeing any of the troublesome bitches ever again wouldn't be the dumbest thing he'd ever done either.

Hell, he had absolutely no idea what he'd do . . . or what he should do. It was painful to picture growing old on Schraft Street; but how could he imagine what a totally new life in Florida would be like? The good news being that he didn't have to decide on this interminable damn flight, at least. Anyway, it sure would be good to see ol' Keith. A thoroughly sane friend. What a concept.

But Keith was only one guy—and Keith genuinely loved women, and vice versa, and accordingly Keith spent a great deal of time in their company. Keith was a totally straight guy who'd had more than his share of quality girlfriends, but who'd also, Jim knew, *enjoyed* numerous platonic relationships with smart and substantive women.

Jim smiled. Moving all the way to Florida primarily to be near Keith Garrity was an absurd idea; maybe even as absurd as the idea of growing old on Schraft Street.

But then Jim grinned broadly when he saw Keith in the terminal, wearing a clownishly oversized chauffeur's cap and holding up an elaborately decorated huge sign that said, "Hardcore Jim Herlihy. Boss of Schraft Street. Welcome to Sunshine and Sanity." Jim couldn't deny that he was genuinely thrilled to see old friend Keith.

Jim had taken an eight a.m. flight, and by the time he slipped into Keith's new sky-blue Corvette, it was almost twelve.

Keith said, "Your call, old bud. We can go to The Meet right now—which doesn't open until five—talk some serious business over sandwiches, and have a stress-laden working afternoon. *Or* we can immediately proceed to Bradley's down on The Waterway, have lunch and a few cold ones at the covered outside bar, savor the soft breezes and these sunny high 70s, and work on the girls. Bartenders, waitresses, and civilians, most of 'em sexy, some of 'em available, even to pasty-white muscleheads like you. And then tend to the serious business tomorrow."

It was indeed eye-squintingly sunny, low humidity, and the breezes off the Inland Waterway were blissfully soft, especially compared to the bitter winds that had been blowing down Schraft Street of late. When he had first gotten on the plane, Jim had thought it made sense to dive right into the business proposal, get the complicated, painful details out of the way, and then really relax with Keith, while mutually pondering the pros and cons over beers and breezes. But after four semi-miserable hours on a packed plane—on top of the last couple frustrating weeks of Schraft Street—there was no way Jim was now gonna pass on an afternoon of sun and beer and gorgeous views—sun-splashed water and suntanned woman—in and around Bradley's.

Keith knew the sexy young bartender, Debbie, manning the covered outside bar, who was obviously quite impressed with the charming young entrepreneur. But she was a friend of one of Keith's 'casuals,' and Keith told Jim she was definitely out of bounds for him.

Debbie was also immediately attentive to Jim, so he said to Keith, "This isn't a setup, is it, ol' bud?"

"No, I wasn't even sure when we'd be here, or who'd be working. I haven't mentioned you to woman one, so you are on your own, just as you prefer. You're always complaining about overly attentive females on Schraft Street, so you shouldn't have any trouble garnering a little attention down here, without any pimping on my part."

Keith somberly commiserated with Jim over the painful coincidences and complications surrounding the sad and violent demise of old teammate Harry, finally saying, "Let it go, Jimbo. Harry chose to live in a dangerous world, and then alcohol got the better of him. Gangster madness. It has nothing to do with you, poor little Amy . . . or the real heart of Schraft Street."

They then lightened things up some by casually talking business for a couple of pleasant beer-sipping hours, interspersed with plenty of reminiscing and catching up.

Just when the beer and conversation and surroundings had Jim marveling over how much he was starting to enjoy this much needed getaway, two women sat down next to Keith, one young and very attractive, the other older and married. A boss taking her number one protégé out for a few mid-afternoon drinks as a reward for a project well done, it would turn out.

When Keith slipped into a focused conversation with those two—obviously working hard on the attractive young and unattached one—Jim had no choice but to turn his attention to Debbie The Bartender, who wasn't busy at all here on a weekday mid-afternoon.

Debbie had been working at Bradley's fulltime for a couple of years, and had aspirations of becoming one of the assistant managers in the near future. When she learned that Jim actually owned a bar—even if small, local, blue-collar, and sports-oriented, about as different from Bradley's as a watering hole could be—she peppered him with questions, enough of them insightful that Jim, for the first time in a long time, started to actually enjoy talking and thinking about Schraft Street Sports.

She served him a couple more beers, and Jim now regaled her with tales of Fat Frankie Leonnetti, The Big A, Eddy Harcharik and his scrawny mug-firing wife, the wildly-out-of-place and newly contentious Gay Guys, and the generally colorful cast of construction and factory workers, cops, sports fanatics, semi-alcoholics, and marginal criminals and lowlifes who frequented his establishment and provided him with part of his marginal living. With a few beers in his tight belly, Jim was a reasonably funny fella, and by the time the growing late afternoon bar crowd stole Debbie away, Jim had her laughing pretty good.

The two women next to Keith left, and Keith headed to the men's room inside. On his way back, he spoke briefly with Debbie, and then sat back down.

Keith gave Jim a big sly grin, and said, "I could tell you like Debbie, and that she likes you even more, which she has just basically confirmed. She gets off at six, and we now have reservations at eight for four at Morton's right down the street. The ladies are both going to meet us there; they're big girls who are accustomed to making their own way in this world. Let's leave now, we want to smell good and be semi-sober for the affairs of what should be a reasonably long and very satisfying evening."

Jim chuckled. "Well, I guess I did just enough to pretend I had some hand in setting this up. If I had any money I'd say the classy thing now is for me to insist on picking up the entire heavy tab at Morton's. But I just got done telling you I don't."

"Yeah, well, that's the thing—you invest your time and your money in The Meet, you'll be able to afford to do the classy thing in the future. Among innumerable other benefits."

It was just a few hundred feet along scenic Flagler Drive on The Waterway to Keith's luxurious condo at Trump Towers—with wall-sized windows overlooking that same Waterway—and just a few hundred yards further to Morton's Steakhouse.

The Morton's steak was, of course, perfect, and the atmosphere calm, quiet, and generally delightful. Debbie knew Keith's date as a semi-regular customer, and the two ladies got along just fine—and were reasonably intelligent and pleasant conversationalists. They also seemed to think Jim Herlihy and Keith Garrity were the two funniest fellas in the history of West Palm Beach.

After Jim and Keith had taken turns telling funny stories about growing up on Schraft, Keith said, "Schraft Street can certainly be nonsensically lively, but, believe me, the lower-middleclass and the blue-collar folk have no monopoly on nonsense. I met this attractive, sophisticated heiress at that great bar at Chuck and Harold's on Poinciana Way over on Palm Beach, and dated her for a short time. She was a little older, very wealthy, had a great condo right across the street from the ocean, and managed a high-end art gallery there on the island. Anyway, she's taking me to this fancy charity shindig at The Palm Beach Country Club, I don't know any of these heavy hitters, I'm pretty nervous, and so I start to have a couple pre-event cocktails to loosen up. But she stops me—'No, no, *no,* Keith, you got to be on your absolute best!' I'm not in the place a half hour, sober as a judge, go to the bar, and two guys there are cussing each other out at the top of their lungs, f-bombs everywhere, and even a couple c-words made a notorious surprise appearance right in the midst of Palm Beach High Society. I myself had to actually help physically separate these two superbly dressed drunken madmen—and sprained my shoulder doing it!"

Jim said, "Well, then, that fancy dame was right, you did have to be at your absolute best . . . you just misunderstood the *why* of it."

Keith picked back up, "Quiet, Jim, I'm not done. So then, about midway through dinner, there's a commotion outside on the patio. An impeccably coiffed and attired society matron has suddenly gone down, unconscious, back of her knees against a chair, short chubby legs sticking straight up in the air. Someone immediately starts CPR, 911 is called, huge emergency response springs into action. But then her half-hammered husband—who it turns out had lugged her out there for some fresh air—comes back from the men's room yelling, 'Stop all that! Stop! Get off my wife! She's not dying. She's just dead fuckin' drunk!' I kid you not—those were his exact words."

"Again it's good you didn't have those pre-event drinks," said Jim. "Otherwise you might not have *remembered* those exact words—and that her legs were short and chubby, and sticking straight up."

Debbie said, "Life sure can be fun and funny down here, Jim."

Jim replied, "Life can be fun and funny up there on Schraft too . . . Schraft just likes to parcel out the 'fun and funny' sparingly, so no one gets jaded."

After the girls had a couple of martinis, they were laughing so hard and loud that Jim and Keith together quietly agreed to table the humor for the rest of the meal. That slowed the lithesome young beauties down some, but they still sometimes laughed loudly despite the fact that Jim and Keith were no longer trying to be funny.

They seemed like nice girls, so Jim was somewhat surprised at how readily they agreed to repair to Keith's gorgeous condo. But, Jim had slowed his drinking to a crawl in anticipation, so by the time they left Morton's he had the beginnings of a mild hangover, and, after watching the sexy Debbie prowl around all afternoon and evening, was more anxious than ever.

So he decided he was now in no shape to render rational (or anywhere near *impartial*) judgment on the changing mores of modern young women.

Leaving, the image from *Cuckoos Nest* of Jack Nicholson encouraging young Billy Bibbit to "Burn this woman down!" popped into Jim's beleaguered skull.

When he was done, thoroughly spent and knowing he was just about to fall into a deep sleep, he chuckled, thinking that Nicholson line was as apt a description as any of what it felt like he'd just done. Thankfully, young Debbie hadn't seem to mind the least little bit.

In fact, she'd whispered, "Wow. Yikes . . . How much of that was me versus life in general?"

"Believe me, lithe young Debbie, you played a major role. Leading lady, and then some."

Fortunately, although Debbie was working late the very next night, she was enthusiastically available for a reprise the following, as was Keith's latest, with the sumptuous start of the evening moving from Morton's to Ruth's Chris Steakhouse, just around the corner from the center of City Place, and from The Meet.

Tonight Jim and Keith would grab a quick meal at City Cellar right across from The Meet, and then spend the evening studying the mid-week happenings at the club, up close and personal.

Before delving into the complicated tasks of the day, they worked out at an LA Fitness Center in downtown West Palm, a short walk from City Place. Keith was a tall, lean, fit, athletic fella who still looked like the competent quarterback he had been in high school, but he was no weightlifter. They went to the gym after the early morning crowd had cleared out, and got two benches side-by-side. On bench presses—and actually, on most exercises—Jim literally worked with twice the weight Keith did, on all sets, so it made no sense to use the same bench, constantly changing the weight. Jim had long since given up busting on Keith about the light weights he lifted. Especially since he himself was so abjectly vulnerable relative to the comparatively very light wallet he wielded these days.

And Jim already knew right well that ol' Keith considered being rich and popular more important than being strong and muscular.

MBA Keith was a gifted financial analyst, and mini-entrepreneur Jim was competent, so they spent the rest of the day compiling numerous 'conservative,' 'likely,' and 'optimistic' permutations and combinations of financial projections for Jim's net cash from sale of his Schraft Street holdings, and then for the next five years of income he'd receive from his resultant share of The Meet.

The bottom line, they finally determined, was that he'd "likely" have from The Meet about twice the cash in hand of his monthly $6k on Schraft Street. And, for the time being, Keith would be more than happy to rent Jim a very comfortable room in his three-bedroom, two-bath luxury condo overlooking The Waterway, at a very reasonable price.

Jim eventually decided that, although Keith obviously had plenty of both male and female friends, business associates, and a plethora of attractive, interested women down here in West Palm Beach, Keith also felt the powerful need for a trusted—and sensible—old friend. Jim would actually have preferred it if Keith had stayed a little more "businesslike" about the whole thing.

Jim was in fact in no position for this to be about anything except what was best for Jim Herlihy—at this point in life he could not afford to worry about what was best for Keith Garrity, Big Bill Donnelly, Dale O'Dell, Amy Jordan, Fat Frankie Leonnetti, or Schraft Street in general.

In the late afternoon, as Jim and Keith were nearing the end of their day's good work, Jim was surprised to get a call on his cell phone from Detective Lou, without Sergeant Carrollton. Jim could tell almost immediately that Lou didn't have anything new, and was just trying to shake him . . . and to create an opportunity to talk to him without Jim's old friend and current tenant Carlton.

Lou soon said, "I understand that that absolutely gorgeous little Amy's in your apartment all the time. You *gotta* be nailing her! And you were convinced degenerating Harry was gonna rape her . . . at least. So you took care of the drunken lowlife. That's illegal, but it's not the worst thing a very tough stand-up guy ever did."

"Just thinking about it's *not* illegal; and like I said about ten times, that's as far as I got. Nailing sweet little Amy wouldn't be illegal either, nor, of course, is that any of your business—but, for the record, that's yet another thing that all I did was think about. And, just between us Detective, I think about a lot of woman that way . . . and actually get to do precious little. *Although*, I did have a good night last night. And I hope you didn't, and are now jealous."

"You are wiseass cool, I'll give you that," growled Lou. "But, be advised, it pisses me off and makes me all the more determined to nail your self-righteous ass . . . Boss."

"Detective Lou—that would scare me if I was guilty. I am innocent, and therefore it does not. I honestly don't know what else to tell ya, Detective."

After Jim hung up, Keith said, "Be careful, Jim. Watch the news—innocent people get wrongfully convicted all the time. How worried are ya, anyway?"

"Can't help being a little . . . but I'm a lot less worried than I'd be absent old friend Carlton."

Keith grinned. "Yeah, ol' Carl's a lot better guy than he likes to let on. He used to bust my balls big time in the locker room after a tough game . . . but on the field there was no one on that team I'd rather have had protecting my blind side."

Later that night Jim and Keith sat together at the long, winding, mirrored bar at The Meet, with Keith pointing out the regulars, the operators, the loose women, the big spenders, the drunks, the few troublemakers, and the known and suspected hookers. Disagreements and even fights were not quite as rare as the sophisticated surroundings and well-dressed patrons might imply, and the club employed several well-trained, competent, and under-control bouncers to discreetly maintain order.

Keith said, "We have location, design, very attractive surroundings inside and out, reasonable prices for what we offer, attractive and well-trained bartenders—male and female, as you can see—and we work hard on promotions, special events, and basically doing whatever it takes to remain a hot spot for young professionals who like to meet people, have a good time, enjoy a few drinks, and who definitely have a few bucks to spend. I personally talk to a lot of customers about what they like and don't like about this place, and we react accordingly . . . what are you chuckling about now?"

Jim stopped chuckling but kept grinning broadly, and said, "My customers like my location, the prices, the TV's, sometimes each other, surprisingly often Fat Frankie, and, it seems lately, especially slurring drunken nonsense into my poor ears. I was just picturing Fat Frankie tending in here. We should fly the burly, bearded, tattooed bastard down one time just to see the customer reaction."

Keith laughed and said, "You don't have to go to all that trouble. Just go take a big dump in the middle of the dance floor, that'd provoke a reasonable facsimile of the likely reaction."

Jim said, "From Schraft Street Sports to The Meet. Talk about a step up . . . at least on the surface."

Keith replied, "Just because someone is attractive and well-dressed and well-groomed and well-mannered doesn't necessarily mean they're shallow, Jim. And, believe me, all of your customers aren't genuine authentics, either. Plenty of 'em really *are* drunken bums or vicious lowlifes, just as they appear."

Jim grinned. "At least plenty."

Two of the most attractive and best-dressed women came over to Keith, and he introduced Jim, acting like this was going to take a while, at least. Keith and Jim had earlier agreed that tonight they'd be, for the most part, very interested observers, and be satisfied with the sexual antics of the night before and the reprise planned for tomorrow. But Jim knew that Keith was absolutely unable to resist the company of reasonably attractive women, even the all-too-common boring ones.

The woman, 'Kimberly not Kim,' who gravitated to Jim proudly told him that, at age thirty, she'd just been promoted to audit partner at the local office of KPMG, the youngest female partner in the national firm's history. Jim thought that was extremely impressive and even interesting, but that he definitely didn't need any more detail. She gave him plenty anyway, while he maintained his usual friendly, inviting politeness.

He couldn't help thinking of the one accountant he knew well, Lloyd Dolson, 5' 6," 130 pounds, coke-bottle specs, earnest, honest, upbeat, well-meaning; and reluctant aficionado of strip clubs and sometime hookers. At Shenanigans Lloyd was always telling Jim, "Don't let me have more than six beers or three lap dances, good bud. I'm counting on ya. And, please, save me from myself, and talk me out of the after-hours activities." Sometimes Jim could, sometimes he couldn't, sometimes he was either too tired or too bored to try. Either way, Lloyd always forgave him.

Kimberly had held the floor long enough, so Jim chanced Lloyd Dolson and Lloyd's colorful clients, and his own Schraft Street holdings on her. Executive CPA Kimberly definitely did not find Jim's insights on his Schraft Street lifestyle as humorous as bartender Debbie had. Jim also did his best to let his genuine respect for Lloyd Dolson and the challenges he faced in providing financial advice to the marginal people and businesses that were Lloyd's 'professional' world shine through. He thought he'd done a decent job of really listening to 'Kimberly not Kim' and understanding her high-level work with substantial companies, and asking some insightful questions for an outsider, and she'd seemed appreciative.

But he thought she was now doing a piss-poor job of reciprocating, and Jim was genuinely surprised and a little disappointed that he could not make the economic aspects of Schraft Street—admittedly of minuscule scale, but still, 'business is business'—interesting to someone like 'Kimberly not Kim.'

Jim started wishing KNK and her friend would drift away, so he and Keith could get back to sipping beer, observing, and discussing potential plans. But soon he could tell that ol' Keith was succumbing to familiar temptation, and KNK was happily back to extolling her own virtues and successes. After a while, although Jim felt for his part he and KNK were hardly connecting on anything remotely resembling a meaningful level, she seemed comfortable with his prowess as smiling, handsome, uncomplaining backboard; and, he guessed, she was becoming increasingly attracted to him.

Jim grinned. He honestly didn't quite understand his attraction for quite a few women. Lack of competition, he generally supposed. And more than one woman had told him it was his hair and especially his winning smile that had captured her heart. Jim grinned even more broadly at that thought, thinking about how deserving that made him feel. At any rate, that attraction certainly had its pros and cons—which, he now supposed, was only fair, given the shallowness of its genesis.

But, what the hell. Boinking an attractive new 'youngest-partner-ever' of a national CPA firm in the guise of a definite 'one-time-only' would be something of a notch on the old belt, at any rate.

Later, in the throes, Jim thought of how Amy, Consuela, and the other pros talked of "being boinked angry," and how sometimes that was exciting, and sometimes it was just painful and scary. And, he once again thought of the ol' "burning this woman *down!*" Over the years, given his surroundings, it would have been impossible for Jim not to have had plenty of up close and personal instruction from a variety of off-duty working girls, and, early on, he had been quite the apt pupil. So, in circumstances such as these, Handsome Jim Herlihy knew what he was doing.

In any event, young superstar CPA KNK, like aspiring bar manager Debbie, did not seem to mind the amorous shenanigans of Hardcore Jim Herlihy at all.

Afterwards, KNK said, "Wow. Brother. Talk about a gentle strength. And are you always that energetic? Or was it at least a little bit me?"

"I'm usually pretty enthusiastic, that I cannot deny. On the other hand, you are my first KPMG Partner."

Jim had the exact same seat on the return as he'd hardly enjoyed on the way down. In fact, he spent about five minutes fantasizing about absolutely beating the crap out of the President of Delta, and then cramming and bending the bloody beaten bastard into a really, really tiny space. Apparently he was smiling broadly while doing so, because a passing stewardess stopped, and leaned in.

"Had a good time in West Palm Beach, did we, Handsome?"

Jim grinned back. "Well, it wasn't that I was having all kinds of fun sitting in this tiny seat, Lovely Lady. Having you stop by, however briefly, is a definite step in the right direction, though."

She gave him a big smile, and a light pat on the thigh. Then she squeezed his quad, and whispered, "Wow."

Jim was relieved that the affairs of the last three nights—he doubted 'Big Papi' himself had ever had a more satisfying 'three-for-three'—now had him sufficiently relaxed that his stew-inspired boner was barely noticeable. The middle-aged matron sitting next to him gave him a funny look anyway. Jim responded with his usual easy, friendly grin, while thinking, "If I'd gone 'oh-for-three' in WPB, ma'am, you'd really have something to look funny about."

He pushed the seductively-smiling, thigh-squeezing stew out of his mind—although knowing right well that she was gonna slip him her number sometime during this three-and-a-half-hour endurance test—to once again review the numbers and the opportunity. But, he pretty much had the numbers memorized, and anyway, the financial comparison was a no-brainer.

That got him to thinking about ol' Keith again. Of course, Jim hadn't met all of Keith's friends. But he suspected he'd met most of them. Jim decided that perhaps Keith didn't have any closer 'guy friends' in West Palm than Jim himself had on Schraft Street. But Keith sure did have a lot of woman friends, including many platonic—and seemingly quite close. In fact, one of Keith's partners, Carol Matthews, had seemed to Jim to be something of a 'big sister' to Keith.

Keith had told Jim that Carol was forty, really, really smart, was a successful lawyer-turned-entrepreneur, and not only owned a substantial piece of The Meet, but she also owned a Beef O'Brady's restaurant, two Tire Kingdom franchises, and three beautiful homes in the upscale 'Olympia' development in Wellington, twenty minutes southwest of downtown WPB. Carol had bought the three homes in foreclosure at a very substantial discount, and then fixed them way up. Two of them she rented, one she lived in with her adorable six-year-old daughter, who Jim had met, and, of course, then immediately thinking of the six-year-old Amy. Jim thought the word 'adorable' didn't do either one of those little girls justice.

Jim had immediately liked Carol himself, and after just thirty minutes discussing plans for The Meet with her had to agree that she certainly seemed unusually bright and savvy indeed. He also found her quite attractive, in a sophisticated, full-figured but very shapely, mature way. Keith had insisted that he harbored no such thoughts himself, and considered Carol solely his mentor and good friend.

When Jim and Carol were alone for a few minutes, she said, "For some reason Keith seems to have his heart set on you investing, moving down here, and working closely with him at The Meet. How serious are you about all this?"

Jim gave her a brief, somewhat sanitized summary of his Schraft Street Situation, concluding with, "I honestly don't know. I'm not sure I even know how to decide. But yeah, sure, I'm damn serious about trying to figure it all out, anyway. And, yes ma'am, I certainly do consider Keith a true friend."

Carol said, "In baseball, tie goes to the runner. In life decisions, anything remotely resembling a tie *usually* goes to the status quo . . . except for those delusional 'things are always greener' type folks, which I can already tell that you are not. I think you'll figure it out, Jim." She chuckled. "*Two* very eligible thirty-five-year-old bachelors cutting a very wide swath through West Palm Beach . . . Keith needs to genuinely fall in love and settle down and have a family before it's too late."

After a few very thoughtful seconds, Jim replied, "I guess I agree. That boy is certainly a ladies man at the moment, but I do believe that deep down he's really a family man at heart."

She laughed lightly again. "I hardly know you well enough to offer any sensible advice regarding what the hell you should do. But you do seem to have a somewhat strange life up there on that Schraft Street."

"Yes ma'am. Everybody on Schraft Street's life is at least somewhat strange. And definitely some more than others. You probably wouldn't even want to visit."

Carol laughed heartily at that. "Actually, I'd love to *visit.* I like to see strange places *once.* Keith had already told me some about you and Schraft Street. Anyway, if you have any questions you'd prefer to run by me rather than Keith call me. Seriously."

CHAPTER ELEVEN

Actually Under A Cloud

JIM HAD TAKEN AN EARLY morning flight, so the cab from Boston's Logan dropped him off on Schraft Street around one. He was planning on a salad and protein shake, and then, hopefully, back deep into the writing. He was really tired after a very unusual three straight nights of sleeping restlessly with company, and would have liked to work out this afternoon and go to bed early; but he reluctantly decided best to hit the gym late, when it would be mostly empty.

Walking into his third floor apartment, he was dismayed to see that he had an amazing fifteen messages on his home phone. Jim's closest 'friends' . . . Keith, Lloyd, Dale, Amy, Big Bill, Fat Frankie, Editor Steve Chadwick . . . had his cell number, and would not have left a message on his home phone. These fifteen had to be problematic, and probably even idiotic. Jim thought of Matthew Broderick being happy to come home to twelve messages, only to find that most of them were from the hilariously twisted *Cable Guy*. Likely culprits Jay and Connie were certainly twisted, but if there were two people further from hilarious than that aggravating pair, Jim hadn't met 'em and sure wouldn't want to.

Anyway, why would anyone in this confounding world be happy to have a whole bunch of damn telephone messages to deal with?

But before Jim could pick up the phone to start the painful checking, there was a very familiar knocking on his door. When no sweet little girlish voice immediately followed shouting shocking obscenities Jim felt a flash of concern.

It was Amy, but Consuela was with her, and for their part they certainly looked concerned.

Inside, Amy said, "Asshole Columbo had me take a lie detector three times! I passed with fuckin' flying each and every, though, and I could tell the little weasel was really pissed that I did. They were gonna make Monstrous Bill take one, but then the idiot confessed that he'd been with not one but two of our compatriots all that fuckin' night. Big jerk had been embarrassed to admit it before 'cause he'd paid 'em top dollar, and you know he likes to pretend he's above sorry shit like that. And I think he didn't want me to find out. I'm sorry to say that I could care less, but please don't tell poor Bill that."

Jim said, "Actually, we both need to start telling him that more convincingly, Amy, for the gargantuan lug's own good."

Consuela said, "Boss Jim, I guess Monstrous Bill was their number one suspect, and so now he's totally in the clear. Obviously, they're gonna make you take the test."

"They can't *make* me take it . . . but I'll take it and I'll pass it. What else?"

"I know a lawyer works pretty cheap, plus he gives good discounts in exchange for free boinks," said Consuela. "For you, Sweet Bossman, I would *literally* put my big ol' ass on the line, multiple times . . . he is a pretty mediocre lawyer, though, but still better than nothing."

"Guilty people need good lawyers. I do not. Thanks for your good heart and generous ass, though, 'Suela."

"Uh oh, 'Suela, my Jimmy *used* to be kindhearted and supportive," said Amy. "But when restaurants advertise *generous* portions, I don't think they mean firm and shapely portions."

Consuela turned around and patted her butt, saying, "Nothing mutually exclusive 'bout generous *and* firm and shapely, young lady."

Jim said, "Indeed."

Amy said, "Seriously, Jim, I just saw this pretty damn disturbing documentary, about those West Memphis Three idiots who spent eighteen years in jail blamed for something *truly* horrific that *they* almost certainly didn't do! That tragic shit happens, My Darling."

Before Jim could respond, there was a loud, authoritative knock on the door. It was Sergeant Carrollton, thankfully alone. Carrollton said, "Scram, Sweethearts. I need to talk to Mad Dog Herlihy alone."

Consuela said, "Not even close to funny, Sergeant Carlton Cockknocker."

On her way by Amy punched Carlton as hard as she could—which wasn't very hard at all—on his very sturdy shoulder. She was at best half-kidding. Carlton said, "Out! Ya feisty little knucklehead."

Competent-Cop-observant Carrollton immediately spotted the fifteen on Jim's blinking land line, and said, "Mind playing those while I'm listening, Boss?"

"For the hundredth, I haven't got a fuckin' thing to hide. Including that I serve in the company of fools."

Carlton grinned sardonically, and replied, "I mostly believe the first, and have abundant firsthand knowledge of that last."

Many of the messages were from both Jay and Connie, Linda had called a couple of times checking on his progress on that damn article, Dale had called saying she wanted to talk about Connie, the cashier at Schraft Street Market apparently wanted to give him the latest Schraft Street scuttlebutt and—surprisingly—Keith's smart and wealthy partner Carol had already called, suggesting that perhaps she and Keith really should visit Schraft Street to help him decide. She said Keith did often talk of a brief visit to his old stomping grounds, and that it might even be interesting for her, like an educational safari to The Galapagos Islands or something.

Having just listened to several messages from Connie and Jay, Jim thought that if Charles Darwin himself had visited a place like Schraft Street after those Galapagos he probably would have gotten so confused he'd have never finished *Origins of The Species*.

But Jim didn't have time to marvel at that last, because of the two messages that Carlton had obviously been looking for. They were from a guy calling himself Bradford Benny, "a good friend of Hoary Harry," who wanted to meet Jim at Shenanigans, "just to talk." Jim remembered Harry mentioning Benny as a scary but smart and straight-shooting guy who Harry considered a good friend. Benny was obviously from Bradford, but he did not hang on Schraft Street, and Jim could not remember ever meeting the guy.

Jim looked at Carlton, who said, "I'm sure our downstairs lovelies told you about the alibying shenanigans of Monstrous Bill. Disappointing, that—there's just no morality left in this world. And that we'd like you to come in and get tested. You ain't much but you're all we got."

"Then you don't just not have much you don't have anything at all. But, set it up then. Tell me about Bradford Benny. And do you have an extra gun you can lend me?"

"We honestly don't know whether they're looking for answers 'cause they really don't know, or if it's a smokescreen for our benefit. And you don't need a gun . . . at least not yet."

Jim said, "Bradford Benny."

"Yeah, he has the potential to be a problem. But, like I said, at the moment he's either just looking for some answers or setting a smokescreen 'cause they know damn well who did it. These guys think they're better detectives than we are. Hey, they may be right."

"Like the Savage Brothers in *Mystic*."

Carlton shook his head. "No. Benny is much, much smarter than the Savage Brothers, or even the grief-stricken Sean Penn character who wasn't any genius either. If you're innocent that's a good thing."

"*Since*, not if, Carl. I gotta write this book, plus I got other complicated shit to deal with. I need my sleep. At this point a gun under my pillow might help."

"There's three cops living on the first floor. I will swear to you, Jim, first that you have nothing to worry about at the moment, *anywhere*; and second that as long as we're living on the first floor you'll never have anything to worry about *here*. They are not gonna come into a cop house, whether we're home or not."

"Alright, I'll take the lie detector. Anything else?"

"Hell yeah. Meet with Benny, and wear a wire. He'll know you might be, might even want you to depending, but at this point he won't check, he'll just be careful with the questions he asks, and he won't really answer any of yours. But we still might be able to pick up something. And we'll have a good undercover in the corner, pretending to be infatuated with that gorgeous little Amy, which shouldn't be hard to do."

Jim said, "Taking lie detectors and wearing wires. What in the Good Christ next!"

"Shit happens, Boss. I suspect you want old friend Harry's killer caught almost as much as we do. And, good fodder for the book, I s'pose, anyway."

"Yeah. Okay. So, what do wired folks do?"

"Be as innocent as you have been with us, stay sober, be polite, listen carefully, don't threaten beyond your gifted natural vibe, and generally keep cool. Sort of just be yourself, I guess."

After Carrollton left, Jim thought about that gifted natural vibe. A good-sized half-drunk guy at The Meet had bumped into him when Jim was coming back from the men's, and the guy had stopped, immediately sporting the ol' alcohol-infused totally confident, sneeringly mean look. Jim had done his best to look semi-apologetic—he was after all considering becoming one of the owners—but while thinking, "Yeah, you got a prayer, fella." The guy had taken his first good look at Jim and then wordlessly hurried off with a stricken look on his face, as if Jim had magically morphed into one of the Klitschko brothers. Jim decided it had been like that, not always, but more often than not, at least since high school.

Jim was far from the biggest or toughest guy in the world—hell, he knew he wouldn't last more than a few seconds against a truly out-of-control Big Bill Donnelly, if such a catastrophic circumstance was even possible—but he was tough enough, smart enough, and especially cool enough that, without ever having to back down too badly, he'd never lost a serious fight in his life. Probably lifetime 20-0, he figured.

So he decided he was undoubtedly overdue for a beat down, all the more reason to continue to be very careful and very cool.

Jim had that salad and protein shake, and listened to those damn messages again, while he generally pulled himself together. Get the hard stuff out of the way first, so he called Bradford Benny, and was very relieved to get voicemail. He left a message saying that all he had for Benny would be a recap of several recent relatively brief conversations with a pretty drunk late and great Harry, but he'd be at the bar at Shenanigans Friday and Saturday night between seven and nine as usual, just about anyone could point him out, feel free to stop by.

He was on a roll—he got Connie's voicemail too, and left a message saying that if Connie would call him back with a description of the help she was getting, he'd consider letting her back in the gym in a few weeks, as long as she agreed to be there only when Jay wasn't, at least for awhile.

He got Linda at work, told her some about his trip to WPB but saying that it was purely to catch up with ol' friend Keith—he obviously wasn't gonna tell her about his two nights with Debbie The Bradley's Bartender or that he'd also managed to squeeze in a very energetic one-nighter with a partner at the prestigious national CPA firm KPMG, and he was *definitely* not gonna divulge that he was considering leaving Schraft Street forever—and then had no choice but to promise to now turn his full attention to that article on The Famous Encouragingly-Less-Fat Foursome. He realized he was thus totally blowing that meticulously crafted daily word count timetable for the damn sequel—and for securing that blessed advance.

He called Dale, and before she could lay any emotional pro-Connie psychology on him, he quickly recapped the message he'd already left for Connie. His pre-emptive strike didn't work—Dale still suggested that it would mean a lot to poor Connie if Jim would take her for a non-alcoholic dinner at The Schraft Street Diner as a concerned friend, and lay plenty of the ol' Jim Herlihy commonsense and good nature on the very troubled young musclewoman.

In the end Jim was amazed that, despite his best protestations that just talking to Crazy Connie for a few agonizing minutes on the phone was way above and beyond, the irresistible Dale finally got him to agree to that dinner. Without so much as one beer to lighten the scary load.

Christ, maybe he should forget about Dr. Dale. Lord knows the hold she'd have over him if he was actually nailing the uppity bitch.

He thought about Keith-Partner-Carol—and whether he should call Keith about her message, or just return her call directly. The hell with it, he'd call her directly, but he'd do it tomorrow. He'd already spent way more than enough time on the damn phone for one weary afternoon.

He pulled out the Delta stewardess' number. She'd told him she lived in Marshfield down on the South Shore, so he'd have to invite her here, where all could see. Forget that. As a considerate gentleman, he considered calling her to explain that he'd purely love to—she had seemed quite interesting, so that would be no lie—but that he just could not at this time. But then he thought the highflying slut probably gave her number out to plenty of guys, and he'd undoubtedly end up as just another of the forgettable 62.5% who never responded, so the hell with it. He balled up the piece of paper, and made the shot halfway across the room, expertly banking the tight little wad off the wall and into the corner wastebasket.

So now he wouldn't even have to get up, proving that sometimes good things really do happen to good people.

Jim woke the next morning—ten hours after he'd hit the hay and briefly reveled in rolling around alone in his top-of-the line king-sized before very quickly falling into a deep, dreamless sleep—feeling just fine. He might yet get Carrollton to set him up with a gun, but it wouldn't be to help him sleep. Jim almost always slept soundly, despite what he'd told Carlton.

(There was actually but one person on Schraft with the power to affect Jim's sleep, and it damn sure wasn't Bradford Benny or any other lowlife gangster. And Jim Herlihy was a pretty pragmatic and tough-minded fella when it really counted, losing much-needed sleep over Dale O'Dell certainly wasn't gonna help him win her heart, so he'd pretty much overcome that problem, too—even though he was every bit as much in love with the lovely lady as he'd ever been.)

The gym had been mostly empty at nine-thirty last night, he'd had a fine upper body, shoulders feeling great even on his heaviest benches, and then he'd really hammered the heavy bag. Newly bruised mitts post-Harry wouldn't prove he was innocent, of course, but they would prove that it *could* have just been the big bag all along. Jim grinned, thinking how proudly he was gonna display those badly bloodied knuckles in a couple of days while passing that lie detector, with, as Amy had said, "flying fuckin,' each and every."

In fact, he'd hammered the bag so long and furiously last night that finally Ronnie Doyle had come over and said, "Hey, Boss, two middle-aged matrons just handed in their membership cards and ran out the door. Said they were gonna go look for a gym where the owner wasn't totally insane."

"Now might not be the best time for jokes about my sanity, young fella."

"Ah, everybody with half a brain around here knows you're the sanest guy on Schraft Street, Boss . . . although, that is a small percentage of the subject population, that I cannot deny. Yeah, best be careful."

Jim grinned. "Sanest guy on Schraft Street. That's like being the best player on the Red Sox, these sorry days."

Walking home, taking a shower, getting ready for bed, Jim had thought about young Ronnie, who was only twenty-three years old. Not much older than Amy, in fact. Ronnie had been coming into the gym for about four years, and working for Jim and Big Bill for two. Jim had always liked him, and figured that if Ronnie was closer to his own age, they might have been pretty good friends, even outside the gym. Ronnie had a good sense of humor, and *at least* half a brain, maybe even 75 percent, which was a pretty good record for this vicinity, to quote the late Captain Quint.

When the company providing cleaning services for the gym had recently raised their rates sharply, ambitious Ronnie—who was already closing the gym most nights, with Big Bill tending at Shenanigans—had asked to take on the midnight cleaning himself, at the outside services company's old rates. And then proceeded to do a better job than they ever had.

Ronnie worked out religiously, even though he had the kind of genetics that didn't allow for much muscle growth or even definition. He was in good shape, though, reasonably strong and with well above average endurance pounding on the bag. He was also a knowledgeable and responsible personal trainer, and had built a decent afternoon and early evening clientele with the average folks, despite the fact that there were so many more impressive-appearing trainers working out of the gym. Like Connie and Jay.

Jim grinned. If he was a beginner, he'd be uncomfortable having Connie working out anywhere near him, never mind putting his joints and his physical well being smack into her veiny man-hands.

That started him thinking about that dinner with Connie that uppity bitch Dr. Dale—who virtually *everybody* liked anyway—had probably already set up. That would be a tense and tricky meeting requiring some serious mental preparation. But then he pushed Connie out of his mind as quickly as he could; that mental preparation would have to wait. He'd be sacking out soon, and bedtime thoughts of Connie Parker were hardly conducive to a good night's rest.

CHAPTER TWELVE

Bradford Benny

A STRANGER WHO HAD TO be Bradford Benny spoke to the Shenanigans bouncer/doorman, who pointed to Jim and then waved with a smile. Jim returned the doorman's wave, and politely asked the guy sitting next to him—who he knew casually, and with whom he'd talked potential Red Sox offseason moves earlier—to find another seat. The guy looked at Benny, and gave Jim a concerned, questioning look. Apparently, the guy at least knew who Benny was, and, of course, he had to have heard the rampant 'Mad Dog' Herlihy scuttlebutt, although he hadn't asked Jim about it. Jim made a mental note, naturally, to ask the guy about Benny later, although he seriously doubted the guy could tell him anything that Carlton hadn't. Or more than Jim would be able to pick up firsthand tonight.

Jim looked at his watch. It was five-of-nine. Mind-gaming Benny had come in right before Jim would have left for his own bar, so Benny would have some stupid little psychological advantage from rearranging Jim's schedule.

Bradford Benny was a short, slight, and generally unimposing guy physically, who still came across as quietly formidable and even scary. He reminded Jim of 5'5" Dan Grimaldi playing twins Patsy and Philly Parisi, *Soprano* subordinates, one of whom got whacked, and one of whom urinated drunkenly and copiously into Tony's swimming pool because he was pissed that his twin had gotten knocked off, for scant cause. Not the most satisfying revenge Jim had ever seen depicted on the tube; but it still had been one hell of a whiz. But then, of course, when it came to just one whiz—no matter how copious—into a pool as big as Tony Soprano's, what you don't know has very little chance of hurting you.

Jim pictured Patsy telling Annabella Sciorra to stop bothering Tony, with very scary smile. But actually, Jim now noted that Benny seemed to him quite a bit handsomer than Grimaldi, although Jim was not the best at figuring out what was attractive to woman. Jim knew plenty of guys that he'd have thought women ought to prefer to himself; but they did not.

He figured Bradford Benny had never been in a fistfight in his life—but probably had killed a few people. Certainly not Hoary Harry, though, at least not directly. Benny would be hard pressed to beat up a healthy twelve year old.

Benny sat, ordered a Beefeater and tonic, and said, "I hate strip clubs. I see a woman naked, I want to fuck her but good, ASAP. What's the point?"

Jim replied, "I don't pay all that much attention myself, or stay all that long. But there's usually someone here not too bad to talk to. Plus, my own place up the street, the whole night is basically Bruins and Celtics. The second half or third period is enough of that for me."

"Fuck the Celtics and Bruins. Fuck Bill Belichick and Tom Brady. Fuck the Red Sox and fuck their fried fuckin' chicken, and their generally gutless play and incompetent management. Who gives a shit, and boy what a rip-off all that is. Ya can't fix any of it no more, so, again, what's the point?"

Jim grinned. "You don't care about strippers or sports, no wonder we never see you on Schraft Street, Benny. Would you come if we built The Schraft Street House of Ballet?"

Benny didn't acknowledge that, just watched the stage for a few quiet seconds, and then looked hard at Jim, and said, "So that's the underage-looking little twat fucked up poor Harry's head, eh. Yeah, she really does look like some perverted asshole's sweet little daughter, alright."

Just about anyone else, Jim would have said something in such a manner that the guy would have been immediately looking for another seat, or more likely, another bar. But Jim knew that Benny was just trying to get a rise out of him, and that Harry had undoubtedly told Benny something about Jim's relationship with Amy.

Jim replied, now looking at the 5'5" Benny as if gun powder had never been invented, "Amy's got an amazingly good heart for someone with such awful luck. She never meant Harry, or anyone else, the least bit of harm. What was she supposed to do, pretend she was in love with the poor smuck?"

"Harry was no smuck to me, Boss. He was a true *friend*."

"Not my closest, admittedly, but I considered Harry a friend too, Benny. I actually miss him. I'm truly sorry he ended up like that; and no I did not beat him to death, wish him ill, or lay an unfriendly hand on him since we were kids."

"The dumpster dunking. Why Harry would challenge someone like you with empty hands I have no idea. But then Harry was never the brightest. Not with money, not with business, not with women, and, obviously in the end, not with friends, enemies, and other associates."

Jim looked the much smaller Benny right in the eye, and said, "What really got him spiraling downhill, Benny? His obsession with Amy had to be a symptom, not a cause."

Jim was obviously feeling a touch of guilt himself, but what he was really asking was, "If you liked him so much, Benny, why didn't *you* help him?"

Benny looked back at Jim like he knew exactly what Jim was asking. Benny then said, "Of course she was a cause. Big, strong, *threatening* law-abiding business owners like you were a cause. All the shit I just said he wasn't too bright about was a cause. And some weak motherfuckers become alkies without any cause. Bottom line, I have no fuckin' idea why my good friend Harry went downhill, and probably never will. At the moment I don't have much of an idea of who beat him to death, either . . . but I sure do intend to find that out. Tell me what *you* know, Bossman."

Jim recapped his latest confusing and confounding conversations with Harry. He thought he was staying reasonably brief and to the point, but soon enough Benny was silently rolling his eyes and giving Jim a mini umpires' finger-twirling home run signal.

Jim held his temper and quickly finished—but he was now fantasizing about doing to Bradford Benny what Bradford Benny may or may not really suspect Jim had done to Hoary Harry. He glanced at Benny again, and stopped fantasizing. In a world where empty hands were the sole option, pulverizing the unarmed Benny would be like beating up a woman. In this world Benny would just shoot him, if not during then later, 'cause Jim wouldn't be able to actually beat anyone all the way to death unless they'd already done him or someone very near and dear serious harm.

Benny hadn't done that, and Jim was still expecting that if he himself stayed cool Benny never would.

Jim then said, "How much did Harry owe ya anyway, Benny?"

"If that's all ya got for me, Boss, I gotta go. Thanks for the time. This fuckin' place sucks, by the way. And your little shithole of a bar isn't any better."

Jim noted that the guy he'd figured for Carlton's undercover left shortly after Benny did. He also guessed that the tape of his conversation with Benny would be of zero value to Carlton and his cohorts; even if they could separate the talk from the loud music in the background. Jim thought Benny had underrated Shenanigans overall, but he had to agree that the constant loud music certainly sucked.

Jim had one more beer, generally gazing vacantly into space, while thinking about how grossly unfair it was that a little weasel like Benny—who would have been absolutely obliterated in, for example, a fair fight with Crazy Connie—could strut around intimidating people just because he was psychotic enough to shoot someone in the back of the head without losing sleep over it. He did admit to himself that Benny had to be pretty clever too—to have so far kept his ass out of jail and his own skull out of that line of fire.

Jim finally decided that Benny's day probably would come soon enough, and that gave him some comfort. He slipped out of Shenanigans before Amy or Consuela could corner him, and that made him feel a little better too.

But then the Gay Guys were once again boisterously making their presence felt in Schraft Street Sports, Eddy Harcharik and The Big A were both there past their bedtimes, and the Bruins were down 3-1 with only six minutes left, all of which made Jim feel bad enough to call it a night. He helped The Big A home first, after telling Fat Frankie in no uncertain terms to handle the rest of it. Without repercussions.

Jim almost never spoke that sharply to Frankie, and the burly fella looked at him like maybe he really was Mad Dog Herlihy. Jim just noted that if he ever really, really had to make Frankie do something, he surely could. But then he'd probably feel so bad about it that it wouldn't be worth it anyway.

CHAPTER THIRTEEN

Writing

THE ARTICLE ON THE 20 percent and counting collective progress of
The Famous Foursome went surprisingly well and surprisingly quickly.
Jim was amazed to find himself grinning often while writing it. He called
Linda several times with unavoidable questions, and she was, naturally,
giddy with appreciation. She told him that they'd just weighed in at 790,
so the collective loss was now at 21 percent, and would be even more by
the time the article was completed. Jim assured her that he would in fact
keep updating that magic number right up until publication, and Linda,
as an unusually competent paralegal, was certainly well acquainted with
the magic of modern word processors, so she believed him.

The hard part was convincing her that no more group meetings at
IHOP would be required until the completed first draft was ready for
their review. And, of course, getting her off the phone.

He would have liked to review the first draft with the Editor of *The
Bradford Bulletin* before showing it to The Foursome; but he finally
decided that would increase the likelihood of him being 'tennis-balled'
between the ladies and that editor. He'd get the ladies halfway happy, and
then go fight with the editor. That would be far, far easier than getting the
160-pound editor happy, and then having to go fight with 790 pounds of
loving but very argumentative womanhood.

The ladies loved the draft of the article, and they all gave Jim huge, teary
hugs—he had really played up their somewhat problematic childhoods,

success as paralegals, and especially their genuine friendship and mutual support.

Linda said, "You wrote more about our childhoods and our careers and especially about our friendship than you did about fitness stuff and your business, Jim. You really listened, you understood . . . and you cared. Thank you."

"Well, you certainly gave me some good stuff, ladies. Good stuff to write about . . . good stuff to think about. Thank *you*."

Despite the somewhat unusual unqualified good feelings all around—Jim figured all The Foursome *liked* him, but a couple couldn't help also resenting a little that Jim was never gonna feel about Linda like she did about him—it still took a very boisterous three hours at the IHOP for The Four to finally agree with semi-professional writer Jim on the final changes.

To finally get out of there, Jim had to tentatively agree on one more group meeting to review the final final, while knowing full well that any such polishing would most assuredly be done by Email.

The Editor of *The Bulletin* loved the finished article too, but he still started to propose some changes, as editors have long been wont to do, starting with callously crossed out pictures on the walls of caves. But Jim had colorfully recapped for that editor the complicated and quasi-painful process of obtaining detailed background for the article, and now Jim just wordlessly pointed to the group picture of the very, very brightly beaming foursome that would accompany the article.

The Editor looked at that picture and just said, "I see your point quite clearly, sir," and then, out of the most unusual goodness of his normally cold, cold, brutally critiquing heart, published the damn thing exactly as the ladies had finally agreed.

That made Hardcore Jim Herlihy feel even better than had making that long distance swish with the slutty stewardess' phone number.

Jim did not receive any payment for the article, but *The Bradford Bulletin* did agree to start it on the first page, include a picture of the superbly appointed neighborhood gym along with that picture of the now even more Famous Foursome, and print the address and phone number of Herlihy's Hardcore at the end of the article, all without charging Jim; although he did agree to in the future pay for a small combined gym and bar ad in *The Bulletin* one day per week. Jim figured he could cover the meager cost of that by drinking one less Shenanigans beer on both Friday and Saturday night, something he ought to do anyway.

Two weeks later Big Bill told Jim that so far fifteen new non-muscleheads had bought one-year gym memberships, citing that article as inspiration. None of The Foursome asked for discounts on their memberships, either, so Jim figured he'd been quite well paid for time spent, although his oversized partner did of course automatically receive 25 percent of the proceeds.

So when Jim took The Foursome to dinner in appreciation and celebration, he made Big Bill come along. Doug Ballard was out of town, so he talked Dale O'Dell into coming too. No one ever minded Dale O'Dell showing up, as long as Doug Ballard wasn't with her. Jim even charged Dale with talking The Foursome into The Schraft Street Diner as venue, so those who were so inclined could have an ice-cold beer with their tasty little steaks.

Jim could hardly talk The Famous Foursome into anything, but Dale O'Dell could talk just about anybody into whatever hit her altruistic fancy, as long as nobody's feelings got hurt in the process. Jim would never say it out loud, but now whenever he saw Dr. Dale, he could not help but think that she was an uppity bitch, but he loved her anyway. That gorgeous, demented little rascal Amy.

Innocent Jim had indeed felt quite calm and confident taking the lie detector test, but apparently he hadn't been quite as cool as he felt, because Carrollton told him at the station that although he'd 'passed,' it hadn't actually been with "flying fuckin' each and every," as Amy's really had been.

Carlton told him, "Man, that Amy was one cool, collected character; especially for such a feisty little madwoman."

"Yeah, Sergeant, it isn't like that little angel hasn't been steeled some by going through about a thousand times more than her fair share by the time she was fourteen," replied Jim. "I thought you kept your eyes open most of the time, sir."

"Yeah, right, sorry; far be it for the likes of me, Boss."

Then the 'Lou-Columbo Hard-Ass' told Jim that his test had been much closer to inconclusive than to "passing with flying fuckin," and that he'd best continue to keep the Bradford Section of The Boston PD informed of all travel plans.

Jim didn't bother to look at the nattily dressed, handsome little prick, instead he smiled slightly at Carlton, and said, "I can't afford to go anywhere else anyway. And apparently West Palm Beach is now gonna come to me."

Carlton replied, "So, that snobby cocksucker Keith Garrity is gonna be slumming on Schraft Street. Good. He's an arrogant prick but I like him anyway."

"Christ, Sergeant, now you're just about quoting the demented little rascal."

"Well, she can grow on ya, Boss."

"Hey Carlton, Keith is gonna be bringing this lady business partner of his, who is about the same age as The Fabulous One, and even reminds me a little of Faye . . . except for about seventy-five points of IQ and fifty damn decibels of vocal cord."

"She reminds you of Faye even the least little bit, then she must be pretty dumb for her IQ," grinned Carrollton. "But then I guess she'd have to be, to bother coming to this place all the way from West Palm Beach, in late November no less. Sounds like I'd enjoy boinking her anyway, in the event you're now offering me a bribe."

"She's all business, Sarge. I don't think Carol's gonna be boinking anybody while she's here. Not even Keith."

Lou-Columbo said, "*Enough,* Carlton." He then turned right back to Jim. "Benny seems surprisingly determined to find Harry's killer. So are we. But so far nobody seems to know anything; the crime scene is mostly clean. Best we can tell, Benny thinks you're a pretty cool customer if nothing else. Whether you're also something of a schizo who went totally ballistic on an unstable and threatening Harry, maybe Benny thinks the jury's still out."

Jim looked at Carlton and said, "I honestly thought Benny lost all interest in me."

Carlton replied, "Probably for now, but no long term promises, Boss."

Handsome little Lou had been staring hard at Jim essentially the whole time, even during the brief interlude on Keith's pending visit. Jim finally could no longer suppress a small sardonic smile in Lou's direction.

Lou said coldly, "Bradford Benny's damn hard to read. Maybe Benny agrees with me that you are too."

Jim shrugged, and said, "I guess I really suck at it, but I'm *trying* to be an open book."

Carlton said, "Alright then. We'll stay in touch, Boss. Make sure you bring ol' Keith by, willya. On the other hand this Carol that reminds of Faye but is all business . . . what's the point, as Benny would say. That much we did pick up on that useless tape."

Jim had that dollop of extra cash from The Foursome-inspired slight surge in new memberships, but he'd spent about half of that on plane fare to WPB, and on the checks for the few beers and meals that he'd been quick enough to snatch away from that arrogant prick Garrity.

Fat Frankie and a few unattractive but formidable female patrons of Sports had long been working hard on him relative to the pungent deficiencies in that beleaguered ladies room. Jim finally got worn down from listening to them, looking at them, and especially from visiting that ladies' so that they could show him exactly what needed to be done and why.

He'd never denied the need. It had just been that given the scant subject population, there'd always been better uses of his meager funds.

But, he finally agreed for Frankie to stop 'nickel and diming' the damn thing, do it right once and for all, and hopefully Jim would never hear another word about it. Unless, of all unprecedented, it was a *nice* word about the Schraft Street Sports ladies.' He knew it wouldn't be, though; not with the preferred speech patterns and sensibilities of Sports' lady customers.

"Wow, June, isn't it nice not to dread having to take a fuckin' piss?"

"Hell yeah, Margaret, remember how that fuckin' shitter *used* to stink to the high heavens. As if every huge drunken whiskey shit you and I ever took in there was immortalized for fuckin' prosperity."

Finally Donna chiming in, "Hey, don't forget me, girls; I took my fair share of beauts that lingered too!"

The good news would be, of course, that he'd just *overhear* that, it wouldn't be shouted in his face, and, best of all, he wouldn't be expected to respond. So, he guessed, the investment would be well worth it.

The problem was, of course, that he didn't have enough cash on hand to pay for it, it wouldn't be fair to make his employee Frankie wait for his dough, and so now he'd have to take on another loan. Jim hated debt, and he owned the three-decker, his 75 percent share of the gym overall, and Sports all free and clear. No debt, except for that monstrous exercise equipment loan that was costing him and Bill $2800 a month. Herlihy's

Hardcore was a gorgeously appointed gym, though, he couldn't deny that; thanks especially to the semi-obsessive passion of his partner, whose head was every bit as hard as it was huge.

Jim grinned, thinking of Big Bill and his loving care of that gym. Bill would storm out from behind the counter—not meaning to be intimidating, just genuinely dismayed—whenever a patron, through either ignorance, carelessness, callousness, or plain over-the-top intensity, would be abusive to the equipment. Woe to those who did not return plates or dumbbells to the proper racks, or even fail to wipe down the bench or stationary bicycle seat.

Bill didn't mean to be so intimidating, but fellas who are 6' 6," 350 pounds, and sport enough muscle to bench well over 600, usually find it difficult not to be intimidating when they are excited and genuinely dismayed.

At any rate, Jim needed some extra cash more than ever; and that promised fifty k advance was more than enough motivation to get him deeply back into the first draft of that sequel.

With two new 'villains,' albeit on opposites sides of the spectrum, based on his unpleasant exposure to Bradford Benny and the hard-assed 'Lou-Columbo' detective.

CHAPTER FOURTEEN

Connie and Dale

DALE O'DELL THOUGHT THAT JIM—AS concerned gym owner and generally kindhearted, responsible leading citizen of Schraft Street—should take Connie to dinner alone. And really listen, emphasize, ponder, encourage, and genuinely try to help. Jim did consider himself concerned and unavoidably somewhat responsible, relative to Connie and to most of the denizens of Schraft Street in general; but he wasn't so sure about that kindhearted. Like most reasonably sane and halfway well-adjusted people he wanted to be kindhearted. But in terms of truly *being* kindhearted, he felt genuinely limited in time, patience, mental energy, personality, judgment, confidence, interest, innate selflessness—and especially in financial circumstance. He knew people did it . . . but how can you be genuinely selfless and kindhearted when you're scraping to keep the roof over your head?

On the other hand he considered Dale herself truly kindhearted. She seemed to have natural, almost effortless genuine empathy and selflessness, and abundant quality time for other people. Even while she worked hard as a P.A., part time but definitely in-demand personal trainer, and Jim knew she had already started seriously studying to be a doctor, even if she could not yet afford to actually enroll in medical school.

Of course, he also knew that Dale wasted zero time and money watching strippers and sports and drinking beer. He guessed that she spent most of her time later in the evenings with that preliminary med school study. At least when that bastard Doug was out of town, which was a lot, especially lately. Thank God for small favors, especially these days.

Jim also thought that Dale had decided that, yes, she was very attracted to Doug physically, as all women were, but also that he had abundant potential to be a good person, potential that she could bring out, and that she, Dale O'Dell *should* bring out. So maybe that was it: she really was attracted to Jim, even almost as much as to Doug, but Jim was already a pretty good guy so current cocksucker Doug needed her help much, much more.

Jim smiled sardonically, pondering that. He wasn't sure that was how Dale felt, but he decided that was as good a way as any for him to consider the puzzling Dale/Doug dilemma, at least for now.

Anyway, after Jim had declined Amy's good-hearted offer to "boink that Doug Babe to show Dale what a phony sleezeball cheater he is," the savvy Amy had assured him that Doug would show Dale his true colors soon enough even without her help, and then the uppity bitch would be Jim's.

Hardcore Jim Herlihy, Boss of Schraft Street, might be halfway sane, concerned, responsible, well adjusted, and even kindhearted, but that did not mean that he was above taking comfort from the counsel of demented little strippers, when such counsel suited his needs.

In the end Dale had reluctantly agreed to accompany Jim to the Crazy Connie dinner, while insisting that she still expected him to do most of the talking. But soon after that she firmly told him that Doug was now going to be all too briefly back in town, and that Boss Jim would just have to handle it himself, as he should be doing anyway.

Then she proudly told him that so-handsome Doug would soon be auditioning for a part in a popular daytime soap opera. She said he probably wouldn't get it, but wouldn't it be great if he did.

Jim asked where that stupid soap was filmed, and Dale said New York; but never mind, Doug probably won't get it.

Jim thought that if Dale moved to New York, that might make it easier for him to move to West Palm Beach, which might just be the right thing for him to do, long term. But he wasn't really any closer to deciding. And, he could not deny, his heart had dropped at the idea of Dale moving away. He also wondered why the apparently well-off Doug wasn't already putting the self-studying Dale through Med School; it had to be either that the hypocritical lothario was too cheap and uncommitted, or that

Dale herself wasn't ready. Or some combination thereof. At any rate, Jim would be thrilled to see the future Dr. Dale officially on her way, but not if it also meant being officially indebted to that bum.

Anyway, for Jim there was that first draft sequel and the fifty k into hand to be accomplished before he could actually pack up and go. Not to mention the ongoing Mad Dog Herlihy cloud complicating the complications.

At The Diner—Jim's treat, of course—Connie and Jim both had two of those delicious little steaks. Jim figured Connie was about 5'9" to his 6,' and about 160 pounds to his 210. She had better definition and less body fat for sure, undoubtedly due in no small measure to the damn steroids, so her body would use almost as much of the protein in those tasty little devils as his would. That actually made him feel slightly better about buying them for her.

She said, "I'm working out at the Powerhouse over in Chelsea, but it means I have to take the fuckin' T. Time and money wasted. Some of my clients are willing to meet me there, some aren't. That's a killer. I've stopped taking the bennies, can't afford 'em any fuckin' way. That plus the strange gym mean my strength and muscle are down some, and I can't tell ya how much I hate that."

"You look great Connie, as least as good as ever." Thinking, of course, that losing a few ounces of muscle should be the least of Connie's problems, but knowing full well that it was a huge issue for her.

"Bullshit, Boss. You never have looked at me; how the fuck would you know? Got a girlfriend who's showing me some yoga, which is boring as shit but I'm doing it anyway, maybe it does help calm me down. Most important is I broke it off with that lying, stealing, cheating, infuriating dickhead Jay. Actually, that's calmed me down a lot more than ditching the speed, and all the dumb twisting and bending, as if trying to lick my own asshole. I can't afford no fucking psychiatrist, though, if that's where you're heading."

"Pretty serious what you did, Connie. Someone easily could have been seriously hurt or even killed."

"Yeah, that's what I've heard about a thousand times now, and I do believe it. So I swear I won't ever do it or anything like it again. There you go. Let me back in so I can make a living, pitiful as it is, Boss."

Connie stared at Jim, looking scarier than ever, no mean feat. When 600-pound-benching Monstrous Bill said even he was scared of Crazy Connie, Jim knew that on some level the big fella was not at all kidding.

Jim said, "Sure you don't have anything in your health insurance that could help with this, Connie? Might really do you some good. No stigma anymore; think Tony Soprano."

Connie snorted. "Fuck Tony Soprano, I know who he is but I've never actually watched him. You think I have money for HBO, Boss? I'm lucky I can still afford my 'roids. And my health insurance basically sucks; nothing for mental. I'd have to get caught doing something really bad to see a shrink; and then I *would* be found fucking competent, believe that. Despite what all the retarded cocksuckers around here are always saying about me."

Connie was now looking at Jim as if the "getting caught" part was the iffy portion of her getting to see a state shrink. She was saying some of the right things, but she was not saying them in a way that made Jim comfortable with letting her back into his gym. Surely not with the truly dangerous precedent she had set. Jim knew that if kindhearted, extra competent paralegal supervisor Linda—the badly bruised innocent victim of Connie's explosive temper—was listening to this and observing Connie from a safe distance, Linda would say, "No way, Jim, no way. I really am sorry, but no freaking way."

Jim now thought that Connie was surely headed for real trouble, and he felt genuinely sorry for her, despite the incredibly hard look she was giving him, with that face that had long been countless thousands of dollars worth of steroids past any hint of feminine softness.

Of course, it also flashed through his head that if Jay had been found dead instead of Harry, this would be one lie-detector-test-taking woman. But Jim had seen Jay hale and hearty at the gym just last night, certainly seeming that his only care in the world was this next set of inclines with 455 freaking pounds. Relative to Connie, Jay just seemed as if he felt well-shed indeed. As, Jim thought, he certainly should; as long as Connie didn't throw any more iron plates at his head—or worse.

Jim was aching to end this ASAP, but he forced himself to stay, bought Connie a couple of pieces of Fabulous Faye's pies for dessert, and even one for himself, working hard on the empathy, and on developing that kind heart that the lovable Dale swore he had.

Nearing the end, Jim could only say, "I honestly understand the problem this is causing you, Connie, I really do. I'm gonna think hard on it, and talk to Big Bill, Ronnie, Linda, and Jay, as I must . . . *say*, you have friends at the gym, and around the neighborhood . . . maybe we could say you have some type of illness, need some help, take up a collection, actually get that serious anger management therapy we're talking about here."

Connie snorted again. "Yeah, all my fuckin' friends. Everybody calls me Crazy Connie, everybody would know what it was for, and the cocksuckers would all gleefully throw in a few pennies, 'Hey, look, we raised fifteen dollars for the crazy cunt. Not enough for anything medical, but it would at least buy a helluva straight razor to cut her fuckin' wrists, and be done with it' . . . I ever do come to that, I won't go alone, Bossman, you can bet on it."

She threw her dirty napkin in his face and stormed out.

Jim sat stunned. This poor woman—who had made his gym her 'home away from home' for years—might well be beyond hope.

Faye came over and gave him a great big hug, saying, "Hang in, Boss, hang in. Your best is all you can do."

Hardcore Jim Herlihy then hurried out of The Schraft Street Diner on the verge of tears. Some Mad Dog he was.

Jim worked legs in prime time the next night, hoping Jay already had one of his young zealot admirers to squat with, and that Dale would be there un-Dougged.

The good news turned out to be that a very high potential young stud was gleefully chasing Jay up the squatting poundage ladder, the two of them whooping and hollering and high-fiving after every steroid-fueled set like they were a couple Alabama linemen who'd just caused a fumble and recovery in the national championship game. Jim grinned. To each his own and good for them.

The bad news was that not only was Ballard there—big handsome smile, bright white teeth, glowing artificial tan, naturally broad shoulders, slim waste and hips, lean muscular legs, just the right amount of bulk to go with that great bone structure for an almost perfect silhouette, spreading his gift of gorgeous charm throughout the gym—but Dale brought Doug over to the leg area, expecting that Jim would provide the sensitive Connie-debriefing in Doug's presence. Jim was dying to talk Connie with

Dale, and he'd already tried her several times on the phone. But he didn't even want to talk about how he'd enjoyed today's quiet, *solo* pre-workout Diner-dinner in Ballard's presence, never mind the potential suicidal-and-or-homicidal tendencies of an apparently *increasingly* Crazy Connie.

He exchanged the usual briefest perfunctories with Doug, politely and skillfully being sufficiently off-putting that Doug did not dare lay any details of the soap opera audition on him.

Jim just told Dale, "The Connie dinner did not go quite as well as hoped. Now is neither the time nor the place. Call me back, willya."

Dale was, as expected, genuinely disappointed. She said, "Oh, I'm so sorry to hear that. Maybe we can go for coffee and dessert at The Diner when you're done working out."

Yikes. She actually wanted Doug to be involved in this Connie madness at some level, presumably as part of some kind of personal development project for the phony, narcissistic son of a bitch. But, Jim was only gonna take this kindhearted nonsense so far, and it was definitely gonna stop far short of Doug Ballard.

So Jim said firmly, "I got work to do yet tonight. But please call me tomorrow, Dale. It is important."

Sergeant Carrollton came in then, and offered to do legs with Jim. Dale and Doug left, Dale promising to call Jim tomorrow, but doing so without the lovely smile. Actually, Jim thought that was the first time Dale had ever parted from his company without at least a small smile. But, between Doug now and Connie earlier, Jim did not feel much like smiling either. In the end he gave his still-beloved Dale his best effort anyway, fortunately catching her eye just before she turned away.

Carlton was perfectly happy to use the exact same weights as Jim on all sets of squats, and on thigh extensions and leg curls too. The sergeant also now had basically the same attitude as Jim on weight training in general: it was a good thing to do, he enjoyed it, kept a reasonably regular schedule, energetic workouts could be a nice, restorative offset to the general frustrations of Schraft Street, and he got self-image satisfaction from being fit and strong—but it was still a means to an end, and far from the most important thing in life. Which were general health, making a living, the work itself, the friends and associates, the local Boston professional sports teams, and finding a good wife. Not necessarily in that order, either in terms of importance, or especially, in terms of degree of difficulty, given Carlton and Jim's somewhat strange shared surroundings.

Jim *thought* Carlton was thoroughly on his side, and if so, was certainly happy to have him there.

Carlton soon said, "You seem even more distracted than usual, Boss. Let Monstrous Bill and Fat Frankie handle some of the shit."

Jim just shook his head sadly, thinking about putting the Connie matter into Big Bill's hands. Bill talked tough when it was Jim's call—"Just ban her forever, Boss, it's a no-brainer"—but if Connie did get to personally appeal to Bill's semi-obsessive love of muscle and all things lifting, Bill would quickly cave. And then forget about it, until disaster struck.

Carlton smiled and said, "Don't tell me you broke down and nailed that sweet but noisy Linda, now did ya? 'Cause I read that love letter you posted to The Famous Foursome in *The Bulletin.* Anyway, I thought you were gonna write another 'good guys and psychos' novel, and finally pay me my overdue?"

"Carlton, as if your midget hardass partner and Bradford Benny weren't enough, now I gotta deal with a certain iron-plate-hurler named Connie Parker, who isn't but could be kin to Bonnie Parker, if ol' Bonnie had been a little more psychotic. You know everything, so I'm sure you know all about this."

Carlton exclaimed, "Holy shit, Boss! I myself cannot deny jerking off many times with that marvelous ass top of mind, but I'd never dream of doing anything with the real thing. Sensible Jim Herlihy my ass!"

"I only had what was supposed to be a counseling dinner with her at The Diner, since I *am* supposed to be Sensible Jim. Of course, we all know I'm only sensible in comparison, present company included in that comparison. But, Connie's been a paying member for a long time, and even brought in some business, plus that body is a good advertisement, at least from a distance. So, I owe her something, I s'pose. What the lovely Dr. Dale tells me, anyway. But in the end, before she threw her napkin in my face and stormed out, Connie seemed to be threatening to off herself, or me, or someone . . . Do you guys worry about Connie?"

Carlton thought for a moment, and then said, "Well, everyone certainly knows Connie and Jay were doing the illegal PEDs, which are pretty expensive, at least relative to what those muscleheads make. Probably some coke just from time to time. She blasted that guy in the nuts at Shenanigans, and roughed up a couple of the girls too, who decided not to press in the end. But, fuck it, let's table the crazy bitch for now, and finish the damn workout. High rep squats are painful enough without adding

Crazy Connie to the mix . . . by the way, why the fuck are we doing 20 reps now, with this lung-busting 315?"

Jim laughed. "Jay told me to."

Carlton laughed too, sweat pouring down his burly cop's big face. "Oh, okay. Now it makes perfect sense."

There was a message from Dale on his land line when he got home, apologizing sincerely for not calling him back sooner, and urging him to call back tonight, "no matter how late you get home. Jim, we have just got to help poor Connie." Of course, he'd come right from the gym, and he'd worked out in prime time with the no-bullshit Carlton, so it was not late at all, only about 8:30.

He recapped everything with Dale, bringing her to tears at the end, when Connie had mentioned offing herself. For now he downplayed the threat to take some people with her.

Dale latched on to the idea of a collection for an unnamed illness . . . maybe some serious internal 'female problem' . . . but Jim mentioned Connie's very real fear of a very well publicized humiliation. Everyone knew Connie, many guys lusted after her regardless of the scary mug—but despite the craziness and drugs, Jim didn't think Connie was particularly promiscuous, and her offer to him had been when she wasn't dating anyone—but Jim and Dale both knew right well that she didn't have many friends. Now that she was on the outs with Jay, Jim couldn't think of any, unless you counted him, Dale, Big Bill, and maybe that forgiving little sweetheart Amy.

Jim finally said, "Dale, I did my best. And who knows, maybe despite the emotional outburst at the end I did some good . . . or at least got some kind of ball rolling. But if we agree a civic collection is the way to go—and we can't seem to come up with any other ideas—then *you* are gonna have to summon up your wealth of feminine compassion and persuasion and sell it to her. Or, at least come with me next time—if there is a next time for me."

That's how they left it for now.

CHAPTER FIFTEEN

Sane and Successful People on Schraft Street Safari

JIM BORROWED BILL'S RICKETY OLD pick-up truck (driver's seat uncomfortably sunken as if a 350-pound man had been intermittently sitting in it for seven years) to pick Keith and Carol up at the airport a few days later, at 10:30 AM. They'd taken the red-eye, leaving WPB at 7:00. Boston had just enjoyed a few days of late November sunshine and unseasonable warmth, but now it was back to gray, drizzly, windy, and generally just teeth-chatteringly raw.

Jim said, "Flying from West Palm Beach to Boston. Three and a half hours of wishing desperately that you'd never been born."

Carol replied, "Actually, Keith had the aisle, I had the window, and the middle seat was empty. I enjoyed the quiet time, nothing to do but read this very entertaining nonsense about time travel and the Kennedy assassination by Stephen King. I read about 200 pages, damn near 20 percent of the monster."

Jim said, "Whew, that there tome is a bulky bastard, maybe even the literary equivalent of our Monstrous Bill; I'm surprised they didn't hit ya with a surcharge for bringing it on the plane. But you flew coach and were comfortable, here in the US of A, and in this year of 2012? That's the most amazing thing I've heard since the Sox came back from three down against the Yanks, way back in ought-four."

"I've visited Boston twice, but totally as a tourist," said Carol. "My business interests have always been local entrepreneurial, so I've never even been here on business. So the downtown, Fanueil, Freedom Trail, Fenway Park, Copley Square, Locke-Ober, Beacon Hill, the Common, the Greenway, that's the kind of touristy crap I've done. I'm looking forward to seeing a Boston blue-collar gritty neighborhood up close, in the hands of a genuine expert."

"You're here for three days and nights. I can show you Schraft Street up close and *very* personal in a few hours. I suppose we can work out and eat and drink the rest of the time, if you want to stay on Schraft for the duration. And, I hope you're one of those straight women who can appreciate watching a very in-shape and athletic, thoroughly unclad young lady do some amazing feats of pole dancing."

"Ah, the acrobatic exploits of the lovely little Amy Jordan!" exclaimed Keith.

Carol said, "I can, I actually can. Remember, I'm on safari. You certainly don't have to be a hunter to enjoy watching big game."

"Seriously, Carol, I'll be amazed if you don't really, really like young Amy," said Jim, smiling almost as broadly as he would if Amy had suddenly appeared in person. "Who knows, maybe *you* can even talk some sense into that gorgeous little skull."

"I am only here for three days, Jim. And given what you and Keith have told me about Amy and her circumstances, maybe she really is doing the very best she can. We'll see."

Keith said, "Carol and I are planning to follow you around and observe the highs and mostly lows of your daily existence, Boss. And then, out of the goodness of our hearts, *help* you compare that insanity to the joys of living and prospering in the sunlight."

Coming out of the terminal, Carol shivered and exclaimed, "Boy does this weather suck though!"

Keith said, "Not even winter yet. Boston in late January is one safari that this adventurer is gonna pass on."

"Yeah, last winter was an incredible reprieve," replied Jim. "Now the long-term prognosis is that we're gonna pay for it this year—and the weather knuckleheads are saying it like that's a good thing."

Carol turned out to be relentless. Jim did indeed take her and Keith with him as he reviewed the gym's finances, and maintenance and equipment needs, and strategized with Big Bill and Ronnie Doyle and Lloyd Dolson, likewise with Frankie Leonnetti and Schraft Street Sports; and then on to Shenanigans and Amy and Consuela.

Jim soon realized, of course, that Carol's constant intense interrogations were primarily designed for his own enlightenment rather than hers.

Carol and Keith had been sworn to secrecy relative to Jim's big decision. Never mind the brutal demise of Hoary Harry and the implications with regard to that—a *compounding* deafening increase in the hubbub of Schraft Street ringing in Boss Jim's ears was hardly going to help him see the future any more clearly.

Carol and Keith read and liked Jim's article in *The Bulletin*, and then met the subject More-Famous-Foursome at the gym, and naturally liked them too. They proudly announced that they were now down to 784, and Linda said that there should be a little block in *The Bulletin* tracking their weekly progress. In the end, Jim had little choice but to promise to publish a brief follow-up article when they reached a collective 700-even, a loss of 30 percent, and an average 175 pounds of fun and good humor per.

Jim tried to picture the beaming, already less-round-faced Linda at her published goal of 135 pounds; she'd started out around fifteen pounds lighter than the others, and she still was, now at 160, at about 5' 6." He figured she'd look pretty damn good, and with that personality should finally have a satisfying romantic life—if she would then keep the weight off. And, maybe quiet down just a tad, while undoubtedly loving life even more than she already did. Then Jim tried to picture her with Monstrous Bill; because, well, you never do know.

Keith and Carol volunteered to give Jim their opinions on his draft so far of that sequel; Jim was seriously tempted, but then decided it was just too early yet.

One night Keith and Carol accompanied him as he helped The Big A home. Neither of them understood one word of 'A-speak' either, dashing Jim's hope that two pairs of fresh ears might be of assistance in that regard. On another night Carol helped him calm Eddy Harcharik's wife, while Keith gently removed the beer mug from her fingers, right in the middle of her wind-up.

Early one evening at the gym, Carol met Dale and Doug Ballard. Jim wanted Carol's unvarnished feedback on Doug, so he'd been non-committal in describing him upfront to her. Other than to say that Ballard was better looking than any guy had a right to be. Carol replied that Jim and Keith were pretty good-looking guys in their own right, and

Jim answered—after an ironic smile, soft chuckle, and small shake of his head—that there were good-sized guys, and then there was Big Bill.

As Dale approached with Doug in tow, Carol whispered in Jim's ear, "Now I see what you mean. I wish this Doug was unattached and liked older women, and that I was a one-night-stand type of girl."

Jim let the black cat halfway out of the bag by whispering back, "Ah, the handsome scoundrel doesn't deserve Dale, and he doesn't deserve you either, Big Sister."

The next night Carol worked out with Dale, sans Doug Ballard, who had gone back to New York. Two women of unusual intelligence, kindness, and overall quality immediately bonding, as such women are wont to do.

Straight-talking Carol interacted substantially with just about all of Jim's friends, employees, acquaintances, and neighbors, and then peppered Jim with serious questions about them; and about Jim's relationship with them.

Jim thought that if she were a detective with the BPD, the Hoary Harry case would have been solved, and he would be in the clear.

In fact, soon after high school QB Keith had caught up with his old honorable-mention-all-state left-tackle Sergeant Carrollton, Carol interrupted—put a very, very wet blanket on, actually—the funny, locker-room-style high school reminiscing by saying bluntly, "Carlton, I can tell clear as a freaking bell that you're a full hundred percent sure that your very good friend Jim here had nothing to do with the tragic murder of your poor old teammate Harry. Why can't you get your damn Detective Lou off our Gentle Jim's case?"

The would-be Detective replied, "Got his *own* mind, does the natty little SOB. Plus, all cops know—and really everyone knows, if they'd admit it—that you can never truly know what someone is capable of, when seriously pushed. So, yes, Carol, I do know right well that my good friend and old teammate Jim would never absolutely pulverize my old teammate and not-so-good friend Hoary Harry . . . but that knowledge still cannot be a full hundred percent. Anyway, *technically* on this case experienced Detective Lou is my boss . . . and once in a great while I have to actually let him be."

Carol said, "Experienced . . . *and* competent and fair?"

"Seems reasonably so, and that is the rep," answered Carlton. "Lou's certainly not gonna frame Jim, or anything close . . . and so far Mr. Schraft Street Cool here doesn't seem all that bothered by the attention."

Jim shrugged, and said, "Bored more than bothered. Although, I'd also very much like to see Harry's killer caught, and so have somewhat mixed feelings about wearing wires and such. Anyway, because of his relationship with me, I gotta believe Carlton's barely able to stay on the case. Let's not get him thrown off now."

Carlton added, "Yeah, Lou really wants me 'cause I know the neighborhood and the people so well; all too well, actually. But, he is also wary of the relationship, and if Jim ever were to move from marginal to prime suspect, I'd be out of it. That ain't gonna happen, though."

Jim said, "This isn't making me feel any better. Let's move on."

"Let's," agreed Keith. "I don't feel like joking about old times anymore, though."

Amy had a night off from Shenanigans, so Carol invited Amy and Dale to join them for dinner at The Diner. She'd also invited Big Bill and Sergeant Carrollton, but they were both working. Still, Jim thought the five of them comprised quite a group as they were.

But they were not five. Amy showed up with one young and good-humored Ronnie Doyle. Jim and Dale exchanged big grins. Why hadn't they thought of that? Well, perhaps because of Ronnie's oversized other boss, and his sentiments regarding Amy. And, Ronnie was sort of an ordinary looking guy, albeit probably a little better looking than average, and certainly in better shape, although he didn't jump out as weight-trained, the way even Jim himself did.

And little Amy Jordan was definitely a head-turner, even when dressed conservatively and with class, as she was tonight. Jim thought maybe Carol had advised her on this unusual look, but then he decided that that wouldn't have been necessary. Carol was always dressed impeccably and appropriately for the occasion, be it a high-level business meeting, the gym, Schraft Street Sports (with Frankie-renovated and now semi-acceptable ladies' room, Thank God,) or Shenanigans.

But Jim thought young Amy Jordan had an innate sense of style that rivaled Carol's.

Jim also thought Carol's expertly honed situational good taste was undoubtedly totally wasted on the denizens of Schraft Street, though. He knew right well that the sole universal thought of these knuckleheads relative to Carol's attire—whatever the venue and appropriate outfit—was basically, "Damn good ass for a broad that age! Damn good!"

Jim was a hundred percent sure of this fact, too, because that's exactly what he'd thought upon meeting Carol.

Anyway, you roll on Schraft Street. So Jim, Keith, and Dale outwardly treated Amy and Ronnie as if they'd been a notable Schraft Street couple for years. But, meanwhile, Jim and Dale, and to a lesser extent ex-patriot Keith, proceeded to very carefully observe the interaction between Amy and Ronnie.

Jim would be absolutely thrilled to see this work out, and he knew Dale would be too. But, that would certainly not happen if Amy continued in her chosen profession—and not just the boinking part. Jim knew Ronnie well enough to know that he was not gonna be seriously dating a practicing stripper, even if she was gorgeous, savvy, funny, and, underneath it all, had a sweet little heart of pure gold.

Jim watched Dale too, and he could tell the wheels were really turning. Jim would help things along wherever he readily could, but for the most part he'd let things unfold as they would; but he knew this was definitely gonna bring out the well-meaning matchmaker in Dale O'Dell. Jim would have to caution her. Jim certainly didn't want to start hearing Amy complaining, "That Dr. Dale is getting uppitier by the day, and now I don't like her so much." And Ronnie Doyle was a good-natured, easygoing young fella, but he definitely had a mind of his own too.

Despite the unexpected company, Carol grilled Dale—politely and skillfully, but it was still a grilling—on Doug Ballard, and Dale's relationship with the unusually handsome and well built model and aspiring soap actor. Jim could tell that Dale was wondering if the interrogation was for his benefit, or perhaps maybe Carol herself had designs on the Doug Babe, as most women did.

Amy and Carol repaired to the ladies' room, without announcing what they were gonna do—just makeup, number one, or number two. Jim only noticed because when Amy was with her primary partner in crime Consuela sometimes they did announce, in some specifics, both thinking it hilarious. Jim didn't think Carol would get the joke, though, so he was glad that Amy had kept things quite properly general this time.

The Schraft Street Diner actually had a very nice ladies' room, which Jim knew firsthand because one night when he closed the place with a late steak and was the last customer, Fabulous Faye insisted he go see it. The Fabulous One had loudly harassed the owner of The Diner into engaging the services of handyman Fat Frankie, and he'd just completed his usual excellent if hardly inexpensive job. Faye was quite proud of herself, too, for seeing after the hygienic interests of most of her fellow workers and half of her customers. Faye was not a regular patron of Schraft Street Sports, but she had used the ladies,' and she had immediately and passionately busted Handsome Jim Herlihy about its pungent shortcomings. The newly completed and impressive handiwork of Frankie at The Diner was another such opportunity.

When Jim had recently caved, the ladies room of The Diner had been the model, although Jim didn't have the resources to let Frankie go all out, as Frankie had in The Diner.

In the absence of Amy and Carol, Jim said to Dale, "There's no ulterior motive here relative to Doug. Carol just doesn't go in for superficial small talk, she likes to get to the heart of things, and she doesn't waste time doing it. I've been under intense interrogation for two days now."

Keith added, "Yeah, and I've been under for two years now. But, I'm used to it, and I like it. Big Sister really makes me think . . . *helps* me to think, too."

"Alright, I like Carol too," replied Dale. "But no offense, guys, Carol's getting to a level where I'd prefer it to be one-on-one, and in confidence. Plus I know you don't really like Doug, Jim, and I don't think you do so much either, Ronnie; although I think you're influenced by your two big knuckleheaded bosses."

Ronnie—sporting his usual engaging grin, an easy, genuine smile not unlike that of Jim Herlihy, and a feature that had undoubtedly contributed to his catching the eye of the lovely Amy—replied, "Yeah, sometimes they can be knuckleheads, one way bigger and far more knuckleheaded than the other—but they're pretty good guys who sometimes tell me what to do but never what to think. I don't really know Doug, and don't have much of an opinion one way or the other. Except that I know he's an exceptionally handsome bastard. I know that only because all the women tell me that, just like I know Boss Jim has an absolutely gorgeous ass, only because Linda tells me so. Why she tells me so often I have no idea . . . but I never know why any of The Foursome do what they do, or say what they say . . . what was the question again?"

Keith chuckled, grinned broadly at Dale, winked at Jim, and said, "It's a trivia game, Ronnie. Name the top ten things that make that Doug Ballard guy a flaming asshole."

Dale knew that Keith had just met Doug, and thus knew only what Jim had told him.

Dale said, "Someone from The Meet just called, Keith. You're due back immediately."

Keith replied, leaning over and gently patting Dale's hand, "Sorry, I'm just jealous on a couple fronts; like every guy who sees you and Doug together has *gotta* be."

Jim added, "Not just guys . . . anyone a'tall who has half-decent vision and a pulse."

"Oh shut up," snapped Dale. "If either one of you guys wastes any time at all being jealous of anyone then you're fools."

Before Jim or Keith could answer, Carol and Amy sat back down. Amy said with an endearing big grin, "Now I know *two* uppity bitches I like anyway. You're really, really smart Carol. You must have a fuckin' PhD. *Dr.* Dale and *Dr.* Carol!"

Carol replied, "Just an MBA from Wharton, but you can call me doctor if it suits ya, Amy. You sweet little thing, you."

Ronnie hugged Amy and said, "She is a sweet little thing, but she'd be even sweeter if she'd smooth out the language."

Amy kissed Ronnie on the cheek, and said, "Oh yeah, I agreed and I promised. Sorry, I forgot . . . which brings me to . . ." She looked at Ronnie.

Ronnie said, "Ah, we've been talking about maybe a new career for Amy . . ."

Amy picked up, "One that doesn't involve my freshly unbearded clam . . . oops, sorry, Ronnie, I already forgot again."

Ronnie said, "Amy could help me with the midnight cleaning . . . maybe even on the desk sometimes, if there's a gap between Big Bill and me . . ."

Amy said, "Dr. Dale, maybe you could teach me about that personal training stuff . . . I don't wanna steal any of your business, of course."

Jim had been trying to get Amy to do something like this for a couple years now, even offered to hire her as a waitress at Sports . . . and Faye was always offering to get her a job here at The Diner. But Amy always balked at the tedious work and especially at the relatively short money. Jim was surprised that easygoing, relatively ordinary and unassuming young Ronnie Doyle could have this effect on Amy . . . but, actually, what did Jim Herlihy really know about such matters?"

Jim said, "At the gym, at Sports, even here at The Diner . . . if the lovely little Amy Jordan wants to be saved, Schraft Street can save her almost as sure as it's been trying unsuccessfully to ruin her."

Dale O'Dell—in her own way every bit as relentless as Keith Garrity's Big Sister Carol—hugged Amy hard, and said softly, "Whatever it takes, little girl, whatever it takes."

The night before Keith and Carol were returning to West Palm Beach, they sat with Jim at a table in a quiet corner of Schraft Street Sports. It was a Wednesday night, and a rare late November evening when neither the Celtics nor the Bruins were playing. So, the bar was far from crowded. That made Sports calm and pleasant, for a change, but it didn't do anything for Jim's wallet. That was one thing he liked about Shenanigans. He could savor it being half-empty and relatively quiet and comfortable, without worrying that the night's light crowd was yet another paving stone in his slow road to financial ruin.

That was only as long as Shenanigans wasn't *too* empty, though, thereby leaving the bored and frustrated entertainers with nothing better to do than to delight in pestering Boss Jim Herlihy to utter distraction.

Tonight at Sports Eddy Harcharik was nowhere in sight. The Big A was in his assigned seat, but he'd come in later than usual, without a trace of foreign load. So he was wide-awake, and, at least for the moment, a competent contributor to the conversation at the bar, without displaying a hint of A-speak. In fact, Jim had no doubt that when 'A' was sober, A-speak would be every bit as foreign to its inventor as it was to everyone else.

The slow night also gave Fat Frankie an unusual opportunity to display his considerable talent for keeping that bar conversation lively, reasonably sensible at least for these environs, and, of course, above all, friendly and non-confrontational.

Carol said to Jim, "Schraft Street. What a unique place. By the way, I can't believe how good the food is in The Diner, the quality of the meats and produce in that little market, the high styling of the clothing in that store; and, I guess I can't deny, even how attractive and in shape and friendly and funny most of the poor strippers are at that sad Shenanigans. Not to mention the amazing equipment in your gym; and the most interesting clientele therein. It's kind of a shame the way you do fit in here, Boss. Like Dale says, 'You're addicted to Schraft Street and Schraft Street is addicted to you.' Not necessarily in that order; I haven't quite figured that part out yet."

Keith said, "Not nearly as much as Bossman here, but I was sort of addicted to it too, *if* you include Boston in general, and exclude the torturous winters. And I do miss it, and I do like to visit; but on the other hand I don't have a hint of a second thought."

Jim said, deciding this just now, but undoubtedly based on the hard thinking that relentlessly inquisitive and analytical Big Sister Carol had been skillfully prompting, "I think I have to see how it plays out with Dale and Doug, before I can comfortably decide. I know it seems to the naked eye that I don't have a chance . . . but if I leave now I surely will have an unacceptable level of lifelong second thoughts to bear."

"It doesn't seem to this naked eye that you don't have a chance, Jim," said Carol. "It seems to this admittedly very biased outside observer that in the long term that gorgeous cardboard character Doug doesn't. I don't quite get the high quality and indubitably substantive Dr. Dale's infatuation with Doug, except that he is the best looking man—maybe even the best looking human being—that I have ever seen. Combination of face, smile, big white teeth, hair, physique, and even skin tone. And it's ruined him, especially since as an adult he's always made a very good living with those looks, not just with the modeling but obviously also with the hairdressing. To be honest, I think he's gonna get that soap or something even better, and that eventually he'll move on even if Dr. Dale doesn't. It's hard to imagine anyone passing on Dr. Dale, because that lady does have it all, but Doug seems to me just the kind of gratuitously gifted knucklehead who has but the slimmest idea of what he has in Dale O'Dell . . . then, Jim, you'd be in place, but you'd have to get over being second choice."

"Christ, Carol, I got over being second choice a long time ago. Otherwise, what the hell have I been doing, hanging around here and passing on all other opportunities."

"Yeah, Jim, but in a long-term relationship with Dr. Dale, eventually in the heat of the day-to-day inevitable ups and downs you'd have to consciously resist the temptation to let the memory of the gorgeous Doug Ballard back into the equation."

While Jim pondered that, Carol excused herself to once again go check out the ladies' room handiwork of the talented Fat Frankie Leonnetti.

Jim said, "Hey Keith, when I first met Carol I certainly did think that that was one very sexy older woman, that would be quite exciting indeed. Now that I've gotten to know her some, I really, really like her—but the sexual thoughts are mostly gone."

"Exactly. Big Sister Carol. But, she has her suitors, too, harbor no doubts on that. But they've been older, very smart, very sophisticated, and very successful guys. I and now you are little brothers to Carol, and that is just fine with me."

"Yeah. One way or the other, Keith, help me stay in touch with that good lady."

When that good lady returned she said, "Of course, Jim, you know that since you're passing on The Meet for the time being, we're gonna have to move ahead with someone else. Our partner is hell-bent on pulling his money out now, and we have to get someone to replace that. Since you're not in, I'm gonna take a bigger piece myself, but not all of it."

"But I'm not giving up on ya yet, ol' bud," said Keith. "They'll always be something for ya in West Palm Beach, as long as I'm there and still kicking."

Carol said, "Yeah, I'll certainly second that."

CHAPTER SIXTEEN

Decisions and New Complications

THE NEXT MORNING FOR THE first time in a long time Jim knocked on the door of his very quirky and unconventional second floor tenants. They knocked on his so often that there'd been no need.

Amy answered, and reflexively started, "Holy Jesus Harold Christ, Boss Jim Herlihy at my fuckin' . . . oops, I promised. Hello, Mr. Herlihy, top o' the mornin' to you, sir."

"Come upstairs, young lady. I can't believe I'm saying this, but I need to stick my nose in."

"I can't believe *I'm* saying this, but they'll be no sticking in of any kind now, sir. You missed your chance . . . Hmmm, even that dumb little joke might be considered breaking my promise to my sweet Ronnie. This is not going to be easy, Mr. Jim!"

Upstairs Jim said, "I really like Ronnie, and I really do love you, Little Sister. So?"

"I hope you know by now, Gentle Jim, that your well-intentioned and no longer degenerate little sister would not be playing with the emotional well being of someone as sweet as my Ronnie. He doesn't physically knock me out the way you somehow do, or *did*, kind sir, but I surely do feel something very good when I see that guy coming. I've always liked him, and always felt something for him, too. Not what I felt for you, but a hell of a lot closer to that than what I feel for my dear Monstrous Brother Bill . . . now that I'm committed to being with Ronnie, I don't quite feel the same about you, either. I hope your feelings are at least somewhat mixed about that, too."

Jim grinned, and gave her his usual brotherly hug, and kiss on the top of her head. "Of course they are, ya gorgeous little rascal."

Then he said, "So, you really are retiring from all aspects of Shenanigans, and not just the boinking?"

"I gave 'em two weeks notice. Ronnie wanted me to just quit on the spot, and of course a lot of girls have done that. But they have been pretty damn good to me; at least for a couple of evil money-grubbing exploiters of vulnerable young women, that is. So little Amy Jordan found herself in the ironic position of explaining to her sweet new boyfriend why the *honorable* thing was for her to continue to showcase her freshly unbearded clam for exactly fourteen days; and *then* said clam would be officially retired, except for when he and *only* he was around."

"And Ronnie's okay with that?"

"He's reconciled. I didn't put it exactly like that, by the way."

Jim said, "Maybe they'll find another girl in less than two weeks, and you can surprise Ronnie by getting out earlier than promised."

"Yeah, if they do I will. And they know I'm gone in two whether they have a replacement or not."

"Got some money saved, have ya, Amy?"

"You'd be surprised. I really am pretty smart; and disciplined when it really matters. No drugs, no booze that I have to pay for, no stupid gambling, no sexually-transmitted medical expenses of any kind . . . it may not have seemed so at the time, but sometimes I did listen to you, and even to Dr. Dale, despite her suspect taste in men."

"*No* drugs, Dear?"

"Pretty much. Once in a while shared a little of her coke with 'Suela, but usually only when she insisted. I'm gonna bug the hell out of that uppity bitch who I like anyway about that personal training, too. I like working out and eating good, I really do. And I like interacting with people; do not dare to make any mean jokes, former love of my life. I bet I bug that Dr. Dale so much about that personal training she's gonna be saying that little Amy is one pesty bitch but I like her anyway."

"If you want a waitress job at Sports, you just say the word. In fact, if you want to take up bartending, I guarantee you the burly bearded bastard I got handling that would be more than happy to teach you; and teach you well."

"Thanks. Let me first see how it goes at your gym, Jim. Boy it's hard to make half decent jokes without being dirty."

On her way out, Amy stopped, turned around, and said, "My beloved Big Brother Bill offered to teach me bartending. But I had to tell him I already knew more than he did, just from having once watched the other bartenders."

"Be nice to Bill, Amy."

"Always."

After Amy left Jim got well back into his sequel, planning to write all day, and then once again work out just before his gym closed. That would also give him a chance to casually follow up with Ronnie Doyle, maybe ask a polite question or two. Jim grinned, thinking of Amy helping Ronnie to clean that gym, after it closed at eleven.

But then he frowned. Uh oh, Amy's career redirection and new romance just might mean she'd no longer have the time or inclination to clean his apartment and buy his groceries, in her free mornings. Especially if her career as a personal trainer took off, which he expected it would, given Amy's natural charm and common sense, and with the help of the equally charming and sensible Dr. Dale.

Then Jim grinned again. Hell, his life probably would be simpler if he just hired a part-time professional maid who looked like Sheriff Andy Taylor's sweet old Aunt Bea; or even Bea's best friend, music teacher Clara.

By late afternoon Jim had made fine progress on the sequel and was counting on making plenty more, before he retired to his gym and then to his bed. He even allowed himself a motivational fantasy of what it would be like to have that temporarily-life-changing $50k in hand, and what he'd do with it. But then he thought about how Bill and Frankie would be inspired anew to pester him to invest in the gym and the bar. Of course, the preferred way to handle that would be the radical and innovative strategy The Cable Guy had recommended Matthew Broderick employ relative to his encounter with the hooker and vis a vis sweet girlfriend Robin—"You don't tell her!"—except that Editor Chadwick had told him that Scribner would want to put a brief blurb in *The Boston Globe* about the sequel's pending release, and the advance might well be mentioned.

Jim decided to table all such thoughts for the time being, and delved well back in.

But then Sergeant Carrollton showed up, this time with Detective Lou-Columbo. They sat at Jim's kitchen table, that ever-helpful Amy had picked out for him, drinking coffee that Amy had bought for him, out of oversized mugs sporting obscene one-liners that Amy had brought home from the classy gift shop at Shenanigans.

To win points and influence people, Jim handed Lou the oversized mug that said, "Caution. Little Prick with Big Dick Drinking." In return he saw the first grin he'd ever seen lighten Detective Lou's handsome little face. Jim grinned back, mostly because he knew that Shenanigans had the mugs made up special, most of the generally nonsensically obscene one-liners had been invented by the strippers, and Detective Columbo was now drinking out of an Amy Jordan original.

Amy had selected most of the furnishings now in Jim's modern apartment at Jordan's Furniture in Reading, since a furniture store was one thing that Schraft Street did not have. Amy had driven and picked out several suitable items for Jim's renovation; and Jim and especially Big Bill had done the heavy lifting.

Carlton said, "Did the late Harry Annunzio ever mention Paul Pagliarani to you, Boss?"

Jim thought for a few seconds, and then said, "Harry introduced Pagliarani to me once; at Shenanigans naturally. Called him Paulie Pags, I think. But I remembered Pagliarani anyway, 'cause when I fought as an amateur lightheavy when I was in high school, Pagliarani was fighting as a very tough heavyweight. From Eastie, as I remember; looked a little like Rocky Marciano, only much, much bigger. Scary kid, scarier guy."

Carlton said, "That's him. Sort of in the same businesses as Harry, loan sharking, bookmaking, and definitely in the drug business, probably a level above Harry. Guess who's been seen with Mr. P?"

Jim shrugged. "Hell if I know. Bradford B maybe?"

Carlton said, "Try Connie P."

Jim said, "Well, buying some 'roids from him? That wouldn't be so surprising."

"We think maybe trading sex for drugs," interjected Lou. "Or maybe they're a couple of sorts, even. One very mean looking couple, if they are. We believe Connie's always done some minor steroid dealing, but now that she's got some kind of relationship with Pagliarani, she's probably notched that well up."

Jim said, "Yeah, that Pagliarani went on to fight pro, as I recall, and that didn't do anything to lighten his looks. If those two went on safari together the lions and tigers would run outta the jungle."

"Lions are in Africa and tigers are in Asia," grumbled Carlton, with an ironic little smile. Then he gently banged his big fist on Jim's kitchen table. "It's thoughtless ignorance like yours, Jim, that's letting our best animals go extinct."

Jim exclaimed, "Goddamn, Officers! I hadn't realized until this very moment just how badly Schraft Street was distracting me from my responsibilities as a concerned citizen of the world!"

Lou-Columbo glared at Carlton, and then at Jim. "Carlton told me our Connie has anger management issues, and you're trying to help her. Maybe you could help us."

"*Ahh* . . . you want me to wear that damn wire again!"

And then Jim had little choice but to describe the preliminary plans he and Dale were discussing to get Connie some help to get her messed up life somewhat back on track; and to at least safely allow her back into his gym, without causing a revolt among the general membership. He swore the cops to secrecy for the moment, until he and Dale could get Connie's approval; if they could get her approval.

Detective Lou said, "If as we suspect Connie's hooking up with Paulie Pags and starting to make some serious dough dealing or even distributing, then she's probably gonna back off that personal training, not care so much about getting back into your little house of muscle, and tell you and this Dale to pound sand with your neighborhood collection and anger management . . . some people need the adrenaline of anger, and Connie Parker's probably one of 'em."

Carlton picked up, "But we're asking you to try to have a meeting with her anyway, just to see what we can see."

"Jesus, that midget Benny was one thing, but this Paulie Pags is another," said Jim, shaking his head. "I couldn't handle that big bastard in a fair fight, never mind what else he might bring to the party . . . and what's drug dealing got to do with me . . . shit, what are you guys thinking anyway?"

Jim was looking entreatingly at Carlton, but Carlton looked away, at least slightly.

Lou said, "We been watching Benny best we can, although he is on to us. He seems suddenly interested in Paulie Pags for some reason, and those guys have not been friends or associates. And a guy like Benny could care less how tough Paulie Pags or anyone like him is with his hands. Benny's a hell of a lot smarter and better connected than Pags; and Bradford Benny is not very scared of anyone who's less connected than he is."

Jim turned from Lou to Carlton, spread his arms, and said, "Still?"

Lou put his hand on Jim's shoulder to turn him back, leaned in and said, "You're still a suspect based on circumstances and potential motive, and there's nothing Carlton, me, you, or anyone else can do about that; except find out who brutally beat Hoary Harry Annunzio to death. Sorry, Boss, but that's just the way it is on Schraft Street sometimes."

"Yeah, that's convenient, you both know right well I had nothing to do with it but I'm still a suspect. Are you really trying to link Connie with Harry . . . and, hey, what's Connie herself got to say now?"

Carlton replied, "Absolutely nothing to us. *We* can't get anywhere near Connie without Pags and his barracuda of a lawyer being there."

Lou said, "Yeah, and that repulsive damn trio averages out even meaner than when it's just Pags and Connie, if ya can believe that."

Jim grinned ruefully, and said, "Yikes. Meaner than Connie and Pags. That's like being bigger than Big Bill."

Carlton now looked into Jim's eyes, and said, "So we need you. They don't call her Crazy Connie for nothing, Jim. You as much as told me so yourself. A couple times, actually . . . Paulie Pags is a bad guy, Boss. We don't want him on Schraft Street."

After the cops left, Jim tried to get back into his writing. He soon decided that anything he wrote tonight would take more time to fix than it would to write it fresh tomorrow. He definitely didn't feel like navigating the tricky interpersonal waters that a prime time workout would entail, so he opted for yet another steak dinner at The Diner. Faye would be busy during dinnertime, and if he was lucky no one else he knew too well would be there.

But the sexy young cashier from The Schraft Street Market came in alone shortly after he sat down, and what could Boss Jim say when she asked to join him? She was interesting to look at and easy to talk to anyway, and the dinner would have been pleasant enough, except that it had now been three weeks since his energetic out-of-town escapades with the bartender and the KPMG partner. So when said sexy cashier discreetly let her immediate availability wink through, that unwelcome royal gatecrasher Sir J. Peter was back in full painful under-the-table glory. Unfortunately, this willing young thing didn't live 1500 miles away, she lived in the Schraft Street 'Strippersville' apartments, not even a half mile from Jim's digs. Not to mention the fact that with Amy's career change Jim might well be buying his own groceries from this very cashier for the foreseeable future, until he could drum up a suitable Aunt Bea. No, though she might be immediately available, Jim knew right well that she was no one-night-stand. At least not a quiet and inconsequential one.

Faye kept leering at him too, even winking a couple times, while nodding at the young cashier from behind. Jim could not help briefly fantasizing about a world where he could just *'grab and dash'* 'em both across the street to his place *right now*, and, in one time and place and fell swoop, burn both these agonizingly enticing women *down* every bit as thoroughly as he had Debbie and KNK over those three lively nights!

That made the under-the-table-throbbing even more painful, so as somewhat soothing distraction he chanced talking about that notable new Schraft Street couple Amy Jordan and Ronnie Doyle. He was nothing short of thrilled when the young cashier turned out to know both Amy and Ronnie quite well, obviously liked each of them, and, by far most important, thought that they'd be a good match.

Jim felt a little bit bad that the earnest and eager young cashier seemed surprisingly disappointed that he hadn't followed up on her unspoken offer; but, overall, he walked out of The Diner feeling better.

It was early December, Schraft Street was now fully decorated for Christmas, and there was even a touch of new, still-clean snow in spots. Recent Schraft Street happenings hadn't been so festive overall, but unusually clear-eyed Boss Jim still took a full Schraft Street Holiday turn that had him feeling better still.

Then, on impulse, Boss Jim went into Schraft Street Clothing, and bought a bright red Santa stocking cap from one of the grinning Gay Guys. Jim donned said bright red, and took yet another full turn of Schraft Street, now making it a point to loudly "Ho ho ho, Merry Christmas!" every citizen he happened upon.

His cold, calculating reasoning in so doing was that even the dimmest denizen of Schraft Street would realize that the brutal killer of Harry Annunzio could never, ever be such an enthusiastic and good-natured purveyor of unbridled Christmas cheer.

Big Bill was getting ready to leave for Shenanigans when Jim walked into Herlihy's to do upper body. Jim talked a little Ronnie-Amy with him, and was relieved to find the huge fella reconciled, and at least starting to feel happy for them. Knowing Bill, he figured soon enough Bill would be hoping for it to work out just as much as Jim was.

Jim said, "Casually wish Ronnie well with Amy . . . and don't say anything about pulverizing him if he hurts her feelings."

"I already did that first, Boss. Won't say another word about it."

Ronnie replaced Bill just as Jim started his benches, happy to be working with one of the young muscleheads who wasn't totally obsessed, and who was also a knowledgeable and enthusiastic Bruins fan. Every now and then Jim would glance around at Ronnie, as the friendly young fella made his rounds encouraging the members, giving equal time to young and overly energetic and to middle-aged and painfully struggling.

Between Ronnie, this very strong young workout partner who nonetheless seemed to have his weight training in its proper place, and his own lifting going quite well, Jim soon found himself feeling on top of the world, as if he had his life totally under control. Which he did for the moment, anyway.

Meanwhile, Doug Ballard returned from New York and took Dale to The Del Frisco Steakhouse overlooking the water at Liberty Wharf, just a ten-minute walk south on Seaport Boulevard from Doug's gorgeous waterfront high-rise condo on Atlantic Avenue; to celebrate Dale's thirtieth birthday.

Sitting at a table overlooking the Harbor, Doug said, "What's all that you're writing?"

"Fine-tuning the diet and exercise routines of The Famous Foursome. I just *gotta* find a way for them to make faster progress; and especially to help those delightful ladies stay fully motivated."

"Do you have to do that now, while I'm laying out big dough for *us* to celebrate your birthday . . . and isn't that sort of an exercise in futility?"

"It's more than sort of my *job*, as their personal trainer . . . and as their good friend. *Any* progress is the antithesis of futility . . . *listen*, huh. And, in case you haven't noticed, I'm kinda strapped for time lately, Dear."

"Yeah. Gorgeous lady with the heart of gold; Schraft Street's own very delectable Angel of Mercy. Keep me in mind too, willya. I yam what I yam and that's all that I yam, ma'am."

"I do keep you *well* in mind, believe me. Can't help myself. Sometimes I wish I could."

"I sense that. I know I can be a touch selfish and conceited, but we are at least working on that. It doesn't help my case when your and everyone else's precious Jim makes it clear he thinks I'm an asshole. As far as I'm personally concerned, he's a magician at hiding a decent case of asshole himself."

"I'm afraid Jim's somehow seriously in love with me, and so of course he's in pain over that, and he's naturally jealous of you, as plenty of guys certainly are. I actually think he treats you neutral, and stays pretty polite about it all. You certainly have the right to think he's an asshole, but you'll be the only one. And that's one opinion I'd advise keeping to yourself."

"Yeah, he's an absolute madman on that heavy bag, I know; and I'd never dream of giving the guy cause to rearrange this face that, I think, we *both* love and admire. But, Christ, he's jealous of me 'cause I'm born handsome and starting to make some serious dough off it, not to mention having you . . . but that bastard inherited plenty of money, and everyone seems to automatically like and respect the grinning musclehead *on sight*. He's got no reason to be jealous of anyone."

"Besides what I'm unintentionally doing to the poor guy, he's juggling quite a few balls himself, at the moment. And relative to keeping that opinion to yourself, I meant that it would be a very unpopular opinion in general, not that Jim has any interest whatsoever in rearranging your pretty face, Doug. Absolutely not even close to his style. And, Christ, maybe he's not even jealous of you . . . I don't really know what Boss Jim Herlihy thinks, except that he's in love with me, and that despite that he knows he's gonna be absolutely fine no matter what I, you, or anyone else does or thinks. I should be in love with Jim, but I am absolutely head over heels in love with *you*. When it comes to Jim Herlihy, Doug, *absolutely* do not let that go to your head. Anyway, My Love, our future is in New York City, not on Schraft Street. Let's keep that in mind."

Doug flashed his gorgeous big white grin, and took her hand from across the table, and kissed it with exaggerated tenderness. "Not sure what to make of all that, Darling. Except I surely do like that 'head over heels' part."

Jim didn't want to wear the wire, but finally decided he had no choice. And if Connie hadn't—and wasn't—getting herself into serious trouble, and was just doing her normal steroid use and minor dealing to support that use, Carlton assured Jim that the BPD had much more important things to spend their time on. So then Jim and later Dale could proceed as planned. If Jim was wearing a wire to that meeting, and if there was any chance that Paulie Pags might show up, which Carlton certainly could not rule out, then Dale O'Dell would not be there. Jim would find a way to finesse that.

If, on the other hand, Connie was headed for serious trouble but hadn't fully arrived yet, maybe the BPD could use info supplied by Boss Jim to actually help her.

And finally, if Connie had already completely morphed into the very bad girl she'd seemed to be threatening Jim with, then he didn't want her on Schraft Street any more than Carlton and Lou did.

Jim called Connie several times, not getting her, and leaving messages saying that he'd been confidentially talking to Big Bill, Ronnie, Dale, and several other people at the gym, they all really were concerned about her and interested in finding a way to help, and that another dinner at The Diner would make sense now.

Brother, Jim Herlihy was now in the position of chasing Crazy Connie Parker.

His visit to West Palm Beach and the return visit of smart, sane, and thoroughly sensible Keith Garrity and Carol Matthews suddenly seemed like months ago.

Connie finally called back, but it was somewhat late on a very bad Friday night.

Jim had had a few beers at Shenanigans, scrupulously minding his own as usual, except for the fact that it was close to Amy's end of notice, and a few burly young drunken strangers had been yelling some extremely unfair and tasteless comments at her. Jim had sat quietly, marveling at how stupid these idiots were, and hoping against hope that they'd shut up. They hadn't, and on the way to the men's Boss Jim couldn't help but offer a polite counseling word. After all, Monstrous Bill was industriously tending, (but it was amazing how hard he was trying and how little he was accomplishing) and blessedly hadn't yet heard a thing. But it was still early, and these three knuckleheads weren't getting any smarter.

The three were drunk, clueless, and bullying-mean-spirited, without a hint of the lay of this land, and how Schraft Street worked. Jim figured they were probably from someplace like Newton, and were big enough and sheltered enough that they'd never had to learn to be observant.

When Jim later left, the three were waiting for him outside. The oversized idiot who'd Jim tried to counsel now gave him an obvious aggressive shoulder bump, and then turned and faced Jim in such a way that he knew the guy wasn't gonna let him quietly walk away. Jim had observed that the Shenanigans bouncer had discreetly followed these bums outside, and was now giving Boss Jim an encouraging wink, and knowing big grin.

Jim had only had three beers, but unfortunately, that was one too many.

He grinned at the big fat youngster, and said, "Well, I'm afraid you're gonna have to throw the first punch, 'cause I surely will be needing that crystal-clear self-defense excuse."

The big burly kid blanched, but he'd committed himself in front of his friends, and threw a right hand that could have done some serious damage, if Jim wasn't virtually sober, and about three thousand hours of training beyond such evil ineptitude. Jim casually ducked, and threw a three-quarter-speed right hand that shattered the kid's cheekbone, and bounced him unconscious onto the pavement.

Shit! Had absolutely not meant to do all that! The dumb drunken kid had leaned right into the punch, practically doubling its force.

The bouncer stepped in to calm things, but Jim's easy right hand and its disastrous consequences had frozen—and immediately sobered—the other two potential assailants.

Obviously, Jim was indisputably officially innocent, but the incident wasn't gonna do anything to lighten The Mad Dog Herlihy load.

And Hardcore Jim Herlihy, Boss of Schraft Street, had long considered himself above hospitalizing twenty-three-year-old guys, no matter how big, fat, stupid, drunk, and mean-spirited.

Christ, maybe he should push it direct and hard with Ms. Dale O'Dell, and if she didn't give him definite hope, sell out and head south before it was too late.

Skipping his own bar, Fat Frankie, The Gay Guys, The Big A, and Mr. And Mrs. Harcharik, Jim was home at an unprecedented 9:30 Friday evening, listening to Crazy Connie Parker say on his machine, "You ain't got a fuckin' thing I really need now, Boss Jim; but what the fuck, call me back if ya want to. By the way, fuck Jay, fuck you, fuck Big Bill, fuck that fat Linda and her great big bruised ass that I could *hardly* be expected to miss, fuck Schraft Street in general; and by far most important of all, fuck poor little old *me* while I'm thinking of it . . . anyway, thank you for calling. And sure, I'll dine with you again, kind sir, 'long as you let me pick the fine wine this time. Have a nice night, sleep well, and don't let the bed bugs bite."

Jim thought, "Hey, even the maddest of Schraft Street women have an ounce of wit about 'em sometimes, at least . . . 'course, most likely she'd just taken something illegal but of a mellowing nature for a change. That delightful addition to Schraft Street Mr. Paulie Pags is undoubtedly broadening Ms. Connie Parker's pharmacological options."

He thought the exciting affairs of the evening, and the fact that he'd had three beers but only three beers, might keep him awake; but they did not.

CHAPTER SEVENTEEN

Crazy Connie Parker and Ferocious Paulie Pags

HAVING GONE TO BED SO early Friday night, Saturday morning Jim got to The Diner before Carlton and Lou could knock on his door. It was so early The Diner was empty, and therefore Jim had plenty of time to tell Fabulous Faye his side of the prior night's Shenanigans notable shenanigan. Jim especially told her that (a) he hadn't started it the least little bit, and (b) the drunken kid had sort of knocked himself out on Jim's fist, and the punch had certainly been nothing remotely like the ocean of vicious blows that had done in Harry.

Jim was meticulous with the exonerating details because telling Fabulous Faye in particular was the same as telling Schraft Street in general.

Then Jim almost got to finish his tasty hot breakfast before Carlton and Lou found him.

Carlton gave Faye his usual warm hug and kiss on the cheek. Best Jim knew they were still a couple, and Faye even seemed to be the only woman in Carlton's life at the moment. Jim wondered about that. He genuinely liked Faye, she meant no harm, had a decent sense of humor, and was still, at forty, reasonably attractive. But she was five years older than Carlton, she wasn't fat yet but obviously would be soon; and worst of all she was *loud*—maybe even louder than Linda and her cohorts, at least individually.

As far as Jim was concerned, there wasn't a woman in the world sexy enough for that loudness not to wear thin; and wear thin pretty damn quick too.

Carlton chuckled. "How're them eggs over, Mad Dog? And let me see that infamous right."

Jim's hand was bruised and swollen, but nothing like it had been when he was truly going nuts on the big bag. Carlton, grinning, twisted it around gently, looking at it from different angles, as if he was a famous hand surgeon.

Jim took it back, and said, "What the hell. Nobody's denying a big drunk kid fell onto me mitt last night, and there's the result. Carlton, you're never gonna make full detective because you don't know when to detect and when not to detect. Not so sweet Lou, isn't that the most important thing in the detective game?"

Lou growled, "We got Bouncing Bobby out of bed this morning, went over the stupid story with him. Juvenile bullshit."

Carlton interjected, "By the way, Boss of Schraft Street, you might want to take Bouncing Bobby in hand, sir. That was one hung over kid, maybe even still a little drunk at seven this morning. They don't let him drink on the job, do they? Lose their ticket over that, and then where would you go to get into trouble?"

"You'd have to define let," replied Jim. "Someone needs to watch him closer. I'm long gone before Bobby starts his particular shenanigans, and Monstrous Bill's always too busy looking up the ingredients for a Jack and Coke to worry what Bobby's doing. I'll have a word with someone, I suppose. Bobby is yet another good Schraft Street kid who's apparently heading for trouble."

Lou said, "Yeah, that big ex-BC-backup-linebacker from Wayland you dropped is gonna be alright; already out of the hospital, cheek fractured but totally in place, minor concussion but he doesn't need to use his squash much anyway. Daddy owns a Ford dealership on Route Nine, kid's an oversized, sloppy-looking car salesman there."

Carlton laughed. "Don't go getting too full of yourself, Mad Dog, you didn't deck much. Knucklehead was a backup linebacker for two years, never played a down in a real game. Practice squad only, didn't travel with the team. First time slumming in Shenanigans; undoubtedly the last. Blood alcohol point-one-three. Alert maybe, but still hammered. His memory of the incident is foggy, and his friends aren't saying much either. Bobby said you tried to walk away, really couldn't. And that your right hand was a spot-on imitation of Ali's infamous anchor punch; if the kid had been sober enough to flinch from it instead of falling into it, you'd definitely have had to hit him again . . . actually, if the kid had been half-sober, probably wouldn't have happened at all."

Jim grinned. "I knew the Bobby part of all that 'cause I was there. Did ya get the kid's grades while you were at it, 'cause I'm into this now."

Lou said, "Paulie Pags was in Shenanigans earlier, Bobby thinks those kids bought some ecstasy or coke from him and took it to their car. He wasn't sure enough for us to get cause to search the vehicle. BC did have a trace amount of coke in him. Anyway, *that's* why we checked him out. Took us nowhere though."

"You broke Friday night routine and home to bed, Dog, so you didn't get to hang out with Pags and Connie at your own bar," said Carlton. "Frankie thinks they were waiting for you, although they didn't tell him that. Just had a couple drinks, kept to themselves, came in around eight-thirty, left around nine-fifteen. Frankie knows Pags a little, said he's dropped into Sports a couple times over the last year, just never when you were there. Frankie don't like Pags much at all; said to tell you to be very careful."

Lou added, "Careful and cool, while still doing your civic duty . . . Boss."

Jim quickly cleaned his plate, said bye to Faye while asking not to embellish please, and took his detecting playmates across the street to listen to Connie's strange message.

When the message clicked off, Lou said, "I think maybe Pags has introduced our girl to something a little less stimulating than steroids and speed. If she's willing to meet she—or they—want something. Maybe it is just back into your little house of muscle . . . on the other hand, since Pags was with her at your bar, maybe it's him wants to see if you know anything of interest."

Jim said, "So I meet 'em at The Diner wearing. What if Pags wants to check me out?"

Carlton said, "Get indignant, say don't touch, big fella, and storm out."

Connie called Jim mid-morning, probably knowing that he'd be back from The Diner by then, and that he usually worked out late. So she was genuinely trying to reach him. She suggested they meet at Sports, but Jim replied that customers would undoubtedly interrupt constantly, so The Diner was preferable. She finally agreed without mentioning Paulie Pags. But something in her tone told Jim that Paulie would be there too.

And he was. She introduced him as Paul, and he acted as though he didn't remember meeting Jim before. Maybe he didn't—a guy in Pagliarani's business met a lot of people, and most of them were a lot more important to him than was Jim Herlihy. Until now, apparently.

Pags didn't check Jim for the wire he was wearing.

Connie handed Jim a piece of paper. It was a letter on the fancy stationary of a psychiatric assistant named Jennifer Pagliarani—who they explained was a second cousin of Paul—and in the brief document the good 'Dr.' Jennifer basically stated that she was treating Ms. Parker for some relatively minor issues with anger and depression, and that meanwhile Ms. Parker was a fine and fully functioning member of society.

Actually, Connie was now dressed in classier attire than usual although the striking musculature certainly did still show through, and she did somehow look markedly more relaxed and in control than normal; but of course Jim agreed with Detective Lou's assessment from the phone message that that was probably due to something in the well stocked medicine bag of 'Dr.' Paul Pagliarani rather than to the therapeutic talents of 'Dr.' Jennifer Pagliarani.

Jim thought that perhaps he should ask to have a word with 'Dr.' Jennifer, then thought, "What's the use, let her back, keep her away from Jay, have Bill and Ronnie keep an eye on her, and hope for the best." And just tell Linda, Dale, and the membership that Connie had shown him an encouraging letter from a certified therapist, whose name he couldn't remember.

So Jim said, "Okay. Jay always works out between five and eight. How 'bout avoiding those times then?"

Pags growled, "Fuck that Jay, I'll . . .

But Connie grabbed his beefy arm, and interrupted, "Fine, I'll work out in the morning. Or maybe I'll come in late and work out with you, Boss. That way you can grab me if I start to pitch any fits. But don't grab my tits, my ass, or especially my cooch, you missed your chance; and my Paul won't like it."

Jim replied, while somehow summoning his best easy, friendly grin, "I'll be happy to work out with you late, Connie, if you don't think I'd slow you down too much. And I'm sure I won't have to be grabbing you anywhere."

Pags said, "Schraft Street scuttlebutt is that you decked some big young punk for insulting the Shenanigans stripper girls; I'd say that's spitting into the wind, Boss, *and* trying to push back the tide. Insulting stripper girls is a right of passage. Sir Galahad here."

"I asked them politely to tone it down, is all. Not so much for the girls' benefit, but I myself was right sick of how loud and how stupid. Then they wouldn't let me walk away."

Pags said, "Boss of Schraft Street. Maybe even murderous avenger of said Schraft, hear Bradford Benny tell it."

"Bullshit, Paul. Benny knows it wasn't me."

Pags replied, looking at Jim harder, and the guy was scary, Jim bet he sure didn't have much trouble collecting his debts, "Benny and the cops still think you might have; I can tell by watching."

"Why bother?"

"'Cause Harry owed me enough money to bother, and, depending on who stomped on him, I just might get the evil culprit to make me whole. That's why."

"Yeah, well, Paul, I have nothing to do with you or Bradford Benny, and nothing to do with this very sad story other than that Harry was a friend of sorts; and one of the investigating cops is a good friend, as well as my tenant of sorts."

"What *do* the cops think, Boss?"

"I have no idea, other than that I know that they know I didn't have anything to do with it. Connie, I'll see you at the gym."

Pags now sneered, with what might have been just about the most angry and hateful look in his eyes that Jim had ever experienced up close, "Bradford Benny and that fuckin' Detective Lou. Little pricks on parade!"

Fortunately, Jim had finished his one small steak, and big man Pags had loudly insisted on picking up the check, so Jim left, no one offering to shake hands. Jim was perfectly happy not to shake Pagliarani's hand—it was almost as big as Bill's and those fingers just might have been even thicker. And Pags was undoubtedly the kind of heavy-handed bastard loved to make other fellas wince.

Bradford Benny and Paulie Pags. Why does *anyone* ever want to have anything to do with these kind of guys? Now Jim was thinking maybe Paulie Pags himself was that evil culprit—and whether he was or wasn't, and whether Connie was or wasn't also involved, Jim could see some serious bruises, at least, in Connie Parker's future, at the powerful hands of her Paul. Connie Parker was one tough lady, but if Jim Herlihy wouldn't stand a chance against Paulie Pags, then against the inevitable wrath of that dark SOB Connie might as well be as big and tough as little Amy Jordan, for all the good it would do her.

After Carlton and Lou listened to the tape, which with the light background noise in The Diner was plenty clear, Lou just said, "You suck at wearing a wire, Boss."

Jim replied to Lou, "I figured Pags wasn't a fan of the detecting profession . . . but he don't seem to like Bradford Benny so much either?"

Lou shrugged, and said, "We already told ya Pags was a bad guy, and none of us want him here on Schraft. *That's* the takeaway."

Carlton didn't say anything then and Jim took that cue. Jim knocked on his door later. Carlton was home alone—no other cops, and, blessedly, no loudly good-natured busybody Faye.

Jim said, "That evil son of a bitch Pags did it, didn't he. Used those great big mitts and all that boxing training to inflict that savage madness on poor Harry."

"Probably. No witnesses, no evidence, though. We'll talk to him but talking to lawyered-up hard cases like him and Benny when we have zip is about as useful as listening to the wired interviews you conduct."

"What about Connie?"

"We don't know. Personally and confidentially, I myself think there was an angry, escalating dispute between Harry on one side, and Pags and probably Connie on the other, involving the usual suspects, drugs and money. Whether Connie was there and got her licks in—maybe. You and a lot of other people said she was out of control, and hooked on speed and steroids, and I know that people on that combo are usually hooked on something else to wind down and sleep. That's a lot of money there."

Jim said, with a small, sad shake of his head, "So whether she was there or not you think she was in the mix anyway."

"Yeah, that's what *I* think, but it's just a theory, Jim. We can't do anything about it for now except keep our eyes and ears open. We will stop bothering you if I have anything to say about it."

"That I would appreciate. What's that natty little prick Lou really like by the way?"

"Got a touch of short man's disease, even though the ladies like his looks and style, such as it is, so he has no trouble there. But make no mistake, Lou surely wants to get the bad guy, and he really doesn't want to seriously mess up any innocents along the way . . . he somehow does honestly think you have a dark side, and he hasn't totally ruled you out even now. Somebody must have told him about the look in your eye when you go nuts on the big bag. That unfortunate nonsense Friday night actually helped you in Lou's eyes, because not only Bouncing Bobby but another witness said you'd been pretty restrained and then genuinely dismayed at the result. Even one of BC's friends basically said that. Pretty ironic."

"Brother. So now what do I do around Connie and Pags?"

"Act like you think they're innocent sweethearts. What else can ya do."

Jim was in late doing legs alone when Connie came in to resume her membership. He didn't have to work out with her though, because Pags came in as her guest, making a particularly nasty face when young and unavoidably daunted Ronnie hesitantly made him pay the eight-dollar guest fee.

Wonderful. Jim's superbly appointed neighborhood gym was likely now a hangout for brutal killers.

Connie was doing benches, and Pags was just spotting her, not working out himself, even though he was wearing workout clothes. That included a tank top, and Jim thought guys even half as hairy as Pags ought not. Christ, looking at the back hair on Pags, Jim made a note to go online and check whether there'd been a full moon the night Harry was killed. And if so, then see what *The Constitution of the United States* had to say about neighborhood gyms banning werewolves without other cause.

Pags was also wearing evil-looking coal-black half-gloves—tops of his amazingly thick fingers bare—and Carlton had told Jim that Pags often wore those gloves, and in fact might well have been wearing them when he beat Harry Annunzio to death; *if*, that is, it was Pags who had done the horrific deed.

Pags was undoubtedly every bit as strong and ferocious as he looked, but not particularly weight-trained. Guys like that usually couldn't lift anywhere near as strong as they really were, especially relative to well practiced 'gym rats,' so they usually did opt out of participating.

Jim was squatting those agonizing 5 sets of 20 reps with 315 that thoroughly obsessed Jay had shamed him into, now mentally cursing Jay right along with Connie and Pags. But Christ, what if Connie really was evil, and eventually siced her new Paulie on her ex Jay? Man, this was not the gym environment he'd envisioned at all.

In between his thigh- and lung-burning sets, Jim saw Connie bench 225 for three reps. That was amazing for a 160-pound woman, who actually looked like a woman—unusually muscular, but still a very sexy woman—from the neck down.

225 pounds. Two forty-five-pound plates on each end of the big forty-five-pound Olympic bar. That got him thinking and grinning about the time he and Bill had watched the 'NFL Combine' with the Linemen benching 225 anywhere from 20 to 50 reps, and then decided to have a 225-benching contest at the gym. Jay had done 40 reps, starting out as if the bar was empty, but eventually hitting the wall when his huge pumped pecs started cramping. Bill had hit 50, and then gotten bored well before reaching his limit. So he rested, and then got an amazing 25 reps with 315. Jim had gotten 25 reps with the 225, and most of the participating young muscleheads were somewhere between 20 and 30. Jim and victorious Bill then took all the contestants to The Diner—which had been warned in advance—for steak dinners, including two steaks for all who wanted 'em, which was virtually everybody.

That was fun and well appreciated, but when Jim and Bill got the check—even with 20 percent volume discount—they resolved never to do anything remotely like it ever again.

Jim was glad to get the high-rep squats out of the way, and looking forward to his solitary session on the big bag. Although he was pretty spent from those 100 total reps with 315 pounds. Fuck Jay, from now on he'd do one or maybe two sets of 20, and back down to 15 on the others.

Suddenly Connie and Pags were there, grinning evilly at him—or so it seemed—and wrapping their hands. Pags had come prepared, and wasn't gonna be a guilty bystander all night.

Pags proceeded to not only hit the bag notably harder than could Boss Jim, he'd obviously been studying MMA tactics, or probably some even nastier and more lethal Navy Seal-type madness. He was hitting the bag with vicious elbows, incredibly powerful leg- and hip-driven backhanded karate chops, and assorted other ferociousness that had Jim worrying about whether the extra thick leather on his top-of-the-line heavy bag might actually split.

Normally Jim would at least have much better endurance than the powerful Pags, but he'd overdone it with those hundred squats. He felt totally outclassed, and Pags—and to a lesser extent Connie—were letting him know it without saying a word.

Surprisingly, Pags observed the big sign prohibiting kicking the heavy bag. But when Connie really got going—Jim figured the look in Crazy Connie's eyes was now notably more disturbing than anything anyone had ever seen in his—she started unleashing some very well-practiced karate kicks.

A hideous image of her kicking a helpless Harry after Pags had put him thoroughly down flashed into Jim's head, unannounced. Jim didn't believe his subconscious knew any more about such things than he did, and immediately pushed the awful image out of his mind.

Connie's kicks, well-practiced as they were, were still nowhere near as potentially damaging as the heavy-handed blows of the ferocious Pags. Still, Jim didn't want to allow any dangerous precedents, so when Connie was done and had a minute to sort of compose herself, Jim politely referenced the no kicking sign. She responded with an evil sneer, but didn't kick the bag during her next frenetic turn.

Pags pounded away for a few more furious minutes. Then he and Connie walked off sweaty-arm-in-sweaty-arm and out the gym door, wordlessly, and without so much as a parting glance at Jim.

Instead of going right home, Jim walked the length of Schraft Street and back to his three-decker, a troubled, rubbery-legged walk of about twenty-five minutes in total. And then, after showering and drinking a big protein shake, it took him a very untypical hour to fall asleep.

CHAPTER EIGHTEEN

Amy Jordan and Ronnie Doyle, Dale O'Dell and Doug Ballard—and Jim

SOMEHOW THE CONTRAST OF DEALING with Carol Matthews and Keith Garrity versus Connie and Pags, and the general recent madness on Schraft Street, and especially the most welcome burgeoning romance between Ronnie and Amy, made Jim feel more in love than ever with Dale O'Dell.

And, it was now almost Christmas. Jim had to employ a very healthy dose of the old Herlihy willpower to keep from picturing Dale and Doug sitting by the fire holding hands on Christmas Eve; and then exchanging presents in pajamas by the tree on Christmas morning.

He even considered getting Dale alone, hugging her, shaking her very, very gently, and saying, "Look, Doug is gorgeous and he's gonna be rich, but you know you're gonna end up hating his guts sooner or later—way, way, *way* worse than the rest of us do now. Take a couple hours and really, really imagine what it's gonna be like being with him all the time, day after day, month after month, year after year. And you *know* if he doesn't break your heart in the short term he'll bore you into utter madness in the long term . . . see the impeccable logic here?"

Jim grinned. Would that it were that easy. Maybe he should sit down with Connie and Pags, look 'em in the eye, and say, "Confess. You'll feel so much better."

He called Dale after a workout, on a night he knew Ballard was out of town. He was excited that she answered, except it sounded like he'd woken her up.

"Hey, you going to Amy's clam retirement party?"

"I don't do strip clubs, thank you very much; and don't appreciate sexist nonsense either, visual *or* verbal. What time is it?"

"Early, around ten, normal people just got back from working out and haven't even showered yet. Pretty special night, ma'am, for a pretty special young lady, warranting exceptions from the exceptional."

"Is she going to perform, or just primly preside over her party?"

"Mostly semi-primly preside, I think, but knowing her she'll perform at least a little. Ronnie will be there, so she won't go too crazy. We don't need to stay long, then maybe you and I can have a talk at Sports."

"Shenanigans and Sports. Sounds like someone who recently got into a little trouble will be drinking some beer."

Jim enjoyed a solitary smile. "What'd ya go and do now, Dale? . . . Seriously, have a drink with me once in a while, please."

"I'm too sleepy to argue. Meet me at Sports at seven, I'm not gonna walk into that ridiculous Shenanigans alone. Call earlier in the future, please, I have to get up at five sometimes." She hung up.

Sensible, knowledgeable Dr. Dale didn't drink much, Jim hadn't dated her that long, things hadn't proceeded too far—he'd never had so much as one beer with this love of his life.

Amy knocked on his door a couple hours before the big event. Jim had been trying to concentrate on his writing, but it had not been going well. He was thrilled to see her.

"Is the uppity bitch I better like anyway now that she's gonna be my mentor coming—and coming with you, kind sir?"

"Yeah, she hates strip clubs, but she loves you, Little Girl. Meeting her first at Sports; she didn't want to walk into Shenanigans alone."

"What did she say when you told her my most cherished going away present ever would be if Dr. Dale would perform just one set in *my* honor. And the perverted denizens of Schraft Street would go absolutely nuts!"

Jim grinned. "I chickened out on that one, Amy, nice thought that it was. Please don't be offended if we don't stay long. I already moved heaven and earth. Don't be offended if she doesn't watch you perform, either.

She plans to be way in the back, talking to Ronnie when you go onstage, sitting side-by-side facing the wall."

"I owe it to the owners, the customers, and most of all to the girls to get up there one last time, Jim. I'm moving on, but I do not reject or disrespect where I've been or those poor women who have given me so much support, and yes, love. I could not have made it without them . . . any more than I could have made it without you. Thank you from the bottom of my heart, Jim Herlihy."

Jim could but hug her, with the usual reverent kiss on the top of her head.

He had no prayer of getting back into the writing. He thought about the gym, but it was approaching prime time, and with that he could not deal right now.

So he considered having a beer at the bar with Frankie. It was certainly early to start drinking, especially on a special night like this; but on the other hand he was Boss Jim Herlihy, universally recognized as one of the most naturally gifted *and* well-practiced pacers in the long history of blue-collar Boston neighborhoods. Never mind the recent unfortunate Friday night circumstances at Shenanigans.

Sports was quiet. Jim knew most of the regulars were already at Shenanigans or soon would be. Plenty of dancers came and went at Shenanigans without much notice, but Amy Jordan was not plenty of dancers. All but the totally clueless knew she was special; and it did not hurt that locally influential fellas like Boss Jim and Big Bill and Sergeant Carlton and even Fat Frankie and the late Hoary Harry and now Young Ronnie Doyle made their opinions on that fact quite obvious.

Frankie said, "I got Tony Cetrone to fill in tonight, Jim, but he's not happy about it. Maybe we should just close, in honor. And because we ain't gonna make any money anyway."

"The hours are the hours, knucklehead. Stop pulling my chain. I'm not gonna stay too long, and then I'm coming back here with Dale for a while, so I'll see just how light it is. If Tony isn't making any money, I'll slip him a few bucks personally."

Frankie chuckled. "Bringing Dale O'Dell back here, Boss? Aren't ya afraid of that Doug Ballard?" Frankie boomed an amazingly loud big, big belly laugh at his own joke.

"Just for an innocent talk about some more pain-in-the-ass Schraft Street nonsense. I'm still nowhere, in more ways than ten, Frankie. As usual, you're hardly helping."

"Harry, Carlton, Detective Lou, Benny, Connie, drunken young louts from out-of-town, and especially that evil Paulie Pags . . . I know I haven't gotten around to being less of a pain in your ass, Boss, but I still thought *I'd* slipped right off your radar. You know right well that if it wasn't for that four-eyed little beancunter Lloyd I'd have stole ya blind by now."

"I don't believe that for a minute, Frankie. I have implicit faith in you being only a little bit crooked."

Coincidentally—Schraft Street was pretty small and self-contained, so coincidences were common—that very same four-eyed little beancunter came up behind and overheard.

Lloyd said, "Your personal accountant and trusted advisor would not want you betting your financial well being on that, Boss, so I continue to watch this Burly-B-Boy very closely indeed. I watch him and Big Bill, you watch me. No more than six beers, three lap dances, and no after hours shenanigans for me tonight; or I really will never forgive you this time."

"I'm leaving early, otherwise engaged. You could get Bouncing Bobby to watch you, except he'll probably be drinking early tonight; or Big Bill, except he's gonna be running ragged, serving everyone fucked-up drinks that they had *better* accept anyway, not a word if they know what's good for 'em. Special night, you should just let yourself go, Lloyd. *Walk* home, though."

Frankie said, "My place is right down the street, feel free to crash on the couch. *Alone.*" Frankie roared with laughter again. "Imagine Marnie coming home and finding skeletal 130-pound Lloyd naked on our couch and covered in 175-pounds of equally naked hooker!"

Lloyd comically widened his big, watery eyes behind the thick specs, and exclaimed, "Are you kidding, Frank! I could never get that drunk. I'm scared just saying hi to Marnie passing her on the street! No offense."

"None taken, Lloyd. I've been married to her for twenty years, and I'm scared saying hi to her on the street myself."

Jim said, "Me three. I got good eyes, I can just about see the entire length of Schraft Street, and I tried innocently crossing well in advance. But she's on to me now."

"You want me teach Amy bartending, Boss?" asked Frank. "She surely would be good, *if* she really *hasn't* picked up any bad habits just being around Big Bill, damage to the profession that monster does on a nightly basis."

Jim replied, "She's gonna *try* the personal training and the cleaning, but the best thing for her probably will be the tending—capitalizing on the natural magical charm, amazing looks and even more amazing personality, once she finally grows up now. Train here, move on to classy downtown bars wouldn't open their doors to the likes of your fat ass as a customer, never mind a bartender. I predict you'll be down there watching her make the big bucks through the window."

"Sure, Boss, I agree, and I hope."

"Me too," said Lloyd. "*I* predict I don't go to Shenanigans so much anymore. I bet I liked that Amy every bit as much as big shot studs like you Jim, and Bill, and Harry. No sense insignificant little prick like me showing it. She'd never dream of going home with me at any price, really never did go home with many guys anyway. I hear one sorta special madman wouldn't take her up on a standing free offer, but I couldn't believe something that bizarre, even if it was true. But she was always nice to me, nicer than any of 'em. Treated me just like she did everyone else, which is all a guy like me can ask around women like that."

Jim gave Lloyd an affectionate hug and gentle noogie on his tiny head, thinking that Lloyd's squash was almost as small as Amy's. And that there was certainly a surprising amount of brains and good intentions squeezed into both those little noggins.

Jim sat in the back with Dale and Ronnie, not watching Amy or any of the dancers.

Ronnie said, "I'll be glad when this night's over. I wish Amy would move in with me right away. I like Consuela, but I'm not sure she's such a good influence.'

"I've been watching Amy and her 'Suela interact for a couple years now, son," said Jim. "'Suela's got fifteen years on her, but my little sister is the big sister in that relationship. 'Suela won't try to get Amy doing anything she shouldn't; and couldn't if she did try. Not to worry."

Dale said, "Give it time, Ronnie."

Ronnie grinned. "What do you know, Dr. Dale. You're dating Doug Ballard."

"Hey, Doug's not bothering anyone tonight," said Jim. "Of course, I can't speak for New York City."

Dale said, "Enough. We covered that with Carol and Keith a couple weeks ago. Tonight is about you and Amy, Ronnie."

Amy came over looking stunning in her old Hooters hot pants—she'd worked there afternoons for a while, until she realized how much money she could make at Shenanigans—and mock-violently pushed Jim over, and squeezed in next to Ronnie.

Amy snarled at Jim, "Stop playing with my Ronnie's balls, ya benevolent ol' perv!"

Jim said, "Amy, your retirement present from me is I'm gonna pay for your PT classes and certification."

"Told ya, Generous Jim, that I've managed my money very well. I can pay my own way . . . but Dr. Dale is certified and smarter than anyone ever . . . why can't she certify me, when the time comes?"

Dale said, "I'll teach you well, little girl, but you still have to take the classes and pass the test to make it official. The customers surely do want their trainers to have that ticket."

Jim said, "Plus it's sort of a tip for all the cleaning, cooking, and savvy shopping you've done for me, 'lo these few years . . . not to mention the considerate stroking of an old man's bruised ego. And I *insist!*"

"Boss Jim's poor bruised ego," said Amy. "Yeah, Dr. Dale, you're the smartest lady I've ever met, or maybe tied with that other uppity bitch Dr. Carol, but in one way you're a fuckin' moron; sorry Ronnie, but it's my party and I'll swear if I have to."

"I thought I said *enough* on that," stammered Dale. "I'm not gonna have to leave right now, am I?"

Amy replied, "You should leave. You should go home with Jim and boink his brains out. I'd lend ya this Hooter's costume to help ya fire him all up 'cept it's too small."

Ronnie said, "Amy! That *is* enough."

Jim grinned at Dale. "You know she'd hardly need that Hooter's costume, Amy, although it certainly would do the trick. Right, Ronnie?"

"Yes, Boss. Amy will be modeling those Hooters hot pants for me later, but not for long, kind sir. Thank you for your interest in this matter."

Dale then hugged Amy, and kissed her gently on the top of her head just like Jim often did. She gave Amy her retirement present—which was three sets of attractive shorts and shirts appropriate for a personal trainer—and said, "Jim and I have to leave now, over to Sports, he's got something important he wants to discuss; something that doesn't involve Doug Ballard, or boinking in any form or fashion, thank you very much."

Amy said, "Probably Connie Parker. Yeah, I sure don't want to be involved in that, not on this day. I thought she might stop by, but she didn't."

Dale said, "Her loss, Amy."

Sports was almost empty. Jim asked Tony Cetrone how he was doing, and Tony said that he wasn't making any money and he wasn't getting to see any naked women either. But both the Celtics and the Bruins were winning.

'A' was at the bar—reasonably sober, and he had been doing better lately—and Jim asked him if he in fact did not like to look at naked woman.

'A' just replied, "Not enough to pay those prices," and went back to watching the Celtics. 'A' had actually been a decent basketball player in his long ago youth, and was a pretty serious Celtics fan when he was sober.

Jim already knew that Eddy Harcharik was at Shenanigans and rolling, and also that young Bouncing Bobby would surely be dealing with Mrs. Harcharik, and probably soon. Fortunately Bobby was always in control, even when he was drinking, which he wouldn't be tonight because the owners of Shenanigans had just promised Boss Jim that they'd do a better job of watching him.

Jim chuckled at the thought of Mrs. Harcharik making a minor scene at Shenanigans. Eddy normally never went there, and Jim doubted that the strong-armed Missus had ever been in there. He figured that all the naked women and the strange surroundings in general would inhibit any mug tossing tonight, but that those same naked women and strange surroundings would sure have Mrs. H sputtering.

He pictured poor Eddy hammered but *all* fired-up by the sounds and sights of the evening, and then trying passionately to get Mrs. H unsputtered and into the sack.

Jim made an important mental note to follow up with Eddy on how all that went, next time he saw him sober.

Jim gave bartender Tony a colorful, professional-looking photo of Amy and Consuela with an arm around each other's shoulders, adorable Amy relatively demure in her Hooters outfit, curvy Consuela making a somewhat stronger statement in pasties and a G-string. Tony asked if he could take it home for later, or did he have to hang it behind the bar. Jim sympathized, but still told him to frame it and hang it for now, and of course there'd undoubtedly be more where that came from. Handyman Fat Frankie Leonnetti was pretty handy with a camera too, and Jim knew right well that Frankie liked to look at naked women, and pictures of naked women.

He also knew that uber-formidable wife nurse Marnie was something of an amateur computer whiz which Frankie was decidedly not, and she'd blocked all porn sites from their home computer, as if Frank was a callow youth, instead of a burly, bearded, tattooed biker-looking bartender.

Frankie had told Jim that at least Marnie herself was quite a sensual woman, and Jim had thought but not said that the world is a very strange place indeed; meanwhile employing every last ounce of his considerable power of mind control to prevent any *very* unfortunate mental images from forming.

Jim gave Tony forty dollars, and Tony said, "Don't have to do that, Boss. Frankie told me slow nights are part of the job for junior bartenders, so shut up about it, or he'd have me just working Monday, Tuesday, and Wednesday *all* the time."

"Tonight is above and beyond, and we won't mention anything to Frankie. Just tell him your night here hadn't been quite as bad as expected. Now I'm gonna be sitting in that corner talking serious business with that lovely young lady, so try to keep anyone from bothering us."

Jim brought over two icy Bud Light drafts—Jim and Frankie were both fanatics about keeping the beer very cold and the mugs frozen—and said, "Connie."

He handed Dale the letter from 'Dr.' Jennifer Pagliarani. Jim had decided that one way or the other the extremely well intentioned Dale would involve herself with Connie, and Dale would be safer if he gave her most of the facts as he knew them. He emphasized that there was no doubt that Paulie Pags was a bad and violent guy, but certainly plenty of doubt on his and especially Connie's involvement with the brutality fatally unleashed on Harry.

Dale finally said quietly, "I feel really, really bad, Jim. Connie was around us all the time, and she got totally lost without us even seeing. Meanwhile, Jay is jumping around all thrilled because his ridiculous quadriceps just measured half an inch bigger. I think that narcissistic idiot is happy Connie's with that Pags devil because now she's totally out of his hair."

"Plenty of people get lost on Schraft Street, Dale, and we all have our own problems and responsibilities. *If* Connie is a hopeless case, Amy and Ronnie, and Big Bill, and The Famous Foursome, and Lloyd Dolson sure aren't. Schraft Street Triage—the hard fact is that ya have to let go of the hopeless cases, and focus on the living. Anyway, *your* number one priority is becoming Dr. Dale for real."

"Long term it sure is. Short term it's training my Amy, and with your help, seeing that she does get certified and build up a nice little clientele for herself. I know you and Frankie think her real future is bartending at some trendy hot spot downtown . . . but why couldn't she and Ronnie do something like, say, own their own gym somewhere sometime? Maybe even buy into yours, depending on what you eventually decide to do. I see those two as a couple young go-getters, who've been smart enough to save their money."

Jim grinned. "Ronnie Doyle, the straight-laced young miser of Schraft Street. All the dough he's making at my gym, between his training, the desk, and now the cleaning, and I don't think he's ever bought a beer in my bar here. Amy doesn't spend much on herself, but 'Suela told me that the normally savvy young sweetheart's been something of a soft touch for a few of the sorrier cases at Shenanigans."

Dale said, "I am so, so happy to see her out of there . . . Jim, don't stay on Schraft Street on my account. I really am in love with Doug. I know he has his shortcomings, but he treats me *great*. Anyway, the heart wants what the heart wants, and I can't totally explain it, and I'm thoroughly sick of trying to. And it hurts a little that most people don't like him; and it hurts a lot that you don't."

Jim was far more prepared and resigned than he was shocked or disheartened; despite what Amy and the very smart Dr. Carol had told him.

He replied, "Liking some people is sort of like believing in God. You want to, but you just don't, and there's nothing you can do about it. I can't leave Schraft Street just now, and there's nothing anybody can do about that either. Dale, please do your best to stay away from Connie Parker for now."

Tony brought over two more icy, icy drafts. Dale took a healthy sip, leaned over and punched Jim's shoulder across the table, and said,

"Benevolent Boss of Schraft Street, you're actually a terrible influence. I really, really like this icy cold beer!"

Leaving Jim hugged her firm, full, and long, and said, "When you get home, go on Youtube and play a little Freddy Fender *Teardrops* for me, willya Dear . . . and know that I mean every word of it, too."

She hugged him back hard, and whispered, "I have to marry Doug, Jim, and I sure hope my Amy marries my Ronnie. But you also know both Amy and I will love you forever too."

CHAPTER NINETEEN

Detecting

PAULIE PAGS HAD STARTED HANGING around Shenanigans between seven and eight on Friday and Saturday nights. He'd barely pay any attention to the girls, who paid even less to him. Jim honestly couldn't think of a less likeable—or especially less approachable—guy. Consuela even told Jim that, although she'd never said one word to Pags, he'd paid absolutely no attention to her, and in fact she'd never even met his dark and foreboding eyes, she'd nonetheless had a couple very scary nightmares about the big devil.

But Pags would usually wind up talking to a group or two of young guys, usually non-regulars who just happened to be in when Paulie was, and who'd inevitably leave not long after Paulie did. Big Bill told Sergeant Carrollton all this so the BPD was discreetly watching, which Pags surely knew. No transactions were taking place in or around Shenanigans, and no one knew specifically what was being set up for later and elsewhere.

Then one Friday night—after, it must be admitted, a pretty long wait—Pags ordered a Scotch on the rocks, and sneered at Bill, "Get it right this fuckin' time, ya big dummy. And how 'bout speeding all the way up to slow fuckin' motion."

Bill snarled, "You're out of here. Don't come back, ever. Piece of shit."

Pags grabbed Bill's left arm hard with his powerful right hand, and said, "Best not be doing *me* that way, Big Fella."

Obsessed gym-owner Bill actually felt worse about what Pags was doing to Connie than anyone except Dale did, and the supernaturally easygoing huge guy also somehow hated Pags on general principle: the way Pags looked, acted, talked, moved, expected everyone to step aside when he walked to the men's room; and that he was undoubtedly setting up drug deals at the very bar Bill was tending. Add in the hideous Hoary Harry suspicions, and Bill had started to silently rage at just the sight of Pags.

Without thinking, Bill reflexively twisted his huge upper body and simultaneously slammed his right hand down onto Pags big hairy forearm to dislodge that very firm grip; in the process he badly dislocated Pagliarani's right elbow. Pagliarani howled in pain, grabbed and held his agonizingly throbbing elbow, and then said, "You're *dead*, you oversized fucking retard."

Monstrous Bill, totally sober but still well beyond thinking clearly, just looked at Pags as if, absent the huge, wide bar between them, Pags himself would be, now and forever, the single deadest demon to ever darken Schraft Street. Pags was ridiculously arrogant but not nearly arrogant enough not to now thank the God he didn't believe in for that huge bar.

Someone called 911, while a middle-aged orthopedic surgeon who almost always stopped just on Friday nights for an hour and exactly three quick beers ran over, expertly slipped Pags' elbow back into place, and wrapped it tightly with a towel one of the dancers had quickly produced.

Two local cops responding to the 911 took Pagliarani to the Mass General Emergency room.

Jim came in just as the cops were helping Pagliarani out.

After being briefed, Jim called Carlton on his cell. Carlton listened, and then said, "Lou and I will be there by and by. Keep Bill and some witnesses handy."

The local cops who'd taken Pags to the Mass General Emergency Room came back to get Bill's side of the story.

Jim listened while Bill gave them the basics, and then Jim said quietly, "Guys, Carlton and Lou will arrive directly. There are complications involved here, and the good detectives are up to speed."

One of the locals replied, "Yeah, that sweetheart Pagliarani said he's not gonna press charges anyway; although he did give a pretty menacing general impression that he's not gonna forgive and forget either. Big Bill, it goes without saying to be careful. But yeah, we're more than happy to let Lou and Carlton take over."

When Carlton and Lou finally came in, Jim said, "What took ya?"

Carlton grinned, and replied, "We took the liberty of temporarily classifying Pags' rude grab as assault starting the altercation, and his oh-so-unfair vulgar disparagement of Large William's professional skills as unwarranted provocation. That created cause to search the dark and demonic cocksucker at the hospital. He somehow had a permit for the Glock he was carrying. He did not have a prescription for the medication he undoubtedly ditched behind a bench in the Emergency Room, but we can't officially tie him to that. We told him that if anything happened to our precious Large William we *would* find a way to make him surely wish it hadn't. How much he took that to heart we cannot be sure."

Jim said, "Tell that devil Schraft Street has a line that cannot be crossed without getting torn limb-from-limb slowly, one way or the other. Consequences be damned."

"I just said that, Boss Dickhead," replied Carlton. "Lou and I get paid for this shit, and we wallow in it day-to-day. Credit due, Jim. Be very careful and continue to stay cool, or you're gonna get us disbarred and yourself thrown out of office permanent."

Lou said, "That guy is crazy bad. Very dangerous. Bradford Benny seems to agree. Be very careful, Bill, you too Boss Jim. Something's gotta give, now that Paulie Pags is definitely on Schraft Street. Carlton and I are thinking preventive medicine, not cleaning up any more tragic messes."

Jim calmly said, "One way or the other, fellas."

And left. Walking home he wondered what in the Good Christ he was doing. On the other hand, probably Dale really was lost to him. So, a few beers to the good, he decided, at least for now, whatever he had to.

Then his eyes hardened some more, as he decided he'd actually done precious little to protect his beloved little lost Amy-waif from Hoary Harry; and absolutely nothing whatsoever to help save old teammate Harry from his own self-destruction—no matter who'd actually killed him.

Jim always smiled at and said hello to everyone he passed on Schraft; but tonight he did not. Several guys he knew casually scurried wordlessly out of his way with very worried looks on their faces.

Jim knocked on Carlton's door the next morning. Absent response, he sauntered across Schraft Street to The Diner, where Carlton was indeed having an early breakfast. Faye, on break, was having coffee and a piece of what she called her own special 'Breakfast Pie' with him. Faye immediately moved over for Jim.

She gave him the usual half-grin, half-leer. "How's the love life, Boss? You cashed in that sexy little cashier yet?"

"Nah, just getting her friendly update on the Schraft Street scuttlebutt. She's *The Boston Herald* half-scurrilous version, as opposed to your *National Enquirer* all-out sensationalism."

"My expertise and interest surely is sex not violence," replied Faye, then abandoning both the grin and the leer. "Scary goings-on lately. You guys be careful. All of you. So, is Ronnie/Amy gonna work out?"

"I bet," said Jim. "But even if it doesn't I really do think Amy's hooking and stripping days are over, and that she will be okay. With both men and with money. In Ronnie's case a decent future goes without saying."

Carlton laughed. "The personable young miser of Schraft Street. We have plenty of veteran cops should be so disciplined . . . including me, I suppose."

Faye slipped back to half-leer, half-grin. "Don't go getting too disciplined on me, Dear. And, boy, I bet Ronnie's now unleashing *all* that pent-up youthful abandon on that ravishing little Amy!"

"*I* prefer to think of it as expressing their tender young love for each other, Faye," said Jim, in his best mock-serious, exaggeratedly soft tone, mostly suppressing his usual smile.

Faye chuckled. "Yeah, just like me and Sergeant Carrollton do."

Jim chuckled back. "Exactly like that. Except for the jungle noises I can hear two floors up."

Faye took his order while she finished the last of her special pie, and then as she returned to Diner duty she repeated, "Be careful, good guys."

As soon as Faye was out of earshot, Jim said, "What's Benny doing these days, Sergeant?"

"Why?"

"You heard the Pags tape. Benny's watching you guys—and he's watching me. He told me he doesn't like Shenanigans or Sports, but I hear he comes 'round now and then asking questions. I can see Pags pretty clear, but Benny's a mystery to me. And I got a right to know."

"If we thought Benny was a danger to you we'd have told ya. If we see him *becoming* a danger to you we will tell ya. When we tell a vicious lone ranger dummy like Pags that we sometimes have special interests that we take very seriously, he might not listen all that well. But Benny does. Benny gets the difference between outside-the-lines guys like Hoary Harry and outstanding citizens like Jim Herlihy and Bill Donnelly."

"Okay, Carlton, I appreciate that, I do. But still, what's Benny doing these days?"

"Benny still wants to know what happened to his friend and debtor Hoary Harry. He is not impressed with the hard evidence we have been able to gather; and frankly neither are we. He does not like Paul Pagliarani, he does not respect Paul Pagliarani, and he is not afraid of Paul Pagliarani."

Jim said, "Then why doesn't Benny eliminate Paul Pagliarani, and the rest of us can get on with our lives, such as they are?"

"Benny has not confided in me about that, and I haven't asked. But I suspect that he's not totally sure, just as we are not. And he does not want to go to Cedar Junction on a murder rap; and he does have his senior advisors to consider, who may not care so much about Hoary Harry or about Paul Pagliarani. Or about the peace and quiet or lack thereof on Schraft Street."

That night, again after prime time, Jim had started warming up on the bench, alone, when Connie came in without Pags. All-out Connie did not like to work out alone, and Jim was now the only guy in the chest area of the gym who wasn't middle-aged or an obvious beginner. So when Connie came near, he asked her to join him, working overtime to muster his usual friendly grin. She accepted, while managing a begrudging semi-smile in return.

Connie was stronger than ever and worked out frenetically, but Jim decided she didn't look good at all. She'd gained at least ten pounds, and it was not all muscle. Jim figured that, with Pags' evil help and influence, she'd increased her steroid usage but added something else new, and something not all that conducive to bodybuilding success—alcohol. She was wearing one of her favorite fitted workout outfits, and it was no longer so well fitted.

In the throes of maximum effort, her masculine face, contorted by adrenaline, speed, and an undiagnosed level of mental illness, was impossibly painful to look at. Jim was further dismayed to see what looked like the last remnants of a couple of healed facial bruises.

He was somewhat amazed to see her bench 225 six times, instead of her usual three. He couldn't help thinking, "Christ, selling your soul and risking your health for three more reps with 225. What nonsense."

But Connie said, "Pretty fuckin' good for a woman, huh, Boss? None of the other bitches around here can bench 200 pounds even once."

Jim chanced giving Connie a friendly very light tap on the shoulder, and said, "Very impressive, ma'am."

He was relieved that she did not snarl something like, "Keep your fuckin' hands off, cocksucker," and in fact just continued to beam proudly. Thank God her workout was going well.

Jim was on his heaviest set too, and got six reps with 365 pounds, the best he'd ever done. Schraft Street had been injecting him with a little extra adrenaline of late, plus he'd been spending more time at home what with the writing, and that had enabled him to eat more carefully and more regularly. He was happy enough about it, but he sure wasn't anywhere close to jumping around and whoopin' and hollerin.'

Connie didn't congratulate him or anything—of course he didn't mention that it was a personal best—but she did say, "I wish I was a fuckin' guy. I'd be benching 500 pounds and be heavyweight world MMA champ. Everybody on Schraft fuckin' Street would cross right over soon as they saw me coming."

Jim said with a friendly smile, "That is a nice thought, Connie," while thinking, "Most people already do cross the street, Connie, for a whole host of reasons."

Jim did his complete upper body workout with her, following chest with shoulders and arms, and then a brief but intense session on the big bag. He kept the conversation on the workout, and encouraged her and complimented her on how hard she was working and on how expert her form was, and how strong she was. At the same time, he was careful not to overdo it.

Jim could tell she really enjoyed all that. When she'd worked out with equally narcissistic and obsessed Jay, he was by definition too into his own workout to worry much about hers. Pags, on the other hand, would come in and spot her and generally follow her around, but obviously neither knew or cared much about it—until it came to going psycho on the big bag. And then he became primarily like Jay, hardly watching when it was Connie's turn.

After the workout Connie sat at the juice bar, having a huge protein shake. Jim chanced sitting next to her, having a shake half that size.

He said, "So, Connie, how's it going in general? Is Paul's second cousin helping you to feel better?"

She didn't look at him, continued staring straight ahead at the small TV, and just said, "That was a helluva good workout, Boss. Thanks."

"Yeah, but really, how are ya?"

Now she looked at him, and said, "Just great, just fucking great, on top of the damn world, actually. Benched 225 six fuckin' reps; you saw it." Her lower lip was quivering.'

Jim quickly finished his shake, and left saying, "That was a damn good workout, Connie. You know I'm usually here this time of night, so let's do it again soon."

Jim completed another troubled turn of the length of Schraft Street, and then again had some trouble falling asleep. At least he did sleep well once he'd fallen.

Jim still had Benny's number on his home phone. In the unfamiliar Schraft Street matter of Harry/Benny/Pags, Jim had so far been careful to follow Sergeant Carrollton's lead. But the matter now seemed like an ever-darkening cloud, and Boss Jim was thoroughly sick of having it hang over everything.

He mentally replayed his meeting with Benny, and what the detectives and Pagliarani had said about him. Benny was undoubtedly a bad guy, but he wasn't psycho and he was far from dumb. And, best Jim could tell, he had cared about Harry and now he cared about what had happened to him. Beyond just the money Harry had owed him.

Jim chanced the call, and was once again relieved to get the machine. He just said that time had passed and things had happened, and he would, of course, be in the usual place at the usual time on Friday and Saturday nights, if Benny had any interest in confidentially swapping updates.

Jim had thought about arranging a more confidential meet, where perhaps the fact of the meet could remain a secret. But he didn't know Benny well enough—or the state of Benny's current suspicions well enough—to chance that. Besides, he didn't really have any idea how to do such things—and then if they did happen to be observed, Schraft Street folks would really be wondering. Now, and especially if anything serious happened in the future. And, he thought, it was becoming increasingly inevitable that something serious was going to happen in the future—and probably the pretty near future at that.

Benny left a return message saying that he might stop by sometime, no promises, and that confidentially meant no wire and no undercover cop sitting alone at that small table three over from the main entrance.

So the next couple weekends Jim was in his assigned seat. Pagliarani had hopefully decided that discretion was the better part of valor, but realistically there was probably some darker reason for his absence, which was appreciated anyway.

But Jim wasn't too surprised to find that even though he was absolutely thrilled that Amy Jordan was no longer at Shenanigans, Jim surely missed her when he was there. Jim now decided that maybe Benny had something when he'd wondered what the hell the point of strip clubs was.

Jim wished the scary little prick would show up soon, so he could finally quit coming here on Friday and Saturday nights.

CHAPTER TWENTY

Amy and Ronnie; Dale and Doug

Dale and Amy had worked quite intensely together for a couple of weeks—Amy was already plenty knowledgeable about exercise and nutrition, so Dale was primarily emphasizing the science of teaching, motivation, and injury prevention, especially in older clients—and now Amy was taking the certification classes that Jim had insisted on buying for her. The gym was cleaner than ever, and Ronnie reported that Amy was doing more than her share. Jim didn't doubt that—Amy had kept his apartment spotless for a couple of years. Not only had he never come close to complaining, he'd even felt compelled to tell her several times that he wasn't planning on eating off of the floor or drinking out of the toilet.

Then he found out that Frankie had hired the Doyle/Jordan Cleaning Company to come in to Sports two nights a week, after they'd finished at the gym.

Jim said, "Frankie, you did *not* buy into this bar when I offered, remember? That means that you are not authorized to commit the bar to new contracts and to new expenditures of funds that the owner has not authorized. What's up now, ya burly bearded bastard?"

"I know how ya feel about Amy and Ronnie, Boss. They gave us a damn good price. Me and the other bartenders will still do our thing, but those two young pros are experts who have better equipment than we do, and they can get everything we miss by just coming in for a couple hours those two nights . . . you're not gonna fire Amy and Ronnie, are ya?"

"What I should do is fire your fat ugly ass, and hire those two slim young sweethearts to do everything around here . . . ah, fuck it."

A few weeks after Amy got her certification, Jim took her and Ronnie to dinner at The Diner to celebrate. Jim had not seen much of Amy since her 'retirement.' He'd knocked on the door a couple of mornings looking for her, and Consuela told him that Amy was spending about half her nights at Ronnie's. Amy rarely brought Ronnie to her apartment, because she had the two roommates, and Ronnie lived alone.

Jim said, "You seem pretty down, 'Suela. Is it just missing Amy, or is there something else, dear?"

"It's just missing Amy, but that's more than enough. I miss laughing, and I miss just watching her. She is doing good though, she really is, Jim." Then she gave him a big hard hug.

She said, "But I got all the other girls. I'll be alright, Boss . . . and you?"

"Sure. I got all of Schraft Street."

At The Diner Ronnie said, "We're cleaning this place now, too, and we hired a couple young girls to help us. Amy's a supervisor now."

Amy said, "I gotta kick those two young ladies good in the butt, keep 'em moving. They're both way bigger than me too. Like just about everybody is."

Jim said, "The Doyle/Jordan Cleaning Company. Other prospects? Shenanigans?"

"I know enough not to mess with the guys clean Shenanigans, *that's* out," replied Amy. "But I'm pounding the pavement all around, and we'll get more businesses, hire more girls . . . have you got your Aunt Bea yet, or are you now living in squalor, 'cause you're not too good at picking up after yourself?"

"No, you guys can do my place, if you give me a halfway reasonable price. What about Carlton and Consuela?"

Amy said, "'Suela does her own cleaning; she's a stripper, not a slob. Anyway, if I ever do help her or let her use our equipment after I officially move out, I'd still never charge my sweet 'Suela a cent. Carlton's too cheap, and anyway Faye picks up after him sometimes. We'll give you a fair price, kind sir; but it won't actually be me doing it 'cause Ronnie thinks I still want to boink ya, and that sooner or later you'd have to cave."

Jim said to Ronnie, "If I wasn't gonna do that before, I'm damn sure not gonna do it now that Amy's with you, son . . . and you know she wouldn't now either."

Ronnie replied, "Amy's supervising and selling, and doing personal training in the daytimes, Boss, so she doesn't have time to do homes, yours or anyone's. Although, some of the middle-aged ladies seem put off by Amy's background, so her training business isn't growing quite as fast as we'd like."

Jim said, "Miz O'Dell can help with that, when she gets back from her New York nonsense."

"I'll get there," said Amy. "I am working with The Famous Foursome three evenings a week, and that really is a lot of fun. They're loud, lord they're loud bitches, but I like 'em anyway. But did I mention they're loud?"

Faye was bringing their drinks, overhead, and virtually shouted, "Loud bitches, you say. I *hate* loud women!" And then she laughed like Fran Drescher on methamphetamine."

Jim left The Diner grinning, and ardently wishing that the population of Schraft Street was nothing but Amy Jordans and Ronnie Doyles, with a few Fabulous Fayes thrown in for boisterous, semi-vulgar variety.

And, man, those little Diner steaks were tasty.

He'd been somehow starving going in there, they'd stayed quite a while, and in the end he'd gotten hungry again, and had a third steak while the others were gushing over Faye's latest new pie invention. On break, Faye had sat down beside Jim, jokingly squeezing up against him, and then staying tightly pressed against his thigh while she had a big piece of her own new pasty creation.

Then, as they were leaving and she was going back to work, and as if Boss Jim not Sergeant Carrollton was her regular right-across-the-street lover, she whispered in his ear, "I'll be home soon, dear, and I am one horny cougar, so have that huge hard-on stoked and waiting."

Boss Jim did not then drop by The Schraft Street Market to see what the sexy young cashier was doing after work, but it had taken every last ounce of the well-honed and battle-tested Herlihy willpower not to. Lord, he needed a girlfriend.

But definitely one closer to his age, level of common sense and responsibility, maturity, and with a more compatible sense of humor. A second choice after the apparently permanently unavailable Dale O'Dell; even if said second choice would unavoidably be light years behind that impossibly lovely first one.

Jim sent what he had so far on the sequel—he estimated he was about two-thirds done on the fast first draft—to Keith Garrity for a semi-valued opinion. Keith was very, very smart, but careful, insightful reading and critiquing was not his real strength. And Jim felt Keith had a subconscious positive bias beyond his control. But, other than Editor Steve Chadwick or Sergeant Carrollton or Dale O'Dell, Keith was his best option. He wasn't ready for Chadwick to see it; at this still early point Sergeant Carrollton would confuse him with too much additional technical detail; and Dale certainly seemed to be moving their relationship to a decidedly less intimate level overall.

Jim hadn't said anything to Keith one way or the other about showing the draft to Big Sister Carol. But she was on conference when Keith called Jim back to review the surprisingly extensive notes Keith had earlier emailed. It quickly became obvious that Carol had been an enthusiastic co-author of those notes.

And then the combination of Keith and Carol was even more surprisingly helpful, as Carol forced Keith to be both more insightful and more critical, even as she was offering her own balance of overall encouragement offset by somewhat startlingly pointed criticism.

When he hung up, he was (a) glad that he hadn't chanced what he had so far on Chadwick, and (b) very well motivated to address the eye-opening changes he'd agreed with, and then finish this damn fast first draft.

And get that fifty k advance into his hands, ASAP—his bar and gym revenues were up quite nicely, but so were his expenses: remodeling the ladies bathroom at Sports, buying 'retirement' presents, unwittingly engaging Doyle/Jordan to clean Sports, buying Connie Parker dinners, and assorted relatively minor but still expensive new equipment for the gym, at the insistent behest of that most formidable and obsessed partner and gym manager.

One brutally cold, windy night in early February, as Jim was scrambling from Diner to Gym, he saw Big Bill heading towards him, lumbering energetically but still painfully slowly from Herlihy's Hardcore to his shift at Shenanigans. Jim grinned broadly, despite the icy, eye-watering wind in his face. Three-hundred-and-fifty-pound Bill was absurdly bundled up—including a ridiculous-looking John Candy-Uncle Buck huge fur hat—making him look from a distance for all the world like a realistically awkward 600-pound sasquatch, relentlessly rolling Jim's way.

As Bill got closer, though, Jim followed Bill's steely gaze across the street, where Paulie Pags—who didn't appear at all suitably attired for the bitter cold—was strolling along casually in the same direction as Bill, and staring back across the street.

When he got close enough, Jim said to Bill, "What in the Good Christ is that demon doing now, here in fifteen-fucking-below wind chill?"

Bill replied stoically, "Fucking with me, fucking with people in general. Crazy-scary dark devil wanders a lot now, beyond the dealing, especially late at night. Just for the fun of it."

"Jesus, Bill. Be very, very careful. Cocksucker's packing. And if there's anyone empty-handed still provides the perfect self-defense excuse, it's your monstrous ass . . . especially dressed like that, ya fuckin' mountain."

"Hey, Boss, I know I'm not the brightest light in the shed. But ya do remember what I did for a living before we opened Herlihy's, don't ya?"

Jim punched Bill lightly on the shoulder. (Given the size of Bill and how he was dressed it would not, of course, have mattered one whit if Jim had hauled off and hit Bill as hard as he could.)

Then Jim said, "I do indeed. Be very, very careful anyway, ya big lug. What happened to Harry was way more than bad enough."

Bill replied with a far away, incredibly scary look in his eyes, "Yeah, it surely, surely was. You be very, very careful too, Jim."

Dale called Jim to say she was back, and to ask about Connie; and Pagliarani. When his immediate response was to ask about her visit with Doug in New York, she sounded sincere in saying that she'd had a fantastic time; but then she sure didn't seem interested in elaborating. He actually got slightly irritated at Dale O'Dell.

He'd certainly a few times been disappointed by—and even a little with—Dale, but this was definitely the first time he'd ever been irritated at her. He guessed that was probably now her intention, at least when it came to her romantic relationship with Doug vis a vis her decidedly non-romantic relationship with him.

He updated her on Connie, honestly best he knew, but he realized he was doing it mechanically and dispassionately, and he could tell that was now irritating her. As it should—bad news casually given, about someone he was supposed to care about.

Jim did his best to rally—he did care some about Connie and immensely about Dale—but it was just that things in these two arenas were going decidedly worse than, say, in the Amy/Ronnie arena, or even in his writing. Dale and Connie represented a couple of very different but almost equally frustrating trends he felt basically powerless to reverse.

Dale finally said, "So, the best we can do is work out with Connie whenever the opportunity arises, and hope for the best relative to the Drs. Pagliarani; and relative to the bruises and drug and now alcohol abuse?"

Jim thought better of mentioning his standing offer to meet with Bradford Benny, not able to offer any reasonable or close-to-specific theory on how in the Good Christ that might help.

So he said, "Maybe we'll get lucky and Carlton will figure out a way to arrest Paulie Pags, and then we can move back in on Connie. But I can't arrest him, Dale; nor can I warn him off. He's made it abundantly clear that he's not afraid of me—nor should he be."

Jim did think but not say, "Maybe the big dark devil should be afraid of Bradford Benny, though."

So, thus ended a hardly encouraging conversation with his beloved Dr. Dale.

CHAPTER TWENTY-ONE

Bradford Benny Reprised

A COUPLE WEEKS LATER BENNY finally showed up at Shenanigans. Jim had gotten even more sick of the place—and especially sick of being around naked women, not because he wasn't interested in them but because he really, really was—and had decided that if Benny did show, it would certainly be after eight, so no sense getting there before then. And then he'd always leave right at nine, having but two light beers in the process.

Pagliarani had resumed his Shenanigans shenanigans, but he no longer sat at the bar. Bill asked, but the owners decided they didn't have proper cause to permanently ban the bastard. After all, he'd only squeezed Bill's thoroughly impervious rock-solid 22" left arm, and in response Bill had practically torn the poor guy's arm in half.

And if insulting Monstrous Bill's bartending was a *banning* offense, not only would Shenanigans be empty, but there wouldn't be any males over twenty-one left on Schraft Street.

Tonight scary-looking half-midget Benny strolled in at eight-thirty, and sauntered around the place, checking out everyone but the naked women. Jim had had to forego looking at them himself, so the careful observer might wonder why these this strange pair was in Shenanigans at all, once Benny sat next to Jim. But Jim had not told Carlton of this meeting, so there were no careful observers, at least not of two guys quietly talking at the bar.

Benny first had Jim walk out back with him, where this time he did check Jim carefully.

Jim said, "Neither the detectives nor anyone else knew beforehand that this meeting was gonna take place, Benny. And I don't want this conversation overhead or recorded any more than you do."

"Bullshit on that last. You don't know half what I know—and you probably don't know *anything* I don't know, which of course makes this meeting a total waste of time for me. I finally guess I don't have anything against ya, Boss, except I find you even more boring than these naked bitches that I'm not gonna fuck tonight. But, I am here. So?"

They were now back seated at the bar. For the first time ever Jim was happy to have the non-stop loud music. Schraft Street's well-toned tongues would certainly be wagging about Bradford Benny and Boss Jim Herlihy briefly sitting in very close conference at the Shenanigans bar, but no one would have overhead a word. And, of course, everyone on Schraft Street knew that these two very strange bedfellows had had such a conference before, and absent major consequence.

Jim replied, "*So* I think Pagliarani did it, he's a very bad and three-quarters crazy guy, and he's apt to hurt some totally innocent, or mostly innocent, people that I care about a lot more than I did about Harry. And I did care about Harry, Benny. I've had dinner with Pags and his new girlfriend Connie, and somehow that's just the impression I got. And I certainly don't consider myself out of Pags' line of fire either."

"Yeah, I know about that dinner, and I'm sure you were wearing a wire, and I'm sure Pags didn't say anything incriminating because the cops aren't getting to him. So you don't know. By the way, that new girlfriend of Pags is one mean and crazy bitch, and that mug of hers does nothing to disguise the fact. But that ass of hers, man oh man! I think there was a medieval maiden just like her, some guy decided that extreme necessity is the mother of invention and carried through on that; and then another guy said, 'Hey, that head cover you just invented would be good for carrying groceries, if you just turned it upside down!'"

Jim couldn't help chuckling. But then he thought it made a lot of sense, actually. Ugly women with shapely asses were certainly around a helluva long time before grocery stores were. So Benny had a sense of humor after all—Jim's earlier wisecracks just hadn't been sufficiently mean-spirited.

But then Jim said, "Connie's a person, Benny, who was doing the best she could, until people like Pags got at her."

"Yeah, guys in my line of work can't afford to think like that, Boss," replied Benny. "And, hey, give *me* credit for giving *her* credit for that ass, at least. Plus, I hate to break it to ya, but she just might be almost as psycho-evil as Pags is . . . but you know that right well, don't ya?"

"I honestly still harbor very real hope that Connie had nothing to do with the brutalization of Harry. Personally, Benny, I'd like to see that demon Pags convinced to relocate. Above ground, but reasonably far from here."

"Feds do relocation, Boss. Witness protection. We don't. 'Cause they eventually come back, with worse ideas than they had when they left."

Jim said, "Man, I'd feel real bad if Pags hurts someone else serious, even Connie, or that oversized bartender there whose eventually gonna bring us a second round, maybe. I'll feel especially bad if he hurts me."

"Here's a news flash. Pags'll either kill ya or leave ya alone, no in between. You don't have enough for him to shake ya down, plus your cop friends. Don't bother offering me money for anything; that's not my business. If and when I'm sure I'll take care of it . . . maybe you could make that easier for me, if the time comes. Maybe not necessary; we'll table that for now . . . Jesus, that monstrous lug never did make it back here, and you're his partner, for Chrissake! Why isn't he manning the door, and someone who operates in real time behind the fucking bar?'

Jim replied, "'Cause he's too scary at the door, the squeamish might not come in."

"He's pretty scary behind the bar too, if you're squeamish about drinking something really fucked up, after a ridiculous wait. I'm outta here."

Connie showed up at the gym with bruises that would have kept any other woman home with the shades drawn. She was obviously addicted to hard exercise, and her membership to the Chelsea Powerhouse had expired. She snarled at both Jim and Dale to just leave her alone, so they had no choice.

Dale was acting like it was Jim's fault, and told him that he had to do something.

Then Dale took another trip to New York to see Doug.

Jim was planning to talk to Carlton about the latest state of Connie, but before he could he ran into Pagliarani on the street, coming the other way.

Jim was walking on the right by the curb, and Pagliarani had plenty of room to pass on Jim's left by staying to his own right, but the big guy tried to force Jim to step into the street, so they bumped shoulders hard. Pagliarani then savagely pushed Jim into the street, snarling, "More than happy to kick the ever-loving shit out of the so-called Boss of Schraft Street, asshole. Right here, right now."

Jim replied calmly, "Yeah, big man, ya got forty pounds on me, *had* seventy on poor Harry . . . and now ya got eighty pounds on Connie, ya gutless woman-beater."

Jim blocked Pagliarani's first couple of blows, and caught him with a couple of hard quick rights against the side of his huge head, but it was no use, Pagliarani was too big, too strong, and almost as skilled a boxer as Jim. A hard right put Jim down, and Pagliarani kicked savagely at Jim's head and his ribs, some of them badly bruising his covering arms, and a few getting through. Pags wasn't going to beat him to death right there on Schraft Street—there were a few witnesses now—so he finally walked off wordlessly.

Frankie ran out of nearby Sports with his trusty baseball bat, fully intending to catch up to Pags and do his damndest—Jim didn't know how that would go, probably Pags would rip the bat away from him, and beat Frankie far worse than he had Jim—but Jim broke free from the people who had helped him up and grabbed Frankie.

Jim whispered, "Not now, Frankie, not now. Soon enough, though."

Frankie whispered back, "One way or the other, Boss, one way or the other."

Jim now had no doubt that Pagliarani had killed Harry. And precious little doubt that Pagliarani would like to kill him . . . especially since he'd decided that Harry'd been right about Benny being basically savvy and straight-shooting—and psycho Pags had certainly stopped leaving Jim alone.

Sergeant Carrollton told Jim, "Not much sense pressing charges; you guys bumped in the street, had words, couple boxers exchanging punches, he had the size, you're not hurt serious except the pride."

"He's crazy dangerous, Carl. Look at Connie."

"We've talked hard to Connie twice now; even got her to let us in once when she was alone. *She* surely should press charges, but she won't. She's crazy, scared, dumb, drugged; virtually unshakably mute. Maybe we'll get lucky and she'll shoot him while he's sleeping."

Jim said, "That would be *good* luck, so it couldn't possibly happen. There's plenty of luck on Schraft Street, but that there particular species hasn't been seen 'round these parts for quite a while."

"Well, it never has been too prevalent, Boss, but it's not extinct. Amy and Ronnie. Don't be paralyzed, but don't be stupid either . . . and remember, Lou's something of a 'by-the-book' little hound dog . . . and he's still my boss."

"Yes, Carl, I think I can remember the tomfoolery thrown my way by the persistent little pest, even though it was *multiple* weeks ago. That big dark devil Pags did kick me in the skull, but fortunately the concussion was minor; and the doc told me I still got a couple years yet before dementia sets in."

CHAPTER TWENTY-TWO

Jim Herlihy, Boss of Schraft Street

KEITH CALLED JIM A COUPLE days later, and said, "I'm hearing bad news, Boss. Dr. Dale moved to New York. I sure didn't see that coming. Some gangster knocked you down. You need a change of scenery, old friend. And you would be more than welcome."

"Amy and Ronnie are doing fantastic, Keith. Gym and bar not so bad, either. Carlton, Frankie, Lloyd, the Monstrous One all say hello. Writing's going good, some thanks to you and that straight-talking Big Sister."

Keith said, "Don't do anything crazy, Jim. Come here."

"Nah. Timing's not right. I'll be fine, Brocefious."

Jim met Bradford Benny at Shenanigans again, the very next Friday night.

Benny said, "Our interests seem to be aligning, Boss."

"Roses are red, and this matter needs to be put to bed, mehaps?"

Benny said, "Yeah. No doubt. That *is* our man."

They walked out back. Benny slipped Jim an absolutely wicked right-hand-only brass-knuck. Heavy little bar to be palmed, discreetly raised knuckles. Jim could not believe how heavy it was.

But then Jim hesitated, and looked from the scary, weighty brass in his hand up to formidable little Benny.

Benny looked up into Jim's eyes, and said, "I do indeed want vengeance very badly, Boss. But I don't have anywhere near the vested interest in *future* Schraft Street developments that you do."

Jim squeezed the heavy, very bad brass into his right front pocket.

"Evil prick has forty pounds on ya," said Benny flatly. "That will make things fair. Idiot's now dealing over on King Street sometimes, not far from the little woods where our poor Harry was found. Cops aren't on to that yet, but soon will be. Fair fight coming, for the duly elected and conscientious Boss of Schraft Street?"

"Give me a couple days to acclimate. Then it will be what it must be."

"Don't take too long, Boss. He's getting stupider, so a meaningless short stint in the hoosegow is beckoning. Let's get this over with."

For the next week, Jim worked harder than ever on the big bag. And he shadowboxed relentlessly in the privacy of his living room, wearing that vicious looking right hand enhancement. Given the frenetic activity, he was thrilled that his shoulder and elbow hadn't developed tendonitis. But they along with his whole body felt far better than fine.

(Jim was a most experienced self-motivator, and a pretty tough-minded fella, through both nature and environmentally-mandated practice. Before each of these sessions, he spent some time reliving the vicious, humiliating, unprovoked beating Pags had unleashed on him, right in the middle of Boss Jim Herlihy's own Schraft Street; given his innate sentiments regarding 250-pound professional boxers beating on any kind of woman, he raised even more energizing adrenaline thinking about what Pags was doing to Connie; it seemed the devil himself was now stalking Jim's beloved Big Brother Bill; and finally what he somehow found most enervating were thoughts of practicing T-ball with Hank and Harry and Harry's dad, when Jim and Harry were six-year-olds, surprisingly innocent and carefree, mostly oblivious of the often desperate struggles inherent in their surroundings—because early-on, when hard-ass Detective Lou had honestly considered Jim a prime suspect, the little prick had 'forced' Jim to look at several pictures brutally and crystal-clearly showcasing the dreadful results of demon Pags' unbridled viciousness.)

Benny gave him the call, on an unseasonably warm early spring night in late March. A few very quiet streets over from Schraft, Jim waited—once again mentally replaying those brutal pictures and silently raging, secreted in the very wood where those awful, awful photos had been taken—until Pags' latest round of young customers had left. Then he walked up to the temporarily-deserted Pags and said clearly and sharply, "You have to answer for Santino, you fucking devil."

The semi-obscure *Godfather* reference momentarily confused Pags, and before he could fully register what was going on, Jim hit him with the hardest and quickest right hand he'd ever thrown, adrenaline fueled, and powerized but not slowed by the vicious apparatus he was wearing. Jim's savage, heavy-handed, perfectly aimed right hit Pags just to the left of his Leno-like chin.

Pags was unconscious before he even started to fall. His huge head hit the granite curbing flush, and he was dead as Dillinger upon that gruesome, sickeningly loud contact. That formidable, weighty squash along with Pags' height of six-three was normally a huge plus in a fist fight, but when he was in the first unconscious freefall of his savagely bullying life, the momentum and the granite combined to do him in.

In the northeast, unlike the rest of the country, the local governments pay a significant premium for granite as opposed to concrete curbing, because the incredibly impervious and just plain ultra-hard granite stands up to both the inclement weather *and* the unavoidable abuse from even the most careful and skilled snowplow drivers.

Given all of the above—most of which was fortuitous rather than planned by the just and aggrieved Boss of Schraft Street—Pags huge skull was finally way overmatched.

Boss Jim had been prepared to follow up violently, but was immediately thrilled to see that he wouldn't have to.

Half-midget Benny and some virtual giants immediately pulled up in a Ram 3500, Benny driving, and Benny said, "Schraft Street Waste Management at your service, Boss. Your civic duty is done for the day; go have a well-deserved beer."

Jim wasn't too surprised that the sudden demise of Pags gave him a lot fewer sleepless moments than had the Schraft Street arrival of that demonic madman. Technically, he supposed, he was a murderer and a dirty fighter. But he did not feel at all like either.

He'd had absolutely no choice, and he found he could live with that, no problem. Or not much problem.

He didn't know what Schraft Street really thought, other than that he was still Boss Jim. No one was saying much yet, but almost everyone he passed on the street smiled warmly while they were nodding.

Then some folks started politely asking Boss Jim what he thought about the sudden Schraft Street appearance of Paul Pagliarani, and the even more sudden disappearance—not a trace.

Jim could have—undoubtedly should have—just said, "I have no idea; just glad he's gone for now."

But he usually said, "Maybe he didn't fit in so good on Schraft Street."

That was universally accepted.

Carlton and Lou came to see him at his apartment, about three weeks post Pags.

Carlton smiled tightly. "Christ, you just barely passed the lie detector on Harry . . . and then in yesterday's test it's almost like you never even *had* any significant interaction with Pags."

Lou half-sneered, "You do remember that Pags absolutely kicked the shit out of you, right out in the open?"

Jim replied with a sad shake of his head, "I grew up with Harry, and underneath all the sorry nonsense I cared about him; and even did feel a little *indirectly* responsible. On the other hand I hated that psycho Pags with every fiber of my being; even *before* he put his hands on me. I'm just glad he's gone for now . . . and that he's sure to get his just desserts in the end."

Lou said, "How you *felt* about 'em wasn't the question."

Jim replied, "But that's all them electrodes can measure, how you're *feeling*, isn't it, Detective?"

Lou grimaced, and said, "You tend to do and say whatever ya want, and not worry overmuch about any of it, don't ya, Boss?"

"On the contrary, Detective, I have long been worrying all too much . . . and, unfortunately, like most people, far too often about things that I can't do anything about. *Or*, wherein I had absolutely no other choice. Worry is a waste, though, so I've now resolved to cut way down . . . you *could* keep watching me, but it will prove quite boring and unproductive."

Lou rolled his eyes, and said, "What'd you and Benny talk about?"

"I asked him if he still thought I might have offed Harry, and he said no, he did not. I said that's good for me. I asked if he thought Pags had done it, and he said he didn't know. He never liked strip clubs and Shenanigans is nowhere near the same for me without Amy, so we figured we wouldn't meet there again. Then we wished each other a nice life."

Lou looked at Carlton, who shook his head, shrugged, grinned, and said, "Schraft Street is a pretty growly damn place, Detective. This here is one Bradford-born-and-bred good-natured and grinning SOB, and yet everyone on Schraft calls him Boss . . . and you're the only one does it sarcastically. Like they said about Babe Ruth, 'Well, what the hell are ya gonna do with a son of a bitch like that?'"

Lou stood up and stared out the window for a few seconds. Then he said, "Ya think we'll ever see Pags on Schraft Street again, Boss? Prevailing is that we won't."

"That is the fervent hope. Who knows, maybe he was just smart enough to know it was time to get out of Dodge."

Carlton said, "Well, no one's even filed a 'missing person' on that lonest of wolves; Connie just said that they hadn't been getting along well at all and she had the bruises to back that up, and that she's not surprised he split and, like the rest of the street, she hopes he never comes back."

"No 'missing persons' we don't have a case to solve, so we don't even have to waste our time talking to hardass Benny," said Lou. "How a dumbass like Paulie Pags was able to beat Harry so badly and still leave such a clean crime scene we have no idea. Well, can't win 'em all. Bye, Boss."

Walking out of Jim's three-decker, Carlton shook Lou's hand, and said, "No hard feelings or repercussions, Detective?"

Lou shrugged, and replied, "Not your fault *or* Herlihy's that we were never gonna pin poor Harry on Demon Pags. And, hell, Demon Pags ain't officially missing *or* unofficially missed, he's just *gone*, which is a good place for him. Schraft Street really isn't all that bad, but I've sure had enough of it for now. Gonna be working in the North End for a while. Good luck, Carl."

Carlton smiled tightly while very slowly heading alone across the street to Diner and Faye. Maybe it had been Jim, maybe it hadn't . . . but, Schraft Street being what it was, and especially that Demon Pags being what he'd become, the big dark devil had been a dead man walking for quite a while before he disappeared.

Then the big cop stopped smiling, and even shuddered a little. What a fuckin' shame that dark son of a bitch hadn't clearly shown his evil hand before it was too late for old teammate Harry.

Sergeant Carrollton's cheeks were slightly damp when Faye sat across from him on break. She didn't ask why, just reached across the table with a napkin to gently dry them.

Connie Parker finally got out of rehab. She'd been sent there not by 'Dr.' Pagliarani, but by a real therapist that 'Dr.' Dale O'Dell had set her up with.

Jim and Dale had mutually organized the Schraft Street collection, and Connie had no reason a'tall to be humiliated by the neighborhood response.

Connie knocked on Jim's door, for the first time ever.

She'd lost about fifteen pounds of muscle, but the fat was also gone. Her face had relaxed some. She was never gonna be pretty, but sometimes just looking indisputably sane is good.

She surveyed the apartment, and said, "Wow, that sweet little rascal did do a nice job, as I'd heard. I'm doing much better . . . Please, please, Jim, just between us . . . do I have to worry that he'll be back?"

"No."

"I was out of my head and on some serious shit, and I did owe Harry money I didn't have, but I was not there, and I did not ask that big dark devil to do that; and I did not know in advance. Paul swore he didn't plan it himself, things just got out of control; I honestly don't know if that's true. Probably not—he whacked me around pretty good, but lucky for me he never totally lost control doing it. He'd have killed me sure, though, if he ever thought I was gonna tell anyone. I swear."

"I'm going to believe all of that, Connie."

"It quickly got so I hated him and I was scared to death of him, and I had to get drunk with him every night just so I could bear sleeping next to him . . . me, Connie Parker, getting fat on fucking alcohol . . . Dale says she'll work out with me sometimes, whenever she comes home here. Can I come back?"

"Of course. Nothing's changed except you got help. I'll work out with you sometimes, too.'

She flexed her right arm. "Thanks. Man, I'm puny, I can hardly bear to look in the mirror. I'll stay off the juice, I swear it, but Christ am I itchin' to get back at that iron. I wonder if I can build much muscle clean? You ever try the juice, Jim?"

"Never. You still have of plenty of muscle, Connie, and you'll get some but not all of it back quick enough. Steroids work, of course, but it's hardly worth the money and the risk."

"Jay makes a half-decent living off it. How is he, by the way?"

"He's Jay. We're not close, but he seems okay. Crazy/lucky SOB's gotta have the sturdiest damn knees in the history of mankind. I have no idea how he's gonna make a living five years from now, though."

Connie grinned. "Won't be my problem, that's for sure. Hey, Amy and Consuela and Monstrous but sweet Bill talked 'em into giving me a trial as a waitress at Shenanigans. Maybe I can stay clean and sane enough to keep it. Amy feels guilty because she picked up a few of my training clients. She asked them if they wanted to switch back to me, but so far they said no. Can't blame anyone but myself for that."

"Sounds great, Connie. Just be glad that Monstrous Bill doesn't handle the service bar."

She chuckled. "Poor Bill. I'm really sorry it didn't work out between you and Dale, Jim. You're a helluva guy, one hell of a guy . . . a lot of people around here think I'm a repressed lesbian, and that that's part of my problem. I gotta tell ya, though, when I look at that damn Doug Ballard, the way the ol' clitter starts a-twitchin,' I sure ain't no fuckin' lesbian."

"Point being, I suppose, that according to your clitoris Mr. Ballard is so attractive that I should not be discouraged coming in second to him. Thank you both."

Connie punched his shoulder. "At the risk of being indiscreet, Boss, the ol' clitterer isn't totally immune to your presence, either. On that note I'd probably best leave."

CHAPTER TWENTY-THREE

Aftermath

JIM KEPT TELLING HIMSELF THAT he'd very likely saved his own life, probably Connie's, maybe even Big Bill's, and obviously gotten justice of a sort for poor old friend Harry, but it still took him a few more weeks before he could effectively get back into the writing. But once he did, it flowed at least as well as it ever had.

When he finally showed the draft to Carlton, the veteran cop said, "Yeah, I see a little more insight this time, now that you got at least a slight firsthand taste of the inside view. I can also see a few more bucks headed my way this time, I surely do hope. But we can sharpen it up some too."

"It's semi-light fictional nonsense, Carl, not an official detective's manual."

Carlton laid a bunch of technical detail on him anyway, while Jim dutifully took notes, figuring he'd use at least a little of it.

At the end Carlton said, "Hey Boss, I notice lately your knucks are looking more like those of a writer/businessman and not so much like those of The Mad Dog Boss of Schraft Street. Figured you've done enough hard hitting for one lifetime, have ya?"

"Nah, I still gotta go absolutely nuts on the big bag every couple days, Carl, in the interest of day-to-day sanity. I just started wearing those evil looking half-gloves under my wraps, in honor of a certain Paulie Pags. Now I can pound away for a full hour; not a scratch."

When he officially submitted the draft to Chadwick in April, Scribner gave him the $50k advance, and did put a notice about the whole thing in *The Boston Globe*. Someone showed it to Fat Frankie at the bar, and that burly worthy immediately waddled a hundred yards west on Schraft to plot with The Monstrous One relative to disbursement of the subject funds.

Meanwhile, Jim headed to New York City to meet with Chadwick to discuss in detail Chadwick's reams of editorial commentary, and to plan for Jim's rewrite/final polish. Which would probably take at least three months, including plenty of additional and painful back-and-forth via phone and Email.

Dale O'Dell was now enrolled in the Columbia University College of Physicians and Surgeons, studying, of course, to be an orthopedic surgeon. Now that Dale and Doug were officially engaged—Jim had already been invited to the damn wedding, which would be at a hall just a couple streets over from Schraft—Doug was obviously helping to bankroll her study.

When Jim called to tell her he'd be in New York, and why, she insisted that Doug wanted Jim to meet them at Sparks Steakhouse. Jim didn't even bother to try to get his Dale to meet him without her Doug.

With her extensive experience working as a P.A. accompanied by her almost equally extensive pre-study—which had been overseen by the prominent surgeon she'd worked with for several years, who had no doubt she'd make a great orthopedic surgeon—Dale was now off and running in med school.

They were sitting at the bar at Sparks, waiting for their table. When Dale went to the ladies' room, Doug said, "I'll take good care of her, Boss, treat her every bit as great as she deserves. I know my life'd be in serious danger if I didn't."

Jim replied, sporting a pretty friendly smile, even if unavoidably not his absolute best, "No one's expecting you'd ever physically hurt her, Doug. Emotionally—well, Dale O'Dell is one very smart and very strong lady who is perfectly capable of making her own way in this world. You *both* have my sincere best wishes, Doug, I do hope we all stay in touch; and, well, there you have it."

Jim bought an hour training session with Amy and Ronnie, mostly just to experience them in action, and also, of course, because with the fifty k in hand he *could*. (He wasn't gonna let Frankie and Bill spend *all* of it.) But, ya never know, with their official training and the latest exercise science, maybe the hardworking youngsters could teach him something he didn't know and could actually use.

Probably not, though. Hardcore Jim Herlihy was a huge believer in the time-tested heavy basics—bench presses, squats, weighted chin-ups and dips, power cleans, curls—as long as aging joints permitted. And fortunately his aging joints still permitted. But, what the hell. This was, after all, Amy Jordan and Ronnie Doyle.

But halfway in, Amy said, "Ronnie and I are gonna visit Dr. Carol and that snobby Keith in West Palm Beach, Florida. See that fancy Meet place, finally."

Ronnie said, "Jim"—Jim thought this was the first time young Ronnie had ever called him Jim instead of Boss—"it's understandable that folks around here, much as most of 'em love my Amy, can't forget her unfortunate background. Amy's been talking to Big Sister Carol about us getting a fresh start."

Truth be told, ever-observant Boss Jim had himself started thinking that perhaps Amy was in need of just such a change in venue. Dale, now Amy and Ronnie—but that was of course the way the world worked. Ask any parent or grandparent.

So Jim said, "Doing what, pray tell?"

Amy said, "Me bartending at The Meet and doing personal training at that L.A. Fitness Center nearby. Ronnie doing personal training and being an Assistant Manager at a Beef O'Brady's sports restaurant that Big Sister owns. Plus maybe we can get a few dollars for the Doyle/Jordan Cleaning Company now, and we both have money saved too. Maybe we can even invest in The Meet since you didn't. Or are ya still?"

"Not right this minute, Amy. Took money upfront, now got a book to deliver."

Amy chuckled. "Yeah, read about ya in *The Globe*. Didn't do ya justice, though. Speaking of doing justice and writing, my Famous Foursome are now at 725, and they say—*they* say—that you promised a follow-up article in *The Bulletin* when they got to an even seven. You don't come through, kind sir, they won't so much be bending your ear as they will mine. 'Cause you're never here when they are, and I'm still training 'em twice a week. And, as you know right well, when those four bend ears, they bend fuckin' ears! Sorry, Ronnie, but sometimes ya have to swear to protect ya eardrums."

"Yes, Dear, I have certainly heard them and now I hear you."

Jim said, "Brother, I'm surprised you youngsters have any clients at all, because you sure do deliver a lot of bad news along with the damn training . . . what's Linda at now, by the way?"

"One-fifty," said Amy, sporting a gorgeous big grin. "And, Big Bill's noticed. He doesn't exactly have a Jim Herlihy six-pack stomach himself, either."

It was an unusually warm night for late April in Boston, and spring was definitely in the air. The Sox were—after missing the playoffs in various creative and frustrating ways the last three years—at least off to a good start, at 12-5. Jim loved walking The Street on a crisp-not-too-cold night in the heart of Christmas season, but then there was always the overhanging cloud that tomorrow night would probably be sleet and freezing rain. And then, of course, that January just might aspire to unprecedented heights of unrelenting, "Boy, does this fuckin' weather ever, ever suck! Fuuuck!" just because the weather gods obviously loved to hear folks cuss in a Boston accent.

So an unusually nice early spring night like this was, overall, the best. Well, except for the fact that his favorite person in the world had just moved away, and now two top young contenders for that recently vacated title were planning to follow painful suit.

But, on the other hand, his lifting was going good, joints feeling fine, he had a few bucks in the bank for a change and gym and bar were not doing too badly either, and, perhaps most important, Schraft Street was essentially psycho-free, at least for the moment.

Also as usual, the familiar long, narrow view of lights and businesses and leafy oak trees and three-deckers housing assorted friends and acquaintances was, for Boss Jim, 20/15-crystal-damn-clear.

So, he walked for a good long while, three full-length turns, soon thinking primarily about playing baseball with his beloved, self-sacrificing dad on long ago, promise-laden nights just like this one. And that—a la both little Lloyd Dolson and Hank Herlihy—sometimes you might as well go ahead and think that life is good just because you felt like it.

EPILOGUE

Many months later, Sergeant Carlton Carrollton guided Jim into a corner table at Sports, and said, "Hardcore Jim Herlihy. Boss of Schraft Street. Wonderful but incredibly shortsighted Dale O'Dell has moved to New York, with a guy who is so unusually good looking that you couldn't believe he'd be an even more unusually huge asshole, but he is. Wonderful but not at all shortsighted Ronnie and Amy have now moved to West Palm, under the loving sponsorship of Keith Garrity and that uppity bitch Dr. Carol, and by all accounts are thriving. I can't believe how much I still like my Fabulous Faye, even if I do know she usually is thinking of you while I'm pounding away. Frankie is, I think, fatter than ever, and Monstrous Bill will never, ever improve as a bartender, not in this life. With all due respect, what in the Good Christ are you still doing here, Mad Dog?"

Jim—naturally sporting the usual easy, friendly grin—replied, "I just met this sort of hotshot sexy lawyer at the gorgeous bar at Del Frisco at Liberty Wharf, who has an absolutely amazing damn condo at International Place, twentieth-floor view of the water. But she still drives her new Mercedes over to have dinner with me at The Diner, and a few drinks here at my Sports, and then she stays over with me right here on Schraft Street. At least for a while, 'cause I really like the idea of finally getting laid on Schraft Street; *and* sans unfortunate consequence. She read both my books *before* she met me, and she says I'm some sort of blue-collar Boston poet, and a down-to-earth handsome, thick blonde-headed and neat-bearded well-built fucker to boot. The best might just be that her sense of humor reminds me of Amy's, now that Ronnie's gotten the gorgeous little rascal to tone down the scatological. This smart and sexy lady really likes me and

I really like her, and she doesn't even know that I now have more fuckin' money than she does, despite where I choose to live."

Carlton grinned. "Hey, that's right, Faye told me you showed up at The Diner with a real babe. Said if you brought that babe by again, she was gonna ask her how you were in bed, and to draw a life-size sketch of your dick on the back of a napkin. Didn't realize it was already getting serious. Well then. What the fuck. I guess you did the best you could, and Schraft Street did the best it could."

Jim smiled, and punched Sergeant Carrollton lightly on the shoulder. "*Both* my books are gonna be movies, Carl. Chadwick gave me the amazing numbers yesterday, Hoss. You got five fuckin' *years* free rent coming."